ADONIS IN ATHENS

KAT MIZERA

Winning Whitney

Losing Laurel

Saving Sara

Chasing Charli

A Very Blizzard Christmas

Tending Tara

The Royal Trilogy:

Nowhere Left to Fall

Nowhere Left to Run

Nowhere Left to Hide

Royal Protectors:

Sandor

Xander

Axel

Dax (*A Royal Protectors/Las Vegas Sidewinders crossover*)

Gunnar (*short story, currently unavailable*)

Inferno:

Salvation's Inferno

Temptation's Inferno

Redemption's Inferno

Tropical Inferno (formerly "Tropical Ice")

Romancing Europe:

Adonis in Athens

Smitten in Santorini

Lucky in Lugano

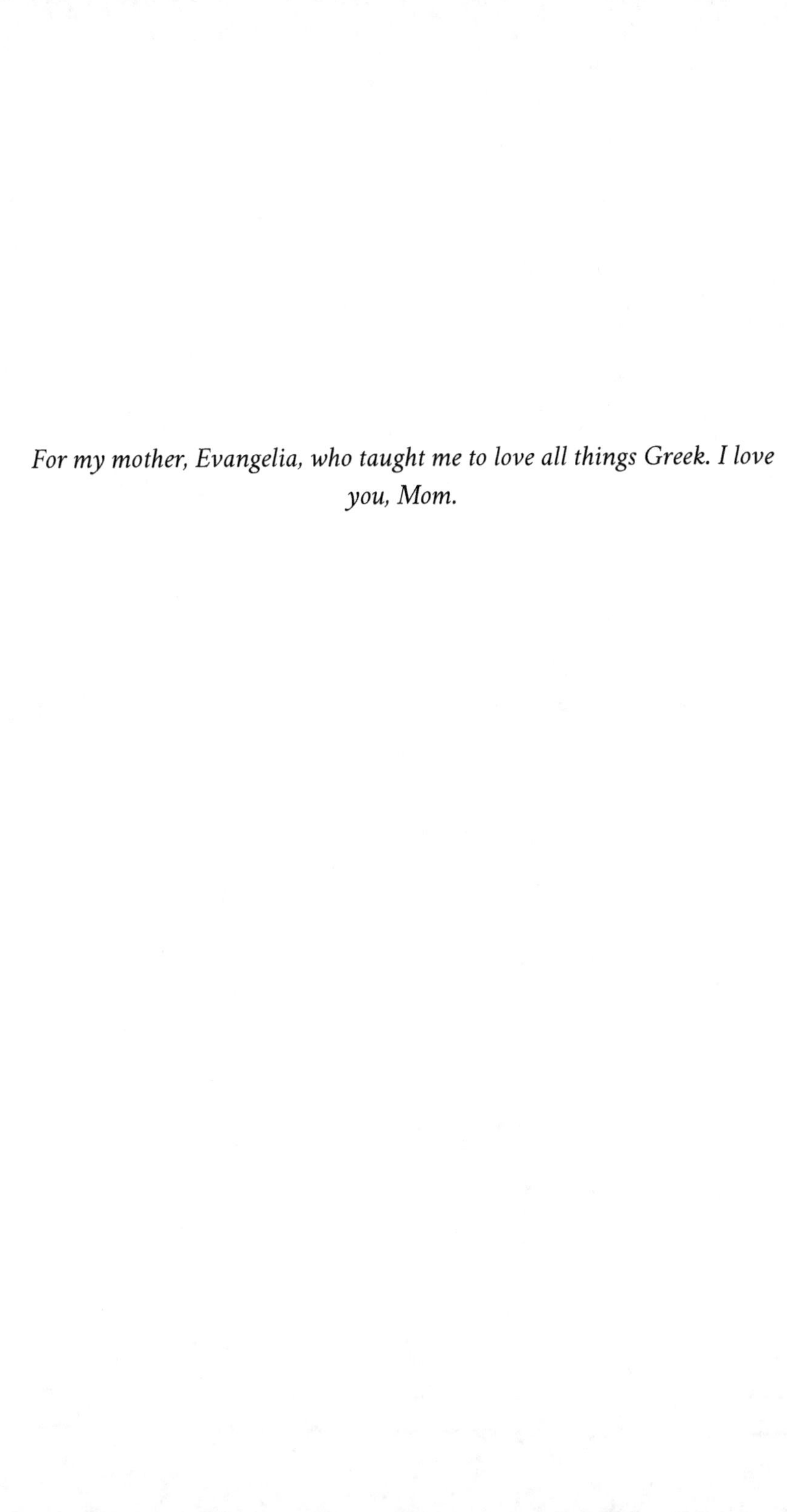

For my mother, Evangelia, who taught me to love all things Greek. I love you, Mom.

———

*P*aige Carter pulled up to the valet and all but snatched the ticket from the young man's hand as she stepped out of her car. She was supposed to be here at 6:00 and it was already 6:10, so she knew her boyfriend would be annoyed. Tom never yelled or got angry when she was late, but she could see the disappointment in his eyes and it was worse than when a parent looked at you that way. It made her uncomfortable, having that much power over a grown man, so she did her best to avoid being in that situation. Today had just been a long day at work and when it was this hot, she felt sluggish.

She didn't mean to fall behind, but somehow it always happened where Tom was concerned. She often wondered if, subconsciously, she did it on purpose. Nothing else made sense, because she was always punctual for work and other appointments. There was something about him, though, that brought out the procrastination and disorganization she usually kept at bay.

Since summer in Las Vegas was hotter than the hinges of the gates of hell probably were, and she could feel the makeup she'd so carefully applied begin to melt off her face, she resigned herself to arriving late, not looking her best and undoubtedly spending half the night apologizing. With a sigh of frustration, she hurried to the entrance.

Pasting a smile on her face, she approached the hostess. "Hi. My boyfriend is probably already here and—"

"Miss Carter!" The hostess's eyes twinkled as she grinned at her. "Oh, yes, he's here! Your whole family is here! Are you totally excited?"

Paige cocked her head slightly, her brows knitting together. "Um, what?"

"Uhh…" The girl's face darkened slightly and she turned away, fidgeting with something on her computer. "Oh, um, maybe I was mistaken. What's your boyfriend's name again?"

Paige had a funny feeling in the pit of her stomach. "Tom. Tom Malone."

"Okay, yes. Um, follow me." She strode into the heart of the restaurant and Paige had no choice but to follow, scanning the tables for Tom.

They walked all the way to the back and the hostess turned with a smile. "You're here in the back room—have a wonderful evening!" She opened the double doors that led into the big room usually reserved for private parties and Paige stepped forward with trepidation.

"There she is!" Tom was grinning broadly as he approached her, and Paige's stomach dropped.

"What's going on?" she whispered under her breath as he brushed his lips across hers.

"Wait and see!" he whispered back impishly.

Paige nearly groaned as she spotted her parents sitting at a table with her sister, Nicky, and her Aunt Sue and Uncle Paul. Her father gave her a thumbs-up while her mother waggled her fingers. She glanced from her parents to Tom and then across the room where she spotted her traitorous best friend, Raegan Warner, who should have warned her that something was going on. Because something was definitely going on.

"Tom!" She squeezed his hand harder than she intended and he turned in surprise, his eyes widening slightly.

"Honey, I know you're always cranky after a long week at work but trust me, okay? You're going to like this!" He kissed her cheek and pulled her along with him to a table at the front of the room, where his parents and sister were sitting.

"Why is everyone so dressed up?" she hissed in his ear. "I'm in capris and a T-shirt!"

"You're gorgeous no matter what you're wearing!" he whispered.

She wanted to roll her eyes but he was being so sweet and earnest, she mentally chided herself as she gave him a little smile. "Thanks—but you know I hate surprises."

"This one is worth it!" he grinned, pulling out her chair and waiting for her to sit down.

"Hi, Mrs. Malone, Mr. Malone." Paige nodded at his parents before turning to his sister, Jean, who hated her. "Hi, Jean."

"Hi." Jean raised her eyebrows. "Nice Duran Duran T-shirt."

"That's what happens with surprises," Paige said lightly. "If I'd known, I would've dressed for a special occasion."

"Since it's not that *special* of an occasion," Jean muttered, "I guess you're dressed fine."

"Jean!" Tom gave his sister a dirty look but she merely shrugged.

He sighed but after a wink at Paige, turned and let out a low whistle. "Excuse me, everyone! Now that Paige is here, I have an announcement."

Paige was getting more and more nervous as she looked up at Tom. Her parents' obvious happiness, Jean's grumpy attitude and the number of friends in the room made his intentions perfectly clear; he was going to propose again and she had no graceful way to refuse him.

"Mr. Carter." Tom took a wireless microphone that seemed to

appear out of thin air and walked across the room to Paige's father, Seth. "You know how I feel about Paige."

Seth smiled. "I think everyone does, son."

No, no, no, Paige thought, her eyes wide, stomach churning as he spoke.

"So after nearly two wonderful years together, I was hoping to get your blessing to ask for her hand in marriage."

Fuck me loud, Paige groaned inwardly. She cut her eyes to Raegan, who was slowly realizing that the shock on Paige's face was not laced with excitement.

"Well, of course you have my blessing," Seth replied. "But I'm not the one who has to marry you. Ultimately, it's Paige's decision."

The guests began to twitter and chuckle, whispers filling the room as Tom walked back towards Paige, pulling a small black box out of his pocket.

I'm going to kill him, she thought, too horrified to move and wondering how the hell she was going to get out of this.

"Paige, would you come down here please?" he asked.

Paige gulped, a roaring in her ears telling her she might start hyperventilating any moment now. She was screwed. There was no way to walk out of here without making a fool of herself, embarrassing Tom, or some combination of the two.

"Honey?" Tom spoke again, his smile faltering slightly.

"Oh, for fuck's sake," Jean muttered. "Just say no and spare us all the headache of watching the two of you make the worst decision of your lives!"

Fuck, fuck, fuck. Paige stood on wobbly knees, struggling to breathe, breaking out in a cold sweat. "T-tom?" Her voice was barely a whisper but her eyes were pleading with him to stop this insanity. He had to know she was going to say no. Why else would he have done it so publicly? This was more than a disaster; this was a nightmare and apparently she wasn't going to wake up before the bad part.

"Sweetheart, I—" He took her icy cold hand in his and pulled her towards him.

"Tom, no!" she whispered frantically. "Please—not here."

His smile fell a little further. "Paige…"

"Put the microphone down," she implored, blinking away tears that were threatening to fall. "I have to talk to you—alone!"

He frowned. "Honey…"

"If you truly love me, you'll do this for me." She was whispering, desperation in her voice and written all over her face.

Tom took a deep breath and let it out slowly, before picking up the microphone and smiling broadly again. "My girl seems to want this part to be private. Can you give us a couple minutes?" He put down the mike amidst boos, cheers and catcalls, and pulled Paige from the room. They walked around the corner and down the hallway where the bathrooms were. Finally, he leaned against the wall and met her gaze. "Why do I get the feeling it's not that you don't want me to propose in there, it's that you don't want me to propose at all?"

She swallowed. "It's not that black and white," she whispered, searching her mind for something she could tell him to make him understand. To make him think about her needs. Hell, to make him stop trying to move so fast.

Raegan told her she was crazy. She worked as a waitress at a casino on the Strip and seemed to meet the very worst possible guys, so Paige thought her opinion of Tom was a bit skewed. Raegan was right about one thing, though: Tom was one of a kind. He wanted to be in a committed relationship and was willing to put in the work to make that happen. He'd already proposed once and she'd had to gently point out that they were both still young, needing time to get to know each other and grow up a little too. He'd been disappointed, but seemed to take her words to heart. He'd bought the house not long after that and seemed intent on showing her how much of a grown-up he was. She just wished he would slow down. Growing up, to her, didn't mean giving up all semblance of youth; it meant living and exploring to find out who you were and what you really wanted in life. Tom was on the fast track to leaving behind every bit of childhood and focusing on retirement.

If she could get him to slow down, to stop rushing all the milestones, it would be easier to love him. She didn't want a mortgage, babies and a dog at 24. She wanted to travel, go to concerts, and get beyond an entry-level position at her job. Tom said he understood, but actions spoke louder than words and his actions said the opposite. He wanted a spouse and a white picket fence sooner rather than later. Paige wanted that too, but later rather than sooner. Was it so wrong to want to enjoy life as an adult without a lot of responsibility for a little while longer?

"Then what is it, exactly?" he asked, his normally easygoing smile turning into a scowl. "I moved too fast the first time, but dammit, Paige. It's been almost two years!"

"Eighteen months," she contradicted, warring with herself about whether to just let him go and get this over with or to try to explain so that he would be patient a little longer.

"Paige, what's going to change at 24 months or 36 months or, hell, 100 months?!"

She bit her lower lip and tried to articulate her reservations. "It's just...I don't..." She couldn't seem to do anything but sigh.

"Do you love me, Paige?" he asked tightly, his brown eyes boring into hers intently.

"I do," she whispered. "But we're at really different places in life right now."

"That again?" he demanded. "Jesus, you want to wait until we're 30? Forty? I mean, how old will be old enough?!"

"It's not about age!" she protested. "It's about lifestyle... You have the big house and the car and the job. You want the wife and babies to go with it, and I'm not ready."

"What do you want to do?" he asked in frustration, calming down now that she'd admitted she loved him.

"I want to focus on my career and get to a point where I feel successful, instead of one step above entry-level. I want to travel. I want to go on adventures… You're only 26, Tom. Why don't *you* want to go on adventures?"

He looked startled, his eyes narrowing a little. "I, um, well, like what?"

"Swimming with sharks in the South Pacific or zip-lining across Costa Rica or excavating shit in the desert in Egypt—I don't know! Don't you dream about anything other than accounting?"

He met her gaze sadly, stuffing his hands—and the box with the ring—in his pockets. "You," he said softly. "I dream about you."

Embarrassment and guilt tore through her, making her want to cry. He didn't deserve a woman like her—he deserved better. He wasn't the kind of guy who dreamed about adventure; his dreams were about reality. Life, love, marriage, children and retirement; that summed up Tom Malone and it was the opposite of everything Paige wanted. There was just no way to explain that without hurting his feelings.

"There's something I have to tell you," she finally said, taking a step away from him and looking anywhere but his face. "I, um, I'm kind of…already married."

"Huh?" Tom looked too confused to even be angry.

"I mean, I think I am."

"What?! You *think* you're married? How can you not know?"

"It was a crazy fling during spring break, three years ago." She looked down. "He was leaving to go back to school the next morning and we couldn't find any papers or anything so we… assumed we hadn't actually done it, like legally, and…forgot about it."

"Forgot about it? *Are you kidding me?*" He was staring at her as though a unicorn horn had just poked through her forehead.

"It was spring break…drinking, partying, carrying on—a too-much-fun overload—and then he was running to catch his flight and eventually going back to Greece… We weren't sure what we'd done. So he left me his information and said to call him. I never did."

Tom was still staring at her. "Let me get this straight. Three years ago you had a wild week with some guy from Greece, whom you may or may not have married, but instead of finding out, you went your separate ways and decided to just ignore it?!"

Hearing it spoken out loud like that, it really sounded dumb, but all she could do was nod.

"Is that your idea of an adventure?"

Her eyes shot up and met his, hurt, guilt and a twinge of anger running through her. "That's not fair," she said hotly. "Name one college student who didn't do something dumb!"

He arched his brows. "I can name at least one."

She scowled. "I'm sorry! I can't help who I am! It's not like I've changed…I've always been this way and you asked me out anyway. I've never lied about who I was and I've tried to compromise, to do some things your way while still doing other things my own way. You just don't seem to want to do any compromising on your end, and now—"

"No compromising?!" He glared at her. "Everything I've done has been a compromise! If it were up to me, we'd already be married and living together! Instead I keep waiting and putting my life on hold so you can grow up!"

"How have you put your life on hold?" She frowned at him, suddenly tired of this, tired of everything. "Your career is on track, you bought the big McMansion in the suburbs, you have a fancy car and the monthly golf date at the country club. How is delaying putting a ring on my finger holding you back?"

"Single guys don't get the corner offices or the partner offers—they're too busy partying to snag the better clients."

"So you need a wife to further your career?" She was getting pissed now, folding her arms across her chest. "All that stuff about dreaming about me was just bullshit!"

"No! Honey, wait." He ran a hand through his thin brown hair and sighed. He reached out and gently put his hands around hers, pulling her closer to him. "Listen, that came out all wrong. I'm sorry."

"Tom, I don't know if I can do this anymore," she admitted. "I love you, but we're in really different places in our lives. Sometimes it feels like you don't know me at all."

"What do you mean?"

"If you wanted me to say yes tonight, this wasn't the way to do it. You know I don't like surprises and gathering all these people stressed me out—even if things were perfect between us, I might've said no because it's just so overwhelming for me."

"I'm sorry."

"And I know you love this stuff. In the end, I don't ever want to be the reason you don't do something. I don't want to hold you back."

"You're not." He looked sad. "But I kind of feel like your heart is somewhere else."

"That's not true!" she protested. "I've never been unfaithful! Never!"

"That's not what I meant. I know that's not who you are…but you're in a different place in life. You want your freedom for a while, to explore the things you feel are missing, and I'm ready to settle down. Maybe…" He met her eyes almost guiltily. "Maybe we need a break."

"A break?" She blinked.

"At the very least, you need to find out, one way or another, if you're married. If you are, you need to do something about it. If you're not, I still think we need some time to think about the future, about where we want to be in a year, five years…ten."

"I…okay." She didn't know how to argue because he was right. Even though it could be different between them, he obviously wasn't willing to find middle ground. He wanted things to be the way he wanted them; her needs and wants weren't his priority, even though he made it appear that they were by spoiling her with gifts she didn't need and the type of overwhelming attention she didn't want.

"Let's take a little time to regroup. You can sort out your… marital status and I can think about the idea of adventures."

She looked up into his handsome face in surprise. "Really? You'll think about adventures?"

He shrugged. "For me to love you, I'd think I'd have to."

"It has to be a choice," she said softly. "Not a burden."

"That's why I have to think about it."

"That's fair." She paused. "Tom, my parents don't know—"

He smiled faintly. "About your possible marriage? I figured. Don't worry. I'll cover for you."

"You will?" She looked at him curiously. "Why?"

"Because you're right—I didn't make tonight about *you*…it was about me. I wanted the big party, the big surprise, the big engagement. I know you, though, and I knew you wouldn't like it. I just hoped you wouldn't be able to say no."

"I'm sorry," she said quietly. "But that's not fair to either of us. I do have to find out, one way or another, whether or not I got married three years ago. And you have to decide if you're willing to put off the white picket fence dream for another year or two, until I've had time to follow some of my dreams too. Once we get married and have kids, everything will change, Tom, and I don't know that I want to give up that much freedom at 24."

"Maybe some time apart will make us see that we're meant to be together," he said.

"Maybe," she whispered softly, leaning up to press a chaste kiss on his cheek.

"Go ahead and go," he said, releasing her hands. "I'll think of something to tell everyone."

"Oh. No, that's not fair. We should tell them together. I can—"

"Tonight was my fault," he admitted. "I never should have put you on the spot like that, so I'll make it right."

"But what will you tell them?"

"That I shouldn't have planned something like this without talking to you first and that you want a private, romantic engagement, not something this big or ostentatious. When they ask where you are, I'll say you're upset with me and that I'm giving you time to cool off. In a few days, we'll tell people we're taking a break."

"And then?" she asked, looking over her shoulder at him.

"I don't know." He met her gaze sadly. "I guess we'll regroup when the time is right."

2

―――――――

The flight to Greece took forever; more than four hours to New York and then another nine to get to Athens. It had given her a lot of time to think and she was even more confused than she'd been before she left Las Vegas. The debacle with Tom had been epic, even for her, and she cringed every time she thought about walking into that room.

Her friends and family were confused because Tom was the kind of guy most women her age were looking for. Not only was he handsome, smart, and funny, he also made an excellent living as an accountant and owned a beautiful home in a gated subdivision. He drove a Mercedes, bought her nice gifts and was generally a good guy. As far as she knew, he'd never cheated, never done drugs and barely drank other than the occasional beer. He'd given her a key to his house, a drawer in his dresser and had asked her to move in repeatedly. He didn't have a single flaw, she thought irritably. Maybe *that* was the problem.

In the 18 months they'd been dating, he'd often surprised her with unplanned weekends away, tickets to shows, and random day trips. His surprise proposal could have been anything from a romantic dinner for two to a formal ceremony where the mayor granted her keys to the city.

She almost snorted at the thought, chuckling at her own sarcasm. Tom was a good guy and she hated being so out of sync with him. Quiet and unassuming, he was always there for her, supportive and as interested in her needs as a guy could be. Maybe too much so, she thought with a grimace. If Tom did have a fault, it was that he seemed to read her mind. If she so much as looked at a purse online, it would appear on her doorstep a day later. If she'd forgotten to schedule an appointment for a haircut, and her hairdresser was booked, he'd make a few calls and an opening would miraculously appear. Sometimes, she wanted to figure out how to afford the purse or get the appointment herself —and he refused to let her. He thought his job was to take care of her, but she just wanted someone who would be there to lend moral support.

Putting her ear buds in as she navigated her way through the airport, she hummed along to the end of Billy Joel's "Just the Way You Are" on the music app on her cell phone. The romantic lyrics made her a little melancholy and she was about to find a different song when the melody of the next song froze her hand in place. The first few bars of Bruno Mars' "Marry You" inexplicably brought tears to her eyes, and for the hundredth time this week, she thought of *him. Apollo.* She could still picture his mesmerizing green eyes, chiseled features and body reminiscent of a Greek god. Literally. Tall, Greek and even-hotter-than-Vegas-in-summer good-looking, she'd done her best the last three years not to think about him. Or the spring break he'd come to Vegas. Or the nights they'd spent dancing and kissing as if nothing else in the world existed, running from casino to nightclub to the gondola ride at the Venetian. Or how he'd brought her body alive in ways that made her shudder just thinking about them.

She was here in Greece specifically to see him, though, so

there was no escaping him, her memories or reality because they were now all rolled into one.

*B*y the time she got her luggage, passed through customs and found the car she'd hired to drive her to her hotel, she was drained. She'd left Las Vegas early yesterday morning, spent four hours wandering around the airport in New York, and then flown all night—through more time zones than she could count—before arriving in Greece at 11:00 in the morning. It was nearly 2:30 by the time she got to her hotel, and she was hot, exhausted and starving. Luckily, she was near Syntagma Square, which was a busy tourist area downtown, just a couple blocks from her hotel. She was too tired to explore much so she went to a kiosk where she bought two bottles of water, a chocolate bar and something called a *tiropita*. It had a fillo crust and was filled with a Greek cheese she'd never heard of called *kasseri*, but it practically melted in her mouth and she all but inhaled it. On impulse, and because at 1.49 euros it fit her budget, she bought another and forced herself to wander the busy winding streets for a little while. If she could make it until about 6:00, she'd sleep for 12 hours and be ready for tomorrow's mission.

Though she was dreading it, she and Raegan had talked for hours about this, and came to the conclusion that she'd be better off getting it over with. Once she faced Apollo and got him to sign the divorce papers, she would be free to enjoy her remaining four days in Greece. She would have done anything to be able to stay longer but flying to Athens in the summer was ridiculously expensive and though she could have found slightly cheaper hotels, she'd wanted to stay somewhere that appeared safe and clean. Greece was generally pretty safe, but as a foreign woman traveling alone, she wasn't comfortable taking any chances. A better hotel meant a more expensive one, which would diminish her already meager budget, resulting in less time here. She simply reminded herself over and over that this was still the trip of a life-time. Well, it would be. Once she got the divorce papers signed.

Three days after her ill-fated engagement party, she and Raegan had walked into the government office where she'd requested a copy of her marriage certificate, stating that she'd lost it. Raegan had been standing behind her, fingers crossed, waiting as the clerk looked it up and verified her identity. Sure enough, on April 3rd, three years ago, she had married Apollo Lakkas. She'd known his last name because he'd given her his business card, but seeing the marriage certificate had left her a little light-headed. Raegan managed to get her outside and got her to drink some cold water, but for at least half an hour, Paige had been shell-shocked. She'd known it was possible, even likely, considering the vague memories she had, but it didn't seem real. Who just walked into a chapel and got married to a guy she met at a club in Las Vegas during spring break? Apparently she did.

After it sunk in, she'd debated calling him, but Raegan thought seeing him in person would be better and give her some sort of closure. Besides, she needed to get divorced and it would be easier to do it in person. That way, she would know it was done and would be able to file everything as soon as she got back. She'd found a lawyer willing to draw up basic divorce papers for a reasonable amount, citing irreconcilable differences and that each party was responsible for their own debts and assets. They would need to have their signatures notarized at the embassy and then it would be over. She could walk away from Apollo Lakkas and their spontaneous marriage without looking back. Then she could enjoy Greece, a place she'd never dreamed she would get to; after all, this was her first true adventure.

Looking up into a clear blue sky, she couldn't help but smile. She was really in Greece, and even though seeing Apollo again was going to be hard, she was as excited as she'd ever been about anything. No one back home had understood why she was suddenly running off to Greece, and she'd had to lie to everyone except Raegan, but this was truly a dream come true for her. Except for that pesky divorce thing. And the hotter-than-hot Greek god she still had to face. She didn't remember a lot about the details of their time together, but she remembered him. Lord, who could forget a guy like Apollo?

Do not think about that, she told herself firmly as she crawled between the cool sheets. She absolutely had to force herself not to think about the way it had felt to have his strong body moving on hers, those amazing lips on her breasts, and his hands...she shook her head abruptly. *No! Stop it!* She closed her eyes and thought about Tom. Kind, patient Tom, who wanted to marry her and give her the kind of life she could only dream of: money, vacations, a beautiful house and a big, wonderful family. Things that a hunk like Apollo probably had no interest in—guys like him didn't do that kind of thing with regular girls like her. Especially when they lived 7,000 miles away. Except, he kind of did. Because they were already married. Sort of. She dozed off remembering the first time he'd kissed her.

*P*aige woke up feeling like a new woman. It was early, just after 7:00, but getting 12 hours of sleep made a huge difference and she was ready to face the day. She dressed in a light summer dress made of white cotton and trimmed with eyelet lace. It fell off the shoulders, leaving them bare, revealing smooth, lightly tanned skin. It was a little short, falling mid-thigh, but showed off her legs and lots more silky skin. She hesitated, looking in the mirror and wondering what Apollo would think. She hoped he wasn't disappointed. Though they didn't have a future together, she didn't want his memories to be that of a plain, boring American girl.

Her ash-blond hair fell just above her shoulders and was parted on the side, all one length—nothing exciting. Her hazel eyes had regular eyelashes that forced her to go out of her way to use lots of lengthening mascara to make them longer. The smattering of freckles across her nose made her crazy, but in temperatures like they had both here and at home, she only wore foundation for special occasions since it was usually gone before she arrived at her destination anyway. Her lips were funky, too, with the lower one slightly larger than the upper. She always tried to use pale colors on them so the disparity was less obvious. Even though Tom said it was sexy, she'd never believed him.

She turned away from the mirror and put the divorce papers, her passport, cash and credit cards into the cross-body purse she'd brought, along with lip gloss, her room key and a map she'd picked up at the front desk. She would take a bus to Piraeus, where Apollo's family's shipping company was located, and then she would walk or take a taxi to the building. It was still early, though, so she planned to take her time grabbing a bite to eat and wandering around the Square. The Greek Parliament House was directly across the street from Syntagma Square, and she'd read that the changing of the guards was something she should see. She'd also heard that feeding the pigeons was fun, so she would do that too. Hopefully it would be interesting enough to distract her from what she had to do.

The Greek Parliament House was just north of the square and she took the time to read a bit of the history in the guidebook she'd grabbed at a kiosk outside the hotel. It said the building had been erected in the mid-1800s and had an austere neoclassical façade. The Tomb of the Unknown Soldier sat out front and was protected by the presidential guard, called *Evzones*. They wore traditional attire called *foustanellas*, which were essentially white skirts that had 400 pleats, representing the number of years the Greeks had been under Turkish rule. The skirts were paired with white, long-sleeved shirts, an embroidered vest and pointed red shoes with large pompoms. It was like nothing she'd ever seen in the U.S. and she took pictures with her phone, hoping she would remember all the details.

The changing of the guards took place every hour on the hour and she waited for the next change to occur. It looked like a slow dance where the soldiers kicked their legs in the air. She found the synchronization of the ceremony fascinating and got in line to take a picture with one of the guards once it was over. She felt a moment of sadness as she handed her phone to the nearest tourist so they could take the picture, wishing Raegan had been able to come with her so they could enjoy this together. She wondered if this was the kind of thing Tom would enjoy, but something told her it wasn't. He was probably more interested in staying at a resort with a golf course than exploring Greek customs and history.

Seeing that time had slipped away, she decided to skip feeding the pigeons that roamed around everywhere, and looked for the bus to take her to Piraeus. Hoping she didn't get lost, she sat at a window and took in every detail of the city. The mix of old and new was incredible, and she wished she'd brought a good camera to get pictures of the dozens of buildings that had such spectacular architecture. She didn't own a camera like that, though, and asking Tom if she could borrow his seemed a bit odd considering they weren't speaking. She hadn't heard from him since the night of his surprise and in a way she was relieved. Despite the fact that he'd said he would think about "adventures," the idea that he had to spend time thinking about it was pretty telling. She didn't have to put any effort into it; she knew instinctively that she wanted to see and do new things. She didn't make a lot of money, but she always spent it on experiences before items.

The apartment she and Raegan shared was filled with hand-me-down furniture and thrift store finds. Though she'd invested in a professional wardrobe since she worked in the sales and marketing department of a professional hockey team, the rest of her clothes were older and bought for comfort; jeans with the knees torn out, concert T-shirts, and yoga pants from Walmart. She'd bought the dress she was wearing today, though, specifically for this trip. Paired with beaded white sandals and silver earrings, it had felt Greek to her, and she thought she looked pretty today. Maybe not pretty enough for a guy like Apollo, but hopefully attractive enough to at least not embarrass herself.

The bus let her off on a busy corner in what appeared to be a shopping area, and the kind gentleman who'd sat next to her got off as well, telling her that the office she was looking for was just a block north. So she headed in that direction, grateful that the numbers on the buildings and shops seemed to be going the right way. When she arrived, she felt the first twinge of fear creep up her spine. What if he was out of town? What if he didn't even work there anymore? What if she'd come all the way to Greece for nothing? Or worse, what if he'd unwittingly gotten married and she was about to completely destroy his life? Somehow, she hadn't thought about that until just now.

She vacillated and stood on the street chewing her lip in a panic. Finally, she reminded herself that he'd been equally responsible for walking away without a second glance and if he hadn't been concerned that he'd possibly gotten married, it hadn't been her job to seek him out. Until now, anyway. Lifting her chin and steeling her resolve, she opened the door and stepped inside, grateful that there was air conditioning. There were three men standing behind a large counter that separated the back of the office from what appeared to be an informal reception area, and they glanced in her direction with obvious interest as she approached. A young man who'd been on the phone immediately disconnected and said something to her in Greek.

"I'm sorry," she said quietly. "I don't speak Greek. I'm looking for Apollo—Apollo Lakkas."

The three men in the back stopped talking and were now listening intently as the young man who'd greeted her cocked his head slightly. "Yes, Apollo. Your name?"

"Paige," she said, swallowing a lump in her throat. "Paige Carter. From Las Vegas."

The man picked up the phone and spoke in Greek, except for her name, and nodded. "He will come. One moment, please."

"Thank you." Paige tried not to think about her queasy stomach or sweaty palms. It would be okay. He would want to get this over with. He probably barely remembered her and would be embarrassed, ready to do anything to make this go away.

*A*pollo was having a shitty day. He'd had to fire yet another receptionist who didn't seem to think she actually had to give the staff their messages, and now his sales team was pissed because they were having to cover the phones and front desk. His father had called him at least a dozen times so far today, trying to keep up with the business he'd been too sick to participate in for the last year. His oldest sister was trying to set him up with one of her girlfriends, and now that they had no receptionist he was thinking his upcoming vacation in Santorini wasn't going to happen.

Drumming his fingers on his desk, he stared out the window at the water. He loved the sea, and loved running his family's shipping company even more, but there were days he just wanted some freedom back. He'd given up a lot to take over after his father's stroke, and most of the time he didn't regret anything at all. It was just once in a while, on a beautiful summer day like today, that he wished he could grab a towel, jump on his motorcycle and drive down to one of the many beaches he loved. He would go for a swim and then lie on the shore soaking up the sun. When he was sufficiently burned and sleepy, he'd go home, shower and take a nap. A day at the beach always relaxed him and when he woke up he'd call a few friends and go out for a beer or coffee, hanging out, flirting with beautiful women and basically enjoying life. Instead, he worked 10-12 hour days, six days a week, and met with his father almost daily during afternoon siesta to update him. Though they were technically closed on Sundays, he usually came in to the office to catch up on paperwork and other things that he was distracted from when the phones were ringing and clients were coming in and out.

Sighing, he sent the younger of his two older sisters a text, asking her to come in and man the phones. She would be annoyed, but that was too bad. He and Melina were close but she'd left most of this to him even though she got her share of the profits. While his father was still the owner and controlling partner, after his stroke, Apollo had been promoted to president and CEO of the company, with a salary that compensated him well. Before he'd taken over, he and his sisters had gotten small dividends from the profits after everyone was paid and all bills were covered. His father had taken a full salary and had begun giving Apollo a bigger share as he'd started grooming him to take over one day. Then he'd had a stroke and Apollo had been forced to sink or swim; since this was his family's legacy as well as his future, he'd busted his ass to keep the company afloat. He'd done a damn good job too, using his double major from Yale in Information Technology and International Finance to bring the company not just into the 21st century, but to also infuse it with new clients and a fresh ideology. It had served them well and his father, though concerned at first, now bragged about how his son was a business genius.

A bored, overworked business genius, he thought in annoyance. He wanted to get out of here today so bad he could taste it, but even if he managed to get away for a few hours, he was expected at dinner at 2:30 and then his father would grill him instead of taking his usual nap during afternoon siesta. By the time all of that was done, Apollo would need to come back to the office. They stayed open until 8:00 on Thursdays even though clients didn't usually come in that late, but they took a lot of calls from the U.S. who were anywhere from 7 to 10 hours behind them. He was setting the groundwork to open a branch of the company in Los Angeles and negotiations were going well, but he didn't trust anyone else to get it started. He wanted to open the office himself, make sure it was done correctly, but that would leave the office here in Greece without a real manager. He didn't trust the sales team to have access to bank accounts and other sensitive information, and while he trusted his sisters, they didn't know the business well enough to handle it. The project was probably going to fall through because there just weren't enough hours in the day, and it was disappointing, but he couldn't be in two places at once and much as his father was getting better, he still had a long way to go.

His phone buzzed and he grabbed it absently, still lost in his thoughts. "*Oriste?*" *Hello?*

"You have a visitor!" Tasos, one of the sales guys, spoke with a hint of mischief in his voice.

"I don't have any appointments," Apollo muttered, glancing down at his desk calendar.

"I'm pretty sure she's not a client," he chortled. "She said her name is Paige Carter."

He mispronounced the American name badly but Apollo still recognized it immediately and froze. *Paige Carter?! His* Paige? What the hell was she doing here?

"I'll be right out," he said shortly, hanging up. Holy shit, the girl he'd been dreaming about for three years was here in Greece? In his office?! What did that even mean? Had she come looking for him? He stood up and tucked his button-down shirt back into his slacks and ran his hands through his too-long hair, thinking he really needed a trim. Damn, he hadn't thought he'd ever see her again, even though he thought of her more often than he wanted to admit.

Curious and just a little bit excited, he strode out to the front office as casually as he could. As he rounded the corner he saw her immediately. Her back was turned and she was reading one of their English advertisements that had been blown up and hung on the wall, but he would recognize those long legs and shapely shoulders anywhere. Her hair was shorter now—three years ago it had hung halfway down her back and he'd wrapped his fist in it while he'd been buried deep inside of her.

Shit! he thought with irritation, changing the direction his thoughts were going. Why was he thinking about sex with her? It wasn't like he lacked in female companionship. They weren't Paige, though, and he'd never had a connection with a woman like he'd had with the sweet American blonde, but that felt like a long time ago. She'd undoubtedly moved on and there was only one reason she could be here. The thought made him sad, but there was no help for it now. So he cleared his throat and spoke her name as calmly as he could.

"Paige? Is that you?"

She turned and nearly took his breath away. Damn, she was still gorgeous, with that luscious lower lip that protruded just a little and her strikingly expressive hazel eyes. When she smiled, it felt like a punch in the gut; it was that magnetic.

"Hi." Her voice quavered slightly, betraying her nervousness, but she put on a brave front. "I hope you don't mind I stopped by without calling."

"Of course not!" He walked out from behind the counter and didn't hesitate to hug her tightly, kissing her once on each cheek, as was the Greek custom.

Paige's breath caught when he wrapped his arms around her and she was helpless to stop herself from hugging him back, breathing in his delicious aftershave and allowing herself just a few seconds to remember the feel of those hard muscles and smooth, tanned skin.

"It's good to see you," he said softly, meeting her eyes. "Come on back to my office and you can tell me what you're doing in Greece." He ignored his gaping employees, knowing he would be grilled within an inch of his life once she left.

"Sure." She followed him down a hallway that led to offices and he opened a door at the end, allowing her to walk in ahead of him. She paused at the view, her mouth falling open slightly. "Oh my gosh, this is gorgeous." Two walls of the corner office had floor-to-ceiling windows and waves bounced and crashed onto the sea wall alongside a pier that was practically steps away.

"It makes it hard to work some days," he admitted, grinning at her obvious pleasure.

"I don't know if I'd ever get anything done if I worked in an office like this!"

He laughed. "I grew up coming in here, but it truly doesn't get old." Instead of sitting behind his desk, he took the chair next to hers and tried not to stare. He still thought she was the most exquisite woman on earth. Maybe not beautiful by celebrity standards, but everything he'd ever wanted in a woman physically. Blond, with big hazel eyes, a mouth made for kissing and a little brush of freckles across her nose that gave her a girlish look.

"You're probably wondering why I'm here."

"I can guess," he said slowly.

"Yeah, so, I almost got engaged and realized I needed to find out one way or another if we'd, you know, really gotten married."

He arched one dark, thick eyebrow, unsure why the idea of her getting engaged made him sad. "You *almost* got engaged?"

She rolled her eyes and shook her head. "It was such a clusterfuck! You wouldn't believe…" Her voice trailed off. "Sorry, you don't need to hear about my life."

He chuckled. "Considering we're married, it might not be a bad idea."

She met his gaze in surprise. "You're not mad?"

"Mad? Why would I be mad? I'm just surprised you didn't check before now. I figured that would have been the first thing you did after I left. Since I didn't hear from you, I assumed we'd been drunk and confused and it didn't happen. Not legally anyway."

She flushed. "I was embarrassed and kind of afraid and then..." She swallowed. "Then my period was late and I was distracted. I did a pregnancy test every single day for two weeks until I finally could be sure that I wasn't."

He wasn't sure why, but he needed to know. "Would you have called me if you'd been pregnant?"

She looked shocked. "Of course! I wouldn't have made any decisions like that without talking to you..." Now it was her turn to hesitate. "Would you have stepped up and been a father?"

His green eyes grew warm and serious. "No question. Even if I'd had to move to the U.S. until you finished school or whatever. We did that together, Paige—we were drunk but not the entire time we were together. I distinctly remember a lot of sober sex..."

She turned bright red but nodded. "Oh, I remember almost everything about those three days...just not the actual wedding part." She sighed and opened her bag. "I, well, I thought it might be time to take care of this but I wanted to see you in person. It felt...*wrong* to send these in the mail." She held out the divorce papers.

Apollo took them slowly, willing the disappointment in his gut to go away. "I see." He didn't even look at them and instead focused on her face. "You want to end it."

She frowned. "Well, I mean...we don't really know each other and live thousands of miles apart. I have a family, a life and a career in Las Vegas. You obviously have a good job here working for your dad and—"

"I don't work for my dad anymore—I'm the CEO now."

She smiled, and not only did it reach her eyes, it seemed to permeate her entire face. "That's wonderful—how exciting for you! But it just drives home my point: this isn't something we could even give a trial run to see if we still like each other. I have to leave in four days and—"

"You came all the way to Greece for four days?" He couldn't

wrap his head around the idea of spending that many hours on an airplane for only four days at the destination.

She flushed. "I can't afford to stay any longer. The flight wiped me out and I hate having credit card debt. The hotel is $200 a night and between the car from the airport, food and a little sight-seeing, I'll be paying this trip off for months."

"But you came in person instead of just calling and mailing me the papers." He cocked his head. "Why, Paige?"

She gave a tiny shrug. "The truth? I think about those three days a lot. I've never had a spark with a guy like I had with you and I've romanticized it in my head for three long years... I figured it was time to see you and get it out of my system." She swallowed. "And I was telling the truth before—we're *married*. Maybe we were young and foolish, and it was a stupid, drunken thing to do, but we're married; legally, willingly married. We consummated that marriage and spent three days laughing and sharing and loving—I don't believe you have to be *in love* to love someone—and that kind of loving relationship deserved a formal, respectful goodbye."

Her words touched him, and ironically, he agreed with everything she'd said. Although they certainly couldn't have been truly in love when they'd drunkenly stumbled into that chapel, they'd shared something special based on chemistry, instinct and at least a little bit of compatibility. Love, even if it was seeded in chemistry, had to have played a part in their subconscious minds because why else would they have done what they did?

"I've thought about you a lot too," he admitted, putting the papers on his desk and staring out at the water again. "I wondered how you were, what you were doing...and if you'd moved on." His eyes met hers with an unspoken question and she looked down.

"Kind of." She couldn't help but be honest. "It was hard not to think about you, wonder if we really were married, and it was always in the back of my mind."

"But you never went to verify one way or the other."

"I was afraid," she admitted softly. "All I had left other than the memories was the possibility that we were still linked by marriage."

"If you'd gone to find out for sure, and it turned out it wasn't legal, or we hadn't done it at all, you would have had to let go of the fantasy."

She nodded, shocked that he'd instinctively understood what she hadn't been able to verbalize.

"Why didn't you want to let it go?" he asked curiously.

She smiled, meeting his gaze without hesitation. "I live a pretty simple existence. Those three days were the most exciting, wonderful days of my entire adult life and, well, the rest doesn't matter."

"Tell me," he pressed. "You came all this way and one signature —" he motioned to the papers on the desk, "—is the end of all of it. You might as well say what you want to say."

"The way you made me feel, the sex, the fun we had—I've never experienced anything like it since and it's probably holding me back."

"From what?"

"Relationships, love…everything. I had to get some closure, remind myself that it was just a silly, albeit wonderful, college fling. Now we're older and live halfway across the world from each other. It's time to let go."

He couldn't explain why he hated the idea of her letting go of her fantasy of him; he loved that she thought about and romanticized their incredibly brief but intensely passionate time together because he'd done it too. He'd never forgotten her; her laughter and zest for life, the way she'd come undone when he'd made love to her—God, he was an idiot. His friends would laugh him out of the country if they knew the way he felt when he thought about her.

"Apollo?" She was staring at him in confusion.

"I never moved past the memories either," he said finally,

standing up and walking over to the picture windows that normally brought him so much joy. "My father started grooming me to take over the company not long after I got back to Greece and last year he had a stroke. I still had so much to learn that I didn't have time for anything else, so I kept the memories of our time in Vegas close. They kept me sane when I was so busy I couldn't breathe, and made me smile when I had dark days. You have no idea how happy I am to see you."

"Really?" She was fighting a plethora of emotions that ran the gamut from excitement to nervousness and confusion. It was supposed to be simple; he would go with her to the embassy, sign the papers and she would walk out of his life, burying those memories forever. Instead, he was making her stomach do funny things and her heart beat in an irregular pattern.

"Do you want to get out of here?" he asked impulsively. "I can't think sitting here in my office and I'm sure the guys are falling all over themselves to figure out who you are."

She smiled shyly. "I'm nothing special—they probably didn't even notice me."

He frowned slightly, walking over to her and reaching out to lift her chin with the fingers of his right hand. "You're beautiful, Paige. Why would you say that?"

"I'm not beautiful!" she laughed. "I'm cute with a very girl-next-door look. No one thinks I'm *beautiful*!"

"I do." He looked into her eyes and saw both pleasure and disbelief, and he wished he could prove to her just how gorgeous she was. If only he had more than four days to do it.

"You're sweet," she whispered in a husky voice, unable to deny that the chemistry was still there, practically sizzling between them.

"Let's go for a drive," he whispered back. "If you keep looking at me like that, I'm not going to be responsible for my actions."

She quickly got to her feet and turned away, nodding. "Yes, okay, let's do that."

He grabbed his keys and opened the door, letting her walk out in front of him again. They'd just gotten to the outer office when his sister Melina breezed in. "*Kalimera!*" she called out. *Good morning!*

"I'm taking the rest of the morning off," he told her briskly, knowing a Greek version of the Spanish Inquisition would start if he didn't make a hasty exit. "Tell Mama I won't be at dinner—my friend from college is here and I'm going to take her for a drive."

Melina's mouth fell open but Apollo had grabbed Paige's hand and all but yanked her out the door the minute he finished talking.

"You're acting weird," she whispered, hurrying to keep up.

"Sorry!" He pulled out his keys and pressed the key fob to unlock the door. "You don't understand Greek families—this is going to be big news within 15 minutes, no matter who I tell them you are. Look at the time. If someone like my mother, my other sister or my friend Xristos doesn't call in the next 10 minutes, I'll give you 20 euros!"

She giggled as he opened the door for her, which made him smile too.

"We'll see how funny you think it is when they're grilling you for two hours about the number of babies the women in your family have had!" he said, putting the key in the ignition.

She laughed outright this time, shaking her head. "It's not like I'm going to meet your family!"

"You just might," he teased. "I could make that happen just because you laughed at me—*then* we'll see how funny it is!"

The thought of meeting his family somehow made everything so real she suddenly didn't know what to say. What was she doing going for a drive with him? He was supposed to sign the papers and let her go back to her brief but exciting adventure.

"We'll drive down the coast," he said, pulling onto the street. "Poseidonos Avenue runs along the beach through a section called Glyfada, which actually has some fantastic shops and restaurants."

"I saw Glyfada on the map and the beaches are supposed to be wonderful," she said. "But I wasn't sure how far down I could go on the Metro."

"It takes you along that route and stops at quite a few of the beaches." He paused. "But I could take you to the beach. If you wanted to go."

"Apollo, I..." She glanced over at him. "You're being very sweet, but I'm not sure what we're doing."

"Getting to know each other again?" He cut a look in her direction.

"For what purpose? In four days I go back to Vegas and you'll be here..."

"I know, but..." His voice trailed off as the devil on his shoulder taunted him to ask her to stay a little longer, give them a chance to get to know each other. The weird thing was, he didn't know why he would even suggest it. With her going back to the States and him tied to the business here in Greece, they had no future. What was the point of getting to know each other if they had no chance of making it work? Except for the tiny little detail that they were *already* married. He couldn't explain it, but the idea of signing those papers made him sick and he had a feeling she wasn't all that keen on it either. Despite her protests about their future, he sensed that she wouldn't have come all the way to Greece if some part of her hadn't wanted to not just see him again, but *be* with him. Even if only for a little while.

3

"Aren't you going to finish your sentence?" she asked after a while, when she couldn't stand the silence or his incomplete thought.

"I don't know what to say," he admitted. "I'm a bit confused."

"About?"

"Everything! Paige, three years ago we spent three fun, passionate days together. For some inexplicable reason, on our last night together, we got *married*. We can say we were drunk, young, foolish—lots of words to describe the act itself, but what words describe the feelings? The subconscious desire to solidify something that should have been nothing more than a college tryst. I've done a lot of drinking in my life, especially in college, and I sure as shit didn't marry anyone else."

"It's easy in Vegas," she pointed out. "There are chapels everywhere, it costs almost nothing and there's no waiting period."

"True. It just feels…intentional. Why didn't I change my flight so I could stay another day and sort out the situation? Why didn't you go get confirmation, one way or another, before now? And when you get married, don't you usually get something in the mail from the state or the government?"

She grimaced. "I've never gotten married before, so I have no idea!"

They both started to chuckle, the absurdity of the whole thing hitting them harder than before.

"Listen," he said when they'd finally settled down. "Spend your vacation with me. I know there probably isn't a future for us, but you talked about closure… Does it seem right to end a marriage without at least solidifying our friendship and maybe making a few more memories along the way?"

She looked over at him suspiciously. "Apollo, I don't think—"

"I didn't mean sex!" he grunted, recognizing the wary look in her eyes. "Jesus, I know we don't know each other very well, but if you think that little of me, why would you have come to find me?"

"I don't think little of you," she protested. "But I have very distinct memories of…*that*."

"*That?*" He couldn't help an impish smile. "Does saying the word *sex* offend you? Would you rather we referred to *that* as making love?"

"I'm not embarrassed," she protested, though her cheeks held a tinge of pink. "I'm just a little overwhelmed. I came here thinking we'd have a conversation, maybe a drink. Then we'd go somewhere to find a notary so we could sign the papers, and we'd say our goodbyes. Now you want to spend time together—why? A guy like you probably has women falling all over themselves to be with you, so I don't believe you're trying to get laid. But even without sex, this has disaster written all over it. We spent three days together, and three years later, we're still fighting this…well, whatever this is."

"Attraction?" he supplied helpfully. "Chemistry? Passion?"

"If in three years we couldn't get over three days, can you imagine how hard saying goodbye is going to be after four more days—four sober days?"

"It just seems to me, if those three days made such an impact on us that we're still feeling the same…*attraction*…three years later, maybe we should explore why. Maybe this is the adventure of a lifetime—for both of us."

She turned to stare at him in shock, her eyes open so wide she was sure she looked ridiculous. Had he just suggested this was an *adventure*? How could he have known? How could he have said the exact word she'd been begging Tom to understand for over a year, after spending just three days with her more than three years ago?

"Do you like adventures?" she whispered when she finally found her voice.

"Of course—doesn't everyone?" He glanced at her curiously.

"Not everyone," she said softly. "Definitely not everyone."

"But you? You're interested in adventures, yes?"

Suddenly it didn't matter that she was certain to have her heart broken. It didn't matter that in four days she would fly out of his life forever. It didn't even matter if he ever signed those stupid papers—the only thing that mattered was the fact that he *knew*. Somehow, someway, he knew her like no one else, and he understood. She didn't know why or how, but she didn't have to. For four days, she was going to have an adventure. *With her husband.* And for four days, she was going to let herself love him. Because deep down, she knew she already did.

"Yes," she said, after a long pause.

"Yes, you like adventures?"

"Yes, I like adventures. Yes, I want to make more memories. Yes, I'd like to spend my vacation with you."

"Yes?"

His smile made her heart feel a little funny, but happy and excited too. "Definitely yes."

"What changed your mind?" he asked curiously.

"You knew about adventures," she whispered, feeling silly but not too embarrassed to say it out loud. "No one else has ever understood, but you do."

He wasn't completely sure what she was talking about, but whatever it was made her happy. Not just happy in general, but happy with him, and for the first time since his father's stroke, he felt truly happy again too.

For a long time after that, neither of them spoke. Paige stared out at the glistening waters on her right, mesmerized by the beauty and a little bit nervous that she'd given him such an all-encompassing *yes*. It didn't feel scary, though, and the comfortable silence between them was so natural she couldn't quite make sense of it. Instead, she focused on the beautiful beaches and the bright blue sky.

"There's a place on the beach nearby that has wonderful food," he said quietly. "Are you hungry?"

"I could eat," she nodded.

"Do you like seafood?"

"Love it! We don't get a lot of fresh seafood in Vegas."

"You're in for a treat then." He pulled off the highway into a large, busy parking lot. "We'll have to walk a little—the beaches are crazy during the summer and parking is limited."

"That's fine." She got out and looked around, loving the sound of the waves crashing nearby and the wind blowing through her hair.

"You look radiant," he said, coming around to look down into her face. "You really are on an adventure of some kind, aren't you?"

"Absolutely!" She grinned up at him. "But *I'm* not on an adventure—*we* are on an adventure."

He chuckled. "So we are." He leaned down to softly brush his lips across hers. Her eyes fluttered closed and he had to resist the urge to wrap his arms around her and press her against the car so he could feel that soft body against his. Damn, he couldn't figure out why he wanted her so much, but he had four days to convince her to let him have her. He didn't know if it was possible to give her whatever it was she was looking for, but he was sure as hell going to try.

"Come on," he said after a moment. He took her hand and led

her up the path that wound along the edge of a line of clubs, restaurants and beach entrances.

"This is so beautiful," she breathed, tugging on his hand to get him to stop walking. "I just…I want to take a minute to breathe it in and suck in as much of Greece as I can because I may never come back."

"Why wouldn't you come back?" he asked.

She shrugged. "Money. Time. Responsibility. Our whole generation is in a hurry to make the big career moves, find the right person, get married, have babies and plan for retirement. It feels like no one wants to enjoy the present because they're so worried about the future."

"I can understand that," he said slowly. "Sometimes you have to worry about the future because the world is a scary place. As the head of the family now, I don't want to have to worry that my parents won't have anything to eat or access to the medicine they need because we didn't plan for the future. However, here in Greece we tend to have a more relaxed attitude about working. Siesta in the afternoon, shorter hours some days of the week…you'll notice that the beaches, cafés and restaurants are packed, despite the struggling economy here right now. It's a different mindset."

"It's lovely," she said. "But I get the feeling that you don't have that relaxed attitude."

"That's not an option for me because of my father's stroke. If I hadn't stepped in immediately, and learned everything I could as quickly as possible, we could have lost everything. After more than a year, I'm still learning, still testing new business models to see what will help us grow in a terrible market." He looked out at the water. "I was just thinking earlier today that I missed the beach and having time to myself once in a while to enjoy life. Then you walked through that door with your silent plea for adventure—and here we are."

"Well, I'm going to need food if you want to adventure me around Greece," she teased.

"Let's go." He threaded his fingers through hers and they walked a few hundred meters to the restaurant. A middle-aged maître d' raised a hand and welcomed them warmly. They were immediately led to a table near the water and Paige just smiled happily as the men chattered in Greek.

"I ordered for us," he said hesitantly. "If you don't like what he brings, we can get other things, okay?"

"Okay." She brushed her hair back from her face, running her fingers through it and letting it fall where it would. Staring out at the sea, she felt as carefree as the wind. She didn't know exactly where she was, what she was going to eat or even what she should say, so she didn't even try. She just watched the waves fizzle out on the shore and the birds swoop down to find food.

Watching her, Apollo wondered what she was thinking that brought such contentment to her face. What was her life like back in Las Vegas that had her yearning for adventure? "So, tell me about your life," he said after they had drinks.

"Well, there's a new NHL team in Las Vegas now, the Sidewinders, and I work in the sales and marketing department, essentially selling ticket packages to companies."

"So the NHL expanded to Vegas," he said thoughtfully. He'd spent five years in New England getting his bachelor's degree and then his MBA, so he was well versed in hockey, though it wasn't a Greek sport. "I thought for sure it would be Seattle."

"That still might happen, but you know how political it can get."

"Do you like working for a sports team?"

"It's a great organization…I work with fun people and my boss is nice."

"And your friend…the one with the pink hair? I can't remember her name."

"Raegan." Paige flushed with pleasure that he remembered her.

"She's still my bestie. We're roommates now, share an apartment about 20 minutes from the Strip. She's a waitress at a casino, getting her MBA."

He nodded. "Good for her! What about you? Are you done with school?"

"I got my bachelor's in marketing, but I needed to get a job because I was tired of being broke. Of course, now my student loans are killing me, but that's a way of life in the U.S. Unless you're really lucky, you wind up with student loans."

"It was expensive," he agreed, "but the education I got made it worthwhile."

"I don't regret getting my degree," she said. "I just wish it hadn't cost so much. It won't be so bad if I start getting more bonuses. I got one in January for reaching 150% of my sales goal and that's how I bought the flight to Greece. I'd put it away for a rainy day, but after some things that happened two weeks ago, I decided this was a worthwhile expense."

"What happened two weeks ago?" he asked as the waiter brought a salad, a basket of bread and a dish of *tzatziki*.

"What's that?" she asked, breaking off a piece of bread and dipping it in a plate of some sort of white dip.

"It's called *tzatziki*," he explained. "Essentially yogurt, cucumbers, dill and garlic—a lot of garlic!"

"Oh my God." She closed her eyes as she chewed. "I'm having a foodgasm."

"A what?" he laughed.

"Foodgasm—combines food and orgasm."

He grinned. "I guess I never thought of it that way, but the food here is truly excellent."

"So far I agree."

"Tell me more about two weeks ago," he said.

"I don't want to talk about me," she said.

"You don't want to talk about you or you don't want to talk

about what happened two weeks ago? Does it have to do with almost getting engaged?"

She sighed, making a face. "Yeah."

"Who proposed?"

"Tom." She stabbed a tomato with her fork and put it in her mouth, thinking about what to say as she chewed. "We've been dating about 18 months and—"

"You're still together?" He couldn't help the rush of jealousy that coursed through his veins.

"No, of course not!" She shook her head. "We'd *been dating* for about 18 months and—"

"*We'd been* is different than *we've been*," he interrupted impatiently.

"Do you want to hear the story or not?" she scowled at him.

He couldn't help but chuckle at the annoyance on her face and had to admit he was being ridiculous. Until a couple of hours ago, he hadn't even realized she was legally his, so he didn't know where this jealousy was coming from. "Sorry," he said contritely. "Please go on."

"He proposed six months ago," she said softly. "And I wasn't ready. Even though it had been a year, it felt... I don't know, it's hard to explain. I can't tell you anything he does wrong. He's handsome, has a good job, works hard, is very sweet and generous with me, but..." She couldn't help the sigh that escaped. "I really can't articulate what I feel but I told him I wasn't ready and he was great about it, said he understood, and that he would ask again when the time was right."

"So two weeks ago..." he prompted.

"He staged this big thing," she said. "He invited our parents, our friends...but I didn't know anything about it. He just told me to meet him at our favorite restaurant. When I got there he went and asked my father for my hand..." She rested her chin in her palm as she recounted the rest of the events of the evening.

"You haven't spoken to him since?"

"There's nothing to say. He has no idea who I am, not really."

"So he's boring."

She sighed, not wanting to say that out loud.

"I guess I owe him one."

"Owe him one? For what?!" she demanded incredulously.

"Whatever happened that night prompted you to come find me," he said quietly.

She met his eyes. "Raegan said you're the reason I wasn't ready to settle down with him."

"What do you think?"

"I think we needed to see each other again."

"Now that you're here, I have to agree."

The waiter arrived with a big tray of food, putting down plates of things Paige didn't recognize and a few she did. When he was gone, she stared in fascination. "That's octopus, right? I've never seen it on a plate like that."

"That poor guy was probably still breathing a couple of hours ago," he said.

"Wow." She stuck her fork into one of the pieces and slowly put it in her mouth. She'd imagined it to be rubbery but it wasn't and the taste held a faint hint of chicken, though that wasn't exactly it. Chicken with a seafood flair? It was different but delicious, and she took another bite. This one was probably part of the head since it looked like a chunk of white meat instead of a tentacle, and she moaned. "Yummmmm."

He delighted in watching her explore the food on the table. From the octopus to calamari, *kasseri* to feta cheese, and both *tzatziki* and *taramosalata*—a spread made from fish eggs—she explored it all and ate with gusto. She didn't eat like most of the American women he'd gone to college with either; she genuinely enjoyed it and ate until she couldn't anymore. When she finally sat back with a groan of satisfaction, she met his eyes almost apologetically.

"I think that's the best meal I've ever had!" she said.

"It was delicious," he agreed. "I used to eat here often, but I don't get down this way much anymore."

"I would eat here every day!" she laughed.

"We'll discuss it again after I take you to George's."

"George's?"

"George's Steak House. It's a place in Glyfada that makes the best damn *biftekia* you'll ever eat."

"What is *biftekia*?"

"Think a cross between a meatball and a hamburger, but no bun or anything—a really big, glorified meatball. But so much more. The place doesn't look like much from the outside, but you won't know what hit you when you taste the food."

She grinned. "Works for me!"

"Would you like to sit here and chat or drive a little further down the coast? I think watching the sunset in Sounion would be fun. We could sit up by the Temple of Poseidon and watch it go down."

"Really?" She almost squealed with glee. "That sounds amazing! Thank you, Apollo."

"For showing you around my country? It's my pleasure."

"But how is this an adventure for *you*?" she asked. "None of this is new—you must be bored."

"Bored?" He chuckled. "I'm on the beach with a beautiful woman, enjoying food I love, interesting conversation and ignoring my phone—I promise I'm not bored!"

"You owe me 20 bucks, by the way!" she giggled.

"It's more like 25 U.S. dollars," he corrected. "But actually, I don't." He held out his phone, showing her a dozen missed calls. "My mother has called three times, my father once, my oldest sister twice, the younger one once, the guys at the office four times and my grandmother—who barely knows how to use a cell phone—once as well."

"Uh-oh."

He shrugged. "They'll get over it. I should call the office back, just in case it's about a customer, but if it's not I'll disconnect immediately. Do you mind?"

"Of course not." She leaned back and enjoyed the scenery as he called the office, trying not to giggle again as his voice grew distinctly annoyed.

He hung up with a huff and rolled his eyes. "The questions were endless."

"What did you tell them?"

"Nothing—I hung up."

"What are you going to tell people like your mother? The ones you really can't hang up on?"

He paused, his dark green eyes meeting hers. "The truth."

4

They were quiet when they got in the car, with Paige ruminating on what he'd said. Why would he tell everyone the truth? Didn't he want to make the break as painless as possible? She had no intention of telling anyone the truth and couldn't imagine why he would. She'd been too shocked to say anything at first and then the maître d' had come back to chat so she'd remained silent. Now that they were in the car, she wasn't sure what to say but felt like she needed to tell him what she thought.

"Apollo, we have to talk about what you said."

"Why? I keep certain parts of my life private—my sex life, for example—but in general, I think lies make things complicated. I don't want to be afraid I'll slip up, or someday when I'm about to get married, have my fiancée discover I was married in a drunken Las Vegas haze…"

She had to clench her jaw tightly at the thought of him being engaged to someone else—even though it was inevitable and she herself had almost gotten engaged. "But they'll probably think I'm some gold-digging bimbo and hate me! The idea was for us to part ways with happy memories, not ugliness from your family or hard feelings because I ruined your life or something."

"You've in no way ruined my life," he said gently. "And no one would ever think you were a bimbo."

She eyed him. "I may never have been to Greece, but I have several Greek-American friends and their mothers are super protective of their sons and extremely critical of the girls they married."

"My mother will certainly be critical—but she won't think you're a bimbo. She might have a thousand other things to say, about language and cultural differences, religion—since I doubt you're Greek Orthodox—and much more, but she won't think you're a tramp. She knows me better than that."

"She could definitely wonder about the gold-digger part, though."

He paused. "I suppose that's a possibility, but that's the case with every girl I've ever dated. My country is struggling economically right now, so we're lucky to be making money and doing well financially. The chance someone is after me for financial stability is nothing new, but since you knew nothing about me when we met three years ago and you came here with divorce papers, that doesn't really make sense, does it?"

"I just don't think we should tell anyone," she said quietly. "I'm only here for a few days and this thing with us—our adventure or whatever you want to call it—is private. I'd like you to respect that. Please."

He hesitated, thoughtful, but finally nodded. "I can respect it while you're here, but I'll certainly tell my family after you've gone."

"That's fair."

"We have about an hour's drive to Sounion. Tell me more about your life."

"I'm boring!" she protested. "You know where I live, what I do at my job and the reason I turned down my ex-boyfriend. What else is there?"

"Your family?"

"Oh. Well, my parents live about 20 minutes away in Henderson. My father is a college professor and my mother is a kindergarten teacher. My sister, Nicky, is a senior at UNLV and is going to be a teacher too."

"Very academic," he said with a smile. "No education career in your future?"

She shook her head. "It's not my thing."

"Teaching doesn't sound that exciting to me, either."

"Your turn," she said. "Tell me about your life."

"Well, I'm kind of boring right now too," he admitted. "My father had his stroke a little over a year ago and I immediately took over the business. I work seven days a week most of the time because I don't trust anyone to do what I do, which is almost everything. The sales guys bring in business, but I negotiate the deals, make sure the contracts are right, take care of the legalities, and keep up with each shipment from the time it leaves port until it arrives at its destination. Once I know it got where it was going, I let the sales guys take care of satisfaction surveys and follow-up unless a customer asks for me specifically, but I handle almost every detail of every shipment."

"That sounds exhausting."

"It is, but I didn't want to disappoint my father and now I'm so deeply immersed in everything, I don't even know *how* to slow down."

"You walked out today without a backward glance," she pointed out.

He nodded slowly. "It's the first time I've ever done that."

"I feel like I should apologize."

"Not at all—it's good for me to step back a little."

"I assume you're close to your family?"

He nodded. "Very. I have two older sisters; Sophia and Melina.

Sophia is 29 and married with a little boy. Melina had just come in as we were leaving today—she's 27 and has been dating this guy on and off since high school but they don't seem to be in a rush to get married. She works at a clothing store part-time and helps out at the shipping company on days like today when we don't have a receptionist. My mother pretty much fusses over my father these days, although he's much better. He still has a little trouble with fine motor skills like writing, but the physical therapy is helping. And my father's mother, *Yaya Thespina*, lives with my parents— she'd love you! She's a pistol."

"I'm sure." She paused. "So what do you do for fun?"

He cut a glance in her direction. "Are you trying to ask about my sex life or whether I'm dating?"

She laughed. "Not directly, no, but generally speaking—do you date?"

"Sure." He made a face. "But not with any regularity. As we discussed, my family's name is well-known because of the company and every father of a marriageable daughter within 50 miles has approached my parents with some sort of dowry and a dozen reasons why we'd be a good match. I avoid that nonsense, and luckily, my parents aren't overly excited about it either. I have an ex-girlfriend I used to see on occasion, but she gave me an ulti-matum about six months ago and I haven't seen her since. I'm busy and the idea of using my precious free time to make small talk feels too much like work, so mostly I don't bother."

"What do you do in your rare free time then?"

He grinned. "If it's summer or early fall, I'm at the beach. My friend Xristos and I both have motorcycles and we like to take off and ride down in this direction until we find a place to stop. Sometimes we meet friends, other times it's just the two of us. We like to swim and lie in the sun, occasionally fish. Other times we head to downtown Athens and go to a couple of clubs, have a few beers. We haven't done anything like that in ages, though. I just don't have the time and he's broke. I tried to offer him a job at the company, but he's proud and doesn't want charity. It's tough right now."

"What does he want to do?"

"He went to school for computers, but there are no jobs right now and though he could probably get one in England, his mother is ill and he doesn't want to leave. Cancer, you know? Her chances aren't good so I think he'll stay until she's gone."

"How sad," she said quietly.

"Yes. Anyway, that's my life. What should we talk about now?"

She laughed. "Anything you want! Tell me about where we are and what I'm looking at."

Apollo seemed enthusiastic about that idea and launched into a lengthy description of each of the little towns they passed and some of the historical highlights. There were hills and houses on the left and miles of clear, azure waters on the right. She longed to put her feet in and told him so.

"Let's go find you a suit," he suggested. "Then we can go for a swim. Mine is always in the car, along with towels."

"I can't really afford—"

"I know," he interrupted gently. "Let me do this for you. I have the money and it was my idea for us to come down here."

"I have a suit at the hotel. We can go to the beach tomorrow."

"Tomorrow I have meetings in the morning I can't miss, and then I want to take you to Monastiraki."

"What's that? I saw the name in the guidebook."

"It's a touristy area, but it's in an old, historic part of the city right near the Acropolis. You could shop—there's a little of every-thing and some of it is dirt cheap. For a couple of dollars you can find Italian Murano glass pendants and items like real leather shoes and handbags for reasonable prices. Not to mention souvenirs. We can eat down there and later in the day, when it's not so hot, we'll climb the Acropolis. So today we should swim."

She looked down. "Okay. But you can't buy me a lot of things.

Tom was always buying me things and it made me feel like I owed him."

"You owe me nothing except four days of your company and that beautiful smile."

"Okay."

"There's just one condition."

She narrowed her eyes. "What?"

"I pick the bathing suit."

She shook her head. "I'm not wearing a thong or going topless or anything like that."

"Not a chance in hell," he said gruffly. "While I appreciate a sexy woman's body, when that woman is *mine*, I don't want anyone else to see that much. Sexy is good, showing some cleavage maybe, but your ass and breasts? That's not for anyone but me."

"Even though I'm not really yours?"

He set his jaw and met her eyes. "Until I sign those papers, technically you're absolutely mine."

She wasn't sure what to say, but had to look away, afraid he would see the flush of happiness that washed over her and warmed her from the inside out. "A lot of guys would go out of their way to take advantage of a situation like this."

"That's not who I am, *koukla mou*."

"What does that mean?" she asked softly.

"Literally, it means *my doll*, but the expression is a term of endearment like *honey* or *sweetheart*."

"I wish I knew some Greek."

"You will by the time you leave!" He pulled off the highway and into a little beachside area. "I think we can find something here. You ready?"

"As I'll ever be!"

. . .

*A*n hour later they were chest-deep in water with the most spectacular view. There were mountains on one side where, if she looked up, she could see the Temple of Poseidon. Hills with white boxes that were actually houses were on another side, with the water's endless horizon if she looked straight out. The sea was warm and as smooth as glass today, and she let her body relax into a floating position, the salt content high enough to keep her buoyant.

Apollo had bought her a gorgeous turquoise one-piece bathing suit that was strapless and high-cut on the sides, well above her hips. It hugged her curves in all the right places, offering the slightest peek of cleavage at the top but covering everything else. She felt sexy and relaxed, and when his strong arms came up under her, pulling her upper body against his chest so that she could rest the back of her head on his shoulder, she didn't even try to hide her sigh of contentment.

"I haven't touched you in three years," he murmured against her temple. "I will absolutely respect your boundaries, but you have to tell me what they are."

"Do I have to decide now?" she asked, covering his forearms with her hands. His arms overlapped just under her breasts, holding her close to him, and she nearly shivered with longing. In the three years since he'd touched her, no one had made her feel so sexy or aroused from such a simple gesture.

"Not about everything." He pressed a kiss to the side of her face. "But you'll probably need to decide about whether or not I can kiss you in the next five seconds."

"I don't need five seconds to make that decision." She turned in his arms and tilted her face up to his. When his lips found hers, they were hesitant, nipping and tentatively caressing, as if waiting for her signals. They'd kissed a lot during their brief time together in Las Vegas, and time hadn't dulled the excitement she felt when he did it.

When his tongue slipped between her lips she instinctively wrapped her legs around his waist so the water didn't move her away from him. Her arms closed around his neck and in that moment, as their tongues came together in a lazy tangle, she could all but feel him taking back what was his. Three years of longing came crashing down on both of them, memories of their intimacy washing over them in a tidal wave of arousal that hit them both at once.

"Fuck," he growled, pulling his mouth from hers. "If sex is off-limits, this has to stop now, because another few minutes and I'm going to be inside you, right here in front of the whole beach."

"That might not be a good idea," she panted, her breath coming in little gasps. "I don't think I'll like Greek jails."

He gave her a sexy grin. "Most likely not, but it'd be worth every damn minute for me."

"Oh, Apollo." She buried her face in his neck, letting her legs drop down and float out behind her.

"What is it, *koukla mou*?"

"I don't want to say no—I don't want to set *any* limits."

"But?"

"But we have to." She raised her head to look into the liquid emerald of his eyes. "Don't we? We're picking up right where we left off and that's just going to make saying goodbye even harder. I cried when you left."

"Did you?" He put his hand on her cheek and used his thumb to stroke it.

"For a *week*."

"I'm sorry, *koukla*."

"I think letting you make love to me would take that to a whole other level of longing... This trip was about closure, not reopening the wound."

"Was it a wound?" he asked softly, staring into her eyes with so much tenderness she nearly started to cry.

"Maybe not for a 22-year-old guy on spring break, but for a

girl like me? You took a piece of my heart with you when you left, and I came here to get it back. If you keep touching me…looking at me like you are now, I'll be lost in you all over again."

"Even horny 22-year-old college students recognize something special when they find it," he said, his eyes never leaving hers. "I missed you. I kicked myself for weeks for just handing you that stupid business card and walking away—why didn't I just ask for your number?—as if a shy, sensitive girl like you was going to come after me!" He rolled his eyes in disgust. "I was so fucking stupid."

"You missed me too?" Her voice was a tiny whisper, her eyes unable to be torn from his smoldering gaze.

"For months," he said. "I kept trying to think of a reason to get back to Las Vegas, but I didn't have your number or know where you lived. I had finals and then there was some family drama…. My parents came for graduation and it seemed like it was better—or at least easier—to let it go."

"Tell the truth," she said intently. "All this time—did you believe we were married?"

"In my heart, I did. I wasn't sure, but since I never heard from you, I told myself I was being silly, that we obviously weren't. I kind of hoped so, though."

"Why?"

"Because then I'd have a reason to see you again."

"You're making this really hard," she whispered.

"Stay with me," he whispered back. "You must have more than four days of vacation. Spend a month here with me. Let's get to know each other. Let's find out what drove two otherwise rational, level-headed college students to walk into a Las Vegas chapel and elope after knowing each other for only a few days."

"Alcohol?"

He shook his head. "I've never known alcohol to change a person's heart. Lower inhibitions? Yes. Make you more daring? Absolutely. Take away a filter? Undoubtedly. But to change who you are at your core? I don't believe it. You see it happen all the time…the guy who's always been in love with the girl but would never admit it for fear of rejection? Then he gets shit-faced and shouts his feelings from the rooftops. The alcohol made him braver, but it didn't change him—he *already* loved her. So we had a reason for doing what we did. Let's figure it out, Paige. Stay longer."

"I can't afford—"

"Shh." He put a finger over her lips. "I have a house. You can stay with me—in the guest room if you want. No pressure, no sex if that's a hard limit, and enough time for us to reconnect."

"I, I can't…my job…" she faltered.

"It's summer," he protested. "Hockey teams can't be busy right now."

"The team isn't, but I sell a lot of season ticket packages in the summer."

"I have a plan on my landline that allows unlimited calls to the U.S. for one flat fee—both at home and at the office—you could work for a while every day to keep up with that. You can use my computer and do what you need to do. Give me a month, Paige."

"I…" She didn't even know how to say no. She wanted him so bad it hurt, and his selflessness made her heart yearn for him even more.

"Thirty days," he whispered against her ear, his lips gently sucking the lobe into his mouth, earring and all.

"Apollo…" His name came out choppy, gooseflesh breaking out on her skin despite the heat.

"I know, *koukla*…I want you too." He brought her legs up around his waist again, adjusting her so that his erection pressed against her crotch. "Look what you're doing to me—you can't leave in four days, Paige."

"I don't think they'll give me a month," she murmured. "I can try to get a couple of weeks."

"We'll take care of that tomorrow," he said, gently untangling their bodies and putting a few feet between them in the water. "Right now, I have to get my dick under control. Later, when we're not in public, we'll talk about this again."

"Apollo…" She reached out a hand and he immediately grasped it in his, pausing to look at her quizzically. "I went three years without your touch—I don't think I could stand not touching you while I'm here."

His eyes darkened with a plethora of emotions she couldn't quite identify, and then he was yanking her against him again, his mouth taking hers like a man possessed. "Keep this up," he growled, "and after I get done with you, we'll be spending your vacation in that Greek jail we talked about."

"I'm beginning to think you were right about it being worth it."

5

They rented two lounge chairs with a shared umbrella and alternated between getting in the water to cool off, sunning themselves, and putting up the umbrella to stave off the midday sun. They talked and ordered drinks, catching up on a lifetime of stories, funny anecdotes from their jobs and random topics that seemed to make conversation flow easily. By the time the sun had gotten a little lower in the sky, they were sunburned and hungry, but Apollo had one more thing he wanted to do before they left Sounion.

"Where are we going?" she asked as they drove up the winding road that led to the Temple of Poseidon.

"I told you we were going to watch the sunset from up there and that's what we'll do."

"It's late—is it still open?"

"It's a quarter of eight and they're open until sundown, which will be in about ten minutes. I may be able to convince them to let us stay a bit longer."

She just smiled, not really caring about the details. It had been a spectacular day, and though the sexual tension was so thick between them it was hard to think about anything else, at some point in the afternoon she'd decided to let it all go. Her doubts about him, concern about the potential for leaving Greece with a broken heart, and her resistance to her quickly growing hunger for him simply drifted into the ether as she lost herself in his deep, slightly accented voice and those damn captivating green eyes.

They parked and walked up another hill, their hands linked between them. Apollo gave the man at the gate some money and they breezed past him, heading up an incline towards the temple.

Standing in front of the large ancient structure, Paige felt a moment of overwhelming awe. She'd known these buildings existed, but being right in front of one was breathtaking. She remembered reading about it in Homer's 'The Odyssey,' and then hearing about its history in high school. She'd been fascinated by the idea of a god of the sea, and though Poseidon was only a mythological figure, she could picture some sort of ethereal being haunting these incredible marble columns.

"What are you thinking with such a serious face?" Apollo asked before wrapping his arms around her from behind.

"Wondering what Poseidon looked like, if he ever existed, and what kinds of parties he would have had in a temple like this."

Apollo smiled at her imagination, captivated by how much his country's history enthralled her. "I'm sure they would have been wild," he chuckled. "Although all those things you hear about the Greeks and Romans being orgy-crazy perverts is mostly untrue. A lot of our ancient artwork depicts plenty of that stuff, but historians are fairly sure it was more fantasy than reality."

"Personally, I think reality probably falls somewhere in between the evidence left behind and the way the historians and scientists interpret it," she said, leaning against him.

"I agree."

"So let's pretend the parties were wild!" she laughed.

"Okay." He let her guide them along, as she circled the building, studying the columns, the pediment and even the cracks in certain pieces of marble. "What has you so fascinated?" he asked.

"Lord Byron—the British poet?—supposedly carved his name somewhere. I hoped to get a picture but we can't get close enough."

Apollo frowned. "I didn't know that." He looked around, wondering if they could sneak past the barriers, but it was strictly prohibited and despite their jokes about going to jail, he knew they could receive a hefty fine if they were caught.

"It's okay." She nudged him, as if she knew exactly what he was thinking. "I have much more exciting plans than spending the night in jail!"

"Yeah?" He looked down at her in amusement. "Like what?"

"Didn't you say something about *biftekia* or whatever?"

He laughed. "Tomorrow. Tonight I was thinking we could order in…relax a little."

"Okay."

They settled on a rock, where he positioned her in front of him between his legs, so they could stare out at the most glorious sunset she'd ever seen. His arms closed around her waist and they were quiet, enjoying the intimacy of their togetherness and the magic of the brilliant colors in the sky. It was a kaleidoscope of orange, yellow and red, adding a surreal glow to the building and the entire area around it. Paige leaned back, lost in the real-life fairy tale she was suddenly caught up in. She'd been almost positive that once she saw him again, and spent time with him, she'd realize how silly her fantasies had been. Instead, reality was so much better than what she remembered and she didn't want this to end. The idea of extending her vacation so she could stay with him was ludicrous, but if she could manage it with work, she was going to. She didn't care that she barely knew him; she needed to be with him for this short time like she needed to breathe. This was her adventure. *The* adventure. Possibly the only one she would ever need.

. . .

*W*hen traces of the sun were almost gone, they headed back to his car and for the first time she realized it was a Porsche. She wanted to tell him how gorgeous it was, but for some reason it seemed irrelevant. The only things on her mind were figuring out how to get an extra week or two of vacation and trying to keep her heart intact while still enjoying every minute she could with him.

"We should stop by your hotel and get your things," he said as they headed back towards Athens.

"I think…" she paused, trying to articulate what she wanted to say. "I think I should stay at my hotel tonight."

"Why? So you can second-guess yourself and get on the first flight out in the morning?" He cut his eyes to her and she could see he was kidding. Mostly.

"No." She reached out to slide her hand into his. "You have early meetings and you probably need to rest. I'm still a little off with jet lag, and I need to sleep too. It would also give us a little time to digest—not run away!" She laughed at his snort. "We talked about all these emotions and three-year-old feelings…let's get a good night's sleep so we can just mull it all over. We're talking about spending an extended amount of time together pretending to be married."

"Not pretending," he said evenly. "We *are* married."

"You know what I mean—we're not married in the true sense of the word."

"We're married in the legal and emotional senses of the word," he said. "We just never had the chance to get to know each other, which is what I suggested we do."

"Tomorrow you're going to walk into your office and be bombarded with questions. Your family is going to call, demanding to know where you were today, and you're going to have to decide what to tell them. I want you to know that if you change your mind—about having me stay, telling them the truth, any of it—I understand. I didn't come here to disrupt your life and it feels like that's what I'm doing."

"What it feels like," he corrected mildly, "is you trying to backpedal. I want you to stay with me, but I don't want to force you. If you're nervous or uncomfortable, I'll sign the papers and let you go home. This adventure only works if we both want it."

"I want it," she whispered. "Just not tonight. I need one night to think about everything that happened today so I can see you again tomorrow with a clear head. The first time, we screwed everything up because we were frantic to do it all... So much passion, sex, alcohol—total chaos that had you rushing off to make your flight. Let's not mess it up this time. If I can get some extra vacation, we'll have a couple of weeks to do all that. We don't have to do it all today. And I'm really, really sleepy."

He smiled, squeezing her hand. "That makes sense, *koukla*."

She closed her eyes, reclining against the soft leather, grateful he was still holding her hand and that he'd understood she needed just a little space to gather her thoughts.

He turned on the radio, wondering what was going on in her head and if she really just needed some time to adjust to the idea of them spending a few weeks together. She was a little skittish, but he couldn't blame her. A young woman in a foreign country by herself, suddenly immersed in an experimental relationship with a man she was married to but didn't really know. It was a little overwhelming for him too, and this was his home, where he had backup if anything went wrong. Not that he would need help, but as a woman she probably felt vulnerable and he understood that. He would give her tonight, but part of him worried that she would run and not give him a chance to prove that he cared for her. He didn't believe in love at first sight, but there had been something magical between them the first time their eyes locked. He'd wanted her physically, but there was a mischief in her eyes that attracted him beyond the bedroom. As soon as they'd started talking he'd known she was different. Sweet and a little bit innocent, but with an incredible sense of fun and a desire to explore the world, he'd convinced her to zip-line over Fremont Street, ride an electric bull and...marry him.

Though he hadn't admitted it to her, he hadn't known if what they'd done was legal, but he'd been positive that they'd done it. He'd fallen hard and fast for the hazel-eyed beauty and he'd spent two days wondering how to get her to go home to Greece with him. The panic in her eyes the next morning, though, had given him second thoughts. She'd been terrified, worried about what she would tell her parents, how she would finish school...so many things he hadn't even considered when he'd teased her into going into that chapel with him. Then the marriage certificate had disappeared and he'd begun to wonder if he'd imagined it—or if they'd gone into one of the many make-believe places in Las Vegas that gave people the experiences they wanted: a gondola ride in Venice, a walk through Parisian gardens, and so much more. So he'd gotten on his flight and figured she would call once she found out one way or another. Instead, that call never came and he'd resigned himself to living with his stupidity. He'd thought she was gone forever. Until she walked into his office this morning and turned his life upside down. He'd wanted her three years ago and he wanted her now, but this time he wouldn't let her go without a fight.

She mumbled something under her breath and he turned. "What, honey?"

"Our song," she murmured. "Turn it up."

He frowned and turned up the radio to hear "Marry You" by Bruno Mars. As he listened, the memories came rushing back and he felt her squeeze his hand. He hadn't allowed himself to listen to this song in three years; it had been too depressing. He could hear her humming along, even half-asleep, and he smiled, knowing that she still considered it their song. Although she didn't know it, it was dancing to this song at a nightclub that had given him the idea of marrying her. Maybe now it would bring him luck again.

· · ·

He woke up early, silencing the alarm on his phone quickly so it didn't wake her. She stirred, though, moving against him like a lazy cat. A smile played on her lips and she nestled closer. "You were supposed to go home," she murmured.

"We both fell asleep," he chuckled. "Sorry."

"What time is it?"

"Six. I've got to get home, shower and get ready for my 8:30 meeting. Can I call you in a few hours?"

She nodded. "I might go for a walk—text me if I'm not here." She handed him her phone, assuming he would know to send himself a text, which he did.

"Go back to sleep, *koukla*," he whispered, kissing the side of her face. "I'll pick you up around one."

"Okay." She flipped onto her stomach and was lightly snoring when he left.

He got to his office at 8:00 and let out a groan when he saw the lights on and several cars in the lot, including Melina's. This would be fun. Or not. But he had two Italian millionaires meeting with him in half an hour for a multimillion-dollar contract, so he didn't have time for games today. He strode into his office in an expensive Armani suit, a tie, Italian leather shoes and his Rolex watch. He normally didn't play up his looks with expensive clothes, but this contract was too big, and there was too much at stake for him to not bring his A game. Even though his mind was back at that hotel with Paige, he knew he wouldn't be able to do anything else until he closed this deal. It would be huge for both himself and the company, and would give them the boost they needed to reach the next level of success in the shipping world.

"*Kalimera!*" Tasos called out, letting out a low whistle. "Aren't you a stud today!"

"This is the biggest deal we've ever had to broker," Apollo snapped back, glaring at his friend. "So knock it off and go put on a tie!"

"*Baba* sent these," Melina said, handing him two thick files from their father. She was dressed in a power suit as well, something that almost never happened, and he gave her a grateful smile, knowing she was prepared to be at his side. Though he knew it was probably killing her, he also sensed that she wouldn't even contemplate asking about Paige until the meeting was over.

"*Efharisto.*" *Thank you.*

She followed him into his office. "*Baba* said to call him as soon as you got in."

"I will." He glanced up. "Thanks for dressing up."

She arched a brow at him. "Did you think I wouldn't be here to help? Don't be ridiculous."

He dialed his father's number and waited for the explosion on the other end. Though he'd texted his sister last night and asked her to tell everyone he'd taken an old friend from college sightseeing, he knew they were all still mad.

"Where have you been?!" the older man roared.

"*Baba*, stop," he said impatiently. "We don't have time for this today. I needed to clear my head yesterday—walk away from everything so I could be fresh this morning. I took a friend to Sounion for the afternoon, dropped her off at her hotel and was in bed by nine. I needed a break in order to be ready today. I've been working on this deal for three months. Don't insult me by insinuating that I was out partying or shirking my responsibilities."

There was a brief silence on the other end. "I understand she was a beautiful distraction."

Apollo chuckled. "Yes. Yes, she was."

"Later you will tell me. Now, what is the plan?"

They talked last-minute strategy and after five minutes disconnected. He glanced at the clock. 8:17. He literally had three minutes. Without hesitation, he dialed the hotel and asked for her room number.

"*Kalimera!*" she laughed, answering the phone. "I'm still in Greece!"

"*Kalimera*, beautiful." He couldn't help but smile at her accented but discernible attempt at Greek.

"Don't you have a big meeting?" she asked.

"In 12 minutes," he said. "But I wanted to hear your voice."

"You promised to give me some space last night," she said, her voice only slightly accusing. "And then you stayed."

"I swear, you got on the bed after we ate and I fell asleep on the chair. I woke up about midnight and I was damned if I was driving home at that point. But I respected your wishes that we not have sex, and I left before you woke up."

She laughed. "Yeah, yeah. I'm not sure I believe all that, but I'm willing to give you the benefit of the doubt. Good luck today, okay?"

"Thank you." He glanced at the time. "I have to run, *koukla*, but I'll text you to let you know how it's going or when it's over."

"Since we're supposed to go to the Acropolis tonight, I was thinking I'd go to the Acropolis Museum this morning—what do you think?"

"I've been multiple times," he nodded. "So that's a good idea. It's within walking distance of your hotel."

"Okay, then have a successful meeting and I can't wait to hear all about it!"

"Thanks, honey. See you later." He disconnected and smiled. Then he picked up the two files on his desk.

. . .

he meeting ran late, the two businessmen asking to see documentation, customs records from different countries, and all kinds of demonstrations about how they did things. At 1:30, Melina ordered lunch and Apollo snuck off to his office to text Paige.

Meeting is still going—I'm sorry. Please do something fun today and don't let me spoil it for you. It can't go more than a couple more hours.

I'm still at the museum—it's amazing and there's so much to see and study. I'm having lunch here at the café. Don't worry about me. Just close your deal and we'll celebrate tonight!

He let out a breath he hadn't been aware he was holding and leaned back against the door of his office, looking out at the water. These guys were breaking his balls just because they could and he sensed he was losing them. He had to do something to turn it around and quickly. He'd taken a gamble once on a sweet girl in Vegas and somehow she'd come back to him; maybe it was time to take more gambles. Doing this by the book didn't seem to be working out and he probably only had one more chance. He took off his jacket and laid it on the back of his chair, loosening his tie at the same time. He rolled up his sleeves, revealing the tattoo of an eagle on his forearm, and stuck his phone in his pocket. If they wanted to play hardball, he could play too.

"Forgive me, *Baba*," he murmured under his breath.

He walked back into the conference room and ignored his sister's wide-eyed surprise and the curious glances from the Italians at his change in appearance. He sank into his chair and leaned back, allowing his sister to set out the food that had just arrived. He waved it away when she put a plate in front of him and feigned disinterest as they ate. Melina and the head of sales, Marcos, kept up a steady stream of chatter, answering questions about the beaches and nightlife in Athens, while he remained aloof. He let the tension build until the food had been cleared away and everyone seemed to be waiting for him to say or do something.

"Did you have more questions?" he asked smoothly, looking from one to the other. "We've shown you everything except how big our dicks are—would that help move things along?"

He could almost feel Melina's startled gasp, but the elder of the two Italians burst out laughing. "Ah, yes, business is often a... What is the American phrase? Pissing contest?"

"I don't really like those kinds of games," Apollo shrugged. "My company has a solid reputation and dozens of references. I've given you my entire morning and you're still undecided. If there is something I can actually show you, or some part of the contract you'd like to discuss specifically, I'll sit here all day. However, if your intention is simply to wear me down or, as you say, compete in a *pissing contest* because you can, I have other aspects of my business to run. We'd very much like your business, but we have done and will continue to do quite well without it."

The two men looked at each other and this time it was the younger man who spoke. "Sometimes we like to see what the men we do business with are made of—beyond the contracts and spreadsheets."

"And are you convinced that I meet your standards?"

"We'd like to have dinner tonight and wrap this up in an informal setting."

"I have plans this evening with an old friend from the U.S.," Apollo said quietly. "She's only here a few days and these plans have been in place for a long time. It would be incredibly rude for me to cancel them."

"This is excellent—since it's a woman, she can join us and the ladies can perhaps chat while we conclude our business."

The look in the older man's eye was almost a dare, as if he didn't believe Apollo actually had an American friend in town. So Apollo smiled and inclined his head. "Then I'm sure she wouldn't mind. What time?"

They finalized plans for the evening and at last the Italians were gone. When Melina started to say something, he held up a hand silencing her. "Not one word until I've had a drink." He strode into his office and sank into his chair, yanking open the bottom drawer of his desk. He pulled out a bottle of aged Kentucky whiskey—a gift one of his fraternity brothers from Yale sent every year at Christmas—and poured two fingers into a tumbler. He tossed it back in one shot, letting it burn its way down his esophagus. Then he opened his eyes and met the curious gazes of Melina, Tasos and Marcos.

"You were brilliant," Melina said softly, surprising him.

He snorted. "Yeah, we'll see how brilliant I am when they take their business to Papaspirou."

"They're not taking their business to those crooks!" Marcos rolled his eyes.

"It's been a long day already," Apollo waved a hand. "Go on home, Marcos. Tasos, you can leave at three. Melina, you don't need to stay either."

She chuckled. "Nice try, little brother. I'm not going anywhere until we talk."

"On that note, I'm going home!" Marcos laughed.

"I've got phones to answer," Tasos mumbled.

When they were alone, Melina strode around behind the desk, pulled out the bottle of whiskey and poured herself a shot. Instead of downing it like he'd done, she perched on the edge of his desk and looked down at him. She took a delicate sip of the whiskey and smiled as it went down, and then held it on her lap as she cocked her head.

"Whatever happened yesterday, you're going to tell me anyway, so why torture both of us?"

He chuckled, knowing she was probably right. He was close to Melina, more so than Sophia. Whether it was because they were closer in age or because they'd both enjoyed going to school in the

U.S. more than Sophia had, he wasn't sure, but he trusted her with almost everything and her support today meant the world to him.

"Who is she?" she pressed.

"If I tell you," he said quietly, not meeting her gaze. "You have to give me your word that you won't tell anyone. Not Mama or *Baba*, and definitely not Sophia. Your word of honor, Lena."

She looked startled. "Of course."

"She's my wife."

6

An hour later he was parked in front of Paige's hotel, watching her come out the front doors. He jumped out of the car so he could take her suitcase. He paused to press his lips to hers and couldn't resist sliding his tongue between them, just enough to get a taste. The answering hitch in her breath made him wish he hadn't agreed to go to dinner tonight, but they were committed now and he grudgingly pulled away.

"I have a lot to tell you," he murmured, putting her suitcase in the back.

"I can't wait to hear all about it." She got into the passenger seat and looked at him expectantly. "Did you close the deal?"

"Not exactly." He explained the way the day had gone. "And when I told them I already had plans tonight, they kind of called me on it. How mad are you?"

"Why would I be mad?" she frowned. "I just don't know if I have anything appropriate to wear. I only brought shorts, T-shirts and that dress you saw yesterday. I don't have anything for an evening with people like that."

"I guess we'll have to go shopping." He glanced over at her. "Will you let me buy you something for tonight?"

She chuckled. "Since it's your fault I have to go, yes."

He grinned. "Did you eat?"

"Yup. I spent the second-best day ever at the Acropolis Museum. I could spend another few hours looking at the reconstructed pieces of the frieze from the Parthenon."

"The second-best day ever?" he asked. "What was the best?"

She grinned. "Yesterday, of course!"

"I'm not sure I can top it, because your first sunset at the Temple of Poseidon is pretty memorable, but I'd like to try."

"You don't have to top anything," she said. "Just being together is nice."

"I think so too." He reached for her hand. "How about we drive to my house, you can drop off your things, and then we'll go shopping?"

"Sure."

He nodded. "The house needs a lot of work, but the architecture and the view blew me away so I bought it anyway. I just haven't had time to get work done."

"You know I don't care about that!"

"The kitchen is a disaster, but I don't cook."

"Me either," she giggled. "I'm good at a lot of things, but cooking isn't one of them. Is that grounds for divorce?"

He laughed. "Nope. Not for me, anyway."

"Oh good."

*I*t took nearly 40 minutes to get to his house with traffic but she was awed as they pulled into his parking space underneath the building. It was a white concrete square shape that appeared to have three floors, and she could see at least one balcony as well as some sort of rooftop space that was lined with a wrought iron fence.

"Is the whole house yours?" she asked in surprise.

"All mine," he chuckled. "Just remember, it needs work."

"Are you trying to impress me, Mr. Lakkas?" she asked, her eyes twinkling.

"Well, Mrs. Lakkas, it's more like I'm hoping you're not overly disappointed."

"Disappointed? You have a three-story house on the beach!" She shook her head. "It's gorgeous! And I'll bet the kitchen isn't that bad."

He coughed. "Okay, sure. Let's go with optimism." He carried her suitcase and she followed with her small carry-on size bag. They walked up a short flight of stairs and he held open the door for her. The main floor was bright and sunny, but he hadn't been kidding about work being needed. The floors were bare concrete and the only furniture was a couch that looked like it had seen better days.

"There's no floor," she joked, giving him a bland look.

"There's a floor," he protested. "It's just not a *pretty* floor."

"Window treatments?"

"Why would I want to block my view of the sea?"

"In case your wife was in here naked."

He leaned against the wall and took his time looking her up and down, his eyes lingering on the swell of her breasts and long legs. "Then I'd buy window treatments...because the only person who gets to see my wife naked is me."

She swallowed at the passion in his voice. Damn, sex was going to happen sooner rather than later and while she'd been fantasizing about it since the last time they'd done it, she wasn't sure she was ready for the intensity she could see in his face.

"Do I make you nervous?" he asked softly, moving closer to her but keeping a little space between them. "You don't have to stay here, *koukla*. We can do the nasty at your hotel."

"It's not nasty," she whispered. "And yes, *you* make me a little nervous, but only because there's so much...*everything*...between us. My memories are of the most amazing sex of my life and I'm afraid..."

"You're afraid that you've built them up in your mind and now the real thing will be a disappointment."

"It's just that every other person I've had sex with has literally been a total disappointment and I don't know why you weren't."

He reached for one of her hands and slowly brought it to his lips. "Because it's us," he said, kissing the back of her hand before turning it over and pressing light kisses on her palm, her wrist and trailing them further up the inside of her arm. "But don't worry, I won't rush you. I'll wait until you're comfortable."

She closed her eyes, enjoying the sensation of his lips on her skin and remembering what it was like when he kissed her in other places.

"Come on. Let me show you the rest of this mess." He squeezed her hand in his and led her up more stairs.

"So that's all there was down there? A living room?"

"Living room, toilet with a clothes washer—washing machine?" He frowned.

She smiled. "Yes. Your English is so good… I've always meant to ask where you learned. You had to have been already fluent to attend a university like Yale."

He nodded. "Yes. My parents sent me to special classes to start learning when I was young—all three of us actually—and then I took it in high school and really excelled. I speak Spanish fluently as well, though I don't use it as often so I've forgotten a lot. I've been losing a bit of my English too, because I don't use it in business as much as I thought I would."

"I used to speak Spanish too, but like you said, when you don't use it, you forget a lot. By the way, *donde está el baño?*"

He laughed. "The bathroom is right over there. One of them anyway. Go ahead and I'll put your bags in the guest room."

She paused, turning to look at him. "We both know that's silly. I'm a little nervous but there's no doubt what's going to happen."

He kissed the side of her face. "Then the guest room will act as a dressing room for you, because I'm sure you like to spread out your clothes and makeup and such."

She just smiled and shut the bathroom door behind her.

He showed her the rest of the house, including his complete disaster of a kitchen. He hadn't been kidding when he'd said it needed a lot of work. The floor was also bare concrete and the sink consisted of one of those giant soaking sinks found in many American laundry rooms. The refrigerator was college dorm-sized and there were no cabinets or usable counters. There was half a counter with an empty cabinet underneath, a folding table against one wall that had a microwave on it, and nothing else except dust bunnies.

Paige gave him a sideways glance. "I can't even make excuses for this room."

He laughed. "Maybe you could give me some suggestions on what to do with it."

She arched a brow. "Refrigerator, stove, cabinets, countertops…tile? Maybe a dishwasher?"

"That's all doable. The problem is time and details. What color cabinets? What type of flooring? Dark or light countertops? Is granite worth the extra investment?"

"Oh, absolutely! Then you don't have to worry about putting a hot pan down—it has to be incredibly hot to burn or damage granite."

"Good to know." He showed her a small dining room and then an odd little room off to the side that appeared to be an office in the making, with a desk, leather chair, file cabinet and bookshelves. There were boxes everywhere, though, and it appeared that other than a phone and a computer, the room wasn't fully functional. "I'd like to be able to work from home sometimes," he explained. "But again, I haven't had the time to get it set up."

"Lots of potential," she nodded. "And there's a real floor!"

"It's odd—the hardwood floors were here when I bought it and it was the only room that had them. I had them buffed and cleaned up and they're beautiful. I was thinking of having them installed in the bedrooms too."

They climbed up to the top floor where there were three bedrooms. The floors were bare, but the master bedroom and guest room both had area rugs and the master bathroom had beautiful ceramic tile. It was the only room in the house that could be considered finished, with a gorgeous tiled shower, the most amazing sink she'd ever seen—made from some sort of multicolored glass that incorporated every color of the rainbow— set atop a brass base, and stunning light fixtures above the mirror. There was a wooden cabinet against the wall opposite the toilet, undoubtedly a place for toiletries and maybe hand towels. It was aesthetically pleasing, modern and functional; it was obvious he'd put a lot of thought into it.

"So..." Her eyes twinkled with mirth. "The bathroom was important to you."

He smiled. "The toilet was nonexistent, requiring me to squat over a hole in the floor to do my business."

She wrinkled her nose. "Really?"

He nodded. "The plumbing, electrical and this bathroom were my priorities because the water pressure was so bad, and the plumbing so antiquated that I got no water up here at all. And honestly, showering, shaving, using the facilities—those aren't optional. I don't have to cook. I don't care if there's concrete on the floor as long as it's clean. I'm not home enough to worry about the living room...but a few things had to be done before I could even move in. The floors will be next. Probably the bedrooms first, then the level with the kitchen, and the bottom story last.

"There aren't any closets," she noted. "I mean, this is like a built-in closet, but it's not what I'm used to." There was what looked like a big piece of furniture that took up one entire wall of his bedroom, with doors, shelves and drawers. It obviously wasn't built in, but something that had been added.

"We don't have the space in Greece," he said. "Although in a stand-alone house like this, I'm not sure why not. If I had the time, I'd like to remodel all of this to add one, but it seems prudent to wait and see if I get married, have kids…" His voice trailed off and he looked at her guiltily. "You know what I mean."

"I do." She nodded, turning away so he wouldn't see the dismay on her face, and strode over to the sliding glass doors that led out to a balcony that overlooked the sea. "Now this is my absolute favorite spot in the house." She unlocked the door and stepped outside. The wind caught her hair, blowing it back behind her as she tilted her face up to the sky.

"This is 90% of the reason I bought it," he admitted, coming up beside her. "The location is perfect, the price was right and this view is sometimes the only stress relief I get."

"I can see why." She leaned against him, sighing when he slid his arm around her waist.

"I never imagined you'd be standing here with me," he admitted.

"I never imagined I'd see you again." She looked up at him, searching his face. "Dear God, Apollo, what are we doing?"

"I'm using every ounce of restraint and good manners I have to keep from throwing you over my shoulder and taking you caveman-style."

She giggled. "Sounds like fun."

He arched a brow. "Paige…"

"I didn't say *no*," she said mildly. "I said I wanted to wait a little —take it slow so we didn't make the same mistakes twice. I absolutely didn't say no."

"You kind of did," he pointed out.

"That was before." She wrapped her arms around his neck. "This is now."

"Oh, hell, Paige." He bent his head and kissed her, surprised that he wanted to savor every minute of it instead of ravaging her the way he'd imagined in his mind.

She opened her mouth and let him in, luxuriating in the sweetness of his touch, the familiarity of the way his tongue swirled with hers and the ease with which they came together. When his hands traveled down to cup her ass, she let out a moan of frustration, wanting him desperately but also still wanting to wait.

"Honey, we can—"

"Apollo! Where are you?" A female voice speaking in English startled them and Apollo groaned.

"Who's here that speaks English?!" Paige stage-whispered.

"My sister," he sighed. He reached down to adjust himself, secretly glad they'd been interrupted because she needed something to wear tonight and he was almost positive once he got her naked, it would be a long time before they left the house. "Don't worry—you'll like Lena." He took her hand and tugged her towards the stairs. "Up here, Lena!"

They went down to the floor with the kitchen and found Melina standing there, a large garment bag in one hand. She smiled at Paige, holding out her free hand.

"Hi, I'm Melina Lakkas, the younger of Apollo's two sisters. You must be Paige."

"It would be incredibly embarrassing if she wasn't," Apollo chuckled.

"Hi." Paige shook her hand, ignoring him. "Yes, I'm Paige Carter."

"I haven't had a chance to tell you," he said to Paige, "but Melina knows the whole story. If there's anyone in my family I can confide in, it's Lena. So don't worry about that."

Paige flushed a little, wondering what his sister must think, but nodded. "It's nice to meet you. This whole trip has been a bit of a whirlwind."

"I'm sure," Lena nodded. She had the same green eyes as her brother and when she smiled, they sparkled like emeralds. "As much as I'd like to take you for coffee and squeeze every last girlie detail out of you, your trip has one more big whirlwind you have to get through first. Since time is limited, I thought maybe I'd bring by a few of my things—we seem to be built about the same —so that you don't have to go nuts looking for something to wear tonight." She looked at Apollo. "Can we use your room?"

"Of course," he nodded.

"Come." Melina motioned with her head and started up the stairs.

Paige glanced at Apollo who nodded. "There's no guarantee we'll find anything that fits, so give it a shot."

She turned and followed Melina, trying not to be too nervous. All they were thinking about right now was the dinner tonight, so Melina probably wouldn't bombard her with questions. The thought relaxed her a little and she stepped back into his bedroom with a smile.

Unprepared for a barrage of questions, her eyes widened as Melina began to speak and pull items out of the garment bag simultaneously.

"I knew," Melina began without hesitation, "that something had changed when he came back from college, but I thought it was a traditional college romance, a girl he'd had to leave behind for whatever reason. It's been three years, though, and although he has more female attention than any guy could possibly need, he's never shown any genuine interest. I have to admit it never occurred to me he'd gotten married, despite the circumstances." She pulled out a white linen pencil skirt with a matching bolero jacket with three-quarter sleeves. "What do you think of this?"

"It's beautiful," Paige responded automatically. "But maybe not for a business dinner with clients. I think something with a little color and not a suit—that's too professional. I need to look classy but this isn't *my* company—I'm the date, not a business associate."

"Do you love him?" Melina asked, nodding and tossing the suit aside as she dug through the stack of clothes on the bed.

"I, um, what?" Paige blinked.

Melina paused and looked up. "It's a simple question, Paige. Do you love him?"

"I don't know," she said quietly. "I've never forgotten him and the moment we were in the same room together, the chemistry between us was so strong it almost knocked me over."

"You're fair, so this would look stunning on you. Is it too sexy?" She held up a red, form-fitting dress that flared at the bottom and had spaghetti straps covered in rhinestones.

"It's not too sexy, but it depends on where we're going," Paige said, holding it up.

"Put it on and we'll ask Apollo."

Paige grabbed it and disappeared into the bathroom, needing a moment to gather her thoughts. Did she love him? Absolutely. She couldn't say that, though. It seemed ridiculous. After a total of four days together, with three years in between visits, how did one build those types of feelings? She felt foolish just thinking it, much less admitting it. But if she didn't, why had she agreed to any of this? If she didn't have feelings that were intense enough to make her want to stay in Greece with him for two extra weeks, she could just go home in three days.

She stepped back into the bedroom and found two sets of emerald-green eyes looking her over.

"Yes," Melina nodded. "It's perfect for where you're going."

"Where are we going?" Paige asked.

"Turn around," Apollo said.

She turned so he could see the back and glanced over her shoulder. "Yes?"

"Yes!" He and Melina spoke in unison.

"So shoes are the only problem," Melina said. "What size do you wear?"

"An eight," Paige responded automatically. "I don't know what that is in European sizes."

"Let me look online," Apollo said, typing into his phone. "Hmm, looks like a 40."

"I'm a 39," Melina mumbled. "Sophia wears a 40, but she'd want to know who was borrowing her shoes and we probably don't want to tell her…yet."

"Where can we go?" Paige asked. "It can't be too hard to find simple black or red shoes to go with this."

"There are shops nearby that would have them, but they're closed now for the afternoon and won't reopen until 5:30 or 6:00."

"It's after four now," Apollo noted. "We'll have a little time to relax and we can be there right when they open."

"What time do we go to dinner?" Paige asked.

"We're meeting at 8:30 so we have a little time."

"Maybe I should shower and do my hair now," she murmured. "In case it takes us a while to find what I need."

"Oh, we have a few minutes," Melina said smoothly. "Let's sit and get to know each other."

"Lena…" Apollo's voice held a slight warning.

She smiled up at him prettily. "Oh stop it—I'm not going to chase her off! God, nothing would make me happier than to see you married off and out of my hair."

He burst out laughing. "Technically, I've been married three years and am still in your hair."

She rolled her eyes. "Yes, but she wasn't here. Now she is…" Her eyes twinkled, further evidencing their closeness.

"We're only married legally," Paige said quietly, putting the dress on a hanger as she came out of the bathroom. "It's not like I'm moving to Greece."

"You wouldn't consider moving to Greece?" Melina looked at her intently.

Paige started. "I don't know. I mean, it's beautiful here, but my job, my family—my whole life is in Las Vegas. I don't know the language here so I probably wouldn't be able to work or anything, and I'm not looking for a rich man to take care of me."

"I know that, *koukla mou*." Apollo reached for her, pulling her close. "Of all the issues here, that isn't one of them. I don't know everything about you, but I know that."

"Honestly, that never crossed my mind!" Melina said quickly, noting how protective her brother was. "The chemistry between you is so clear—anyone can see the attraction—it seems that you'd be thinking of ways to make this work."

"I..." Paige's voice trailed off. "I don't, uh..." She stared at Apollo helplessly.

"We haven't gotten that far, Lena," he said gently, surreptitiously squeezing Paige's waist. "The idea was for us to spend time together, get to know each other on a more intimate level and see what happens. What's the point of making plans when we don't know if we even have feelings for each other?"

Melina snorted, standing up and starting to pack up the garment bag. "That's some bullshit if I ever heard it! You two are so far gone for each other you might as well have it tattooed on your foreheads. The only thing you should be thinking about right now is the logistics of how to be together. Everything else is already there!" She leaned over to hug her brother and then reached out her arms to Paige. She kissed her on each cheek and squeezed her tightly. "He's a really, really good guy," she whispered against her ear. "And he adores you—don't let him go."

"Whatever you just said," Apollo grunted, "better not scare her away!"

"*Skase!*" *Shut up!* She laughed, waved and bounded down the stairs.

"*Efharisto!*" Paige called after her.

"Your pronunciation is pretty good," he commented.

"*Efharisto.*" They laughed together before she hurried to lock herself in the bathroom. She didn't want to think about logistics or anything else; she wanted to make herself as beautiful as she could tonight and help him impress his clients. There was time to think of that other stuff after he closed this deal.

7

They arrived at the restaurant at 8:25 and let a valet take the car. They were meeting at the five-star restaurant within the Hotel Grande Bretagne, and Paige felt a wave of nausea as Apollo took her arm. Dressed in the beautiful red dress with brand-new red heels that matched perfectly, as well as a new coordinating evening bag, she momentarily panicked. This wasn't her world and these were possibly the most important clients of Apollo's career. If she messed things up for him, she would never forgive herself.

"It's going to be fine," he soothed, taking her arm and leading her inside. "You're beautiful, intelligent and work in sales—that's essentially what this is. No one expects you to know about the shipping industry, so any thoughtful comments about business in general is the extent of what you'll need to contribute. I know you well enough to know you're smart and care about your career, so your sales and marketing knowledge can only be a bonus. Don't worry."

"I don't want to screw this up for you!" she whispered. "And what's our relationship?"

He smiled. "Since you don't have a ring, and I told them I was dining with a friend, let's say we had a college romance if it comes up and that we've rekindled it. That way, we're covered if I find it necessary to take you into the restroom and bend you over the sink!"

She nudged him with her elbow. "Not tonight, big guy—all you should be thinking about is closing this deal. And maybe—" her eyes danced with mischief, "—you'll get something like that later if you do."

He kissed her full on the mouth, careful not to smear her lipstick. "Promises, promises."

The Italian businessmen were already seated with their wives and Paige scanned them quickly. The older couple, Pio and Clara Carozo, were probably in their mid-50s and seemed both classy and austere. Clara was dressed elegantly but not overdone, and Pio wore a simple suit without a tie. The younger couple, Fabrizio and Maria Romano, screamed arrogance and new money. She guessed them to be in their late thirties, but it was hard to tell with the amount of makeup and obvious plastic surgery she'd had and his almost too-noticeable attempt to be casual and modern. Her dress was so low-cut her breasts nearly spilled out of the top and her lips had so much filler they didn't look right with her tiny nose and eyes that had already been lifted to the point they seemed to be squinting.

Keeping her smile friendly but reserved, Paige sat next to Maria and three seats down from Clara. They were strategically placed so that the couples were next to each other, but since the table was round they would be able to converse freely. Apollo was on Paige's other side and he rested his arm on the back of her chair as they ordered wine and exchanged pleasantries.

"What do you do, Ms. Carter?" Pio asked, genuine interest on his face.

"I work in the marketing department for a professional sports team in Las

Vegas," she replied, grateful she could pick up her wine glass and take a sip.

"The new hockey team?" Fabrizio actually focused on her now. "They just won a championship, did they not?"

"They did." She nodded.

"Ticket sales must be soaring."

She nodded again. "Absolutely. It's quite a feat for a team that's only been in existence for two seasons."

"Did you study marketing at university?" Clara asked, her English slightly more stilted than her husband's or his partner's.

"I did. I love it."

"Don't most American women go to college to find a husband?" Maria asked, her eyes almost pitying as she met her gaze.

"Maria…" Fabrizio murmured under his breath.

"It's okay." Paige pretended to think it was funny. "You're right —a lot of women go to college with the hopes of finding a husband. I come from a family of academics, though, so I had a bit more pressure to get the degree."

"We dated long-distance in college," Apollo spoke up without warning, his voice completely level though a vein in his neck began to throb. "So she really didn't have the chance to go husband-shopping since she had a boyfriend."

"But you didn't marry her," Maria pointed out, a smile playing on her lips as she blatantly looked him over.

"We had a disagreement," he shrugged. "I'm a year older and I was in an accelerated program, so I was finishing my master's while she was finishing her bachelor's. She had a job opportunity she wanted to take while I had to come back to Greece to start working in the family business. We were young and foolish, but I'm hoping to rectify that this time around."

"Are you planning to move to Greece then?" Pio asked. "I'm sure your marketing background would be useful to Lakkas, International."

"We hadn't discussed it," Paige began.

"She probably doesn't know the first thing about international shipping," Maria laughed. "And what woman wants to be involved in such a stodgy industry anyway? She'd be smart to get herself pregnant!"

"Actually, I find the industry fascinating," Paige said sweetly, ignoring the sarcastic insinuation that she wasn't smart enough to work for the company. "As I started to say before, we haven't discussed my becoming involved in the company itself, but just yesterday I was telling Apollo about my ideas for a new marketing campaign that could modernize their branding and capitalize on the fixed prices of the modified repurchase structure..." That was a lie, of course, but Maria was rubbing her the wrong way and she wouldn't stand for it.

Apollo almost choked on his wine, listening to her explain an idea she had to be coming up with on the fly. There was no way she'd had time to do any research and she'd spent maybe five minutes in the reception area of the office. Pio and Fabrizio were listening to her intently, obvious respect on their faces as Maria sat back in her seat with a huff.

After nearly 15 minutes of Paige holding court and completely selling his company—and her new branding ideas—to the businessmen, Apollo was ready to drop to his knees and ask her to stay with him forever. His spring break fling from Las Vegas was much, much more than a pretty face, sexy body and sweet personality. She was an absolute barracuda in business, and he knew without a doubt she'd just sealed the deal for him. Even though her ideas had nothing to do with their contract or the agreement they'd come to, it was beyond obvious that she'd impressed them enough to solidify the deal because he'd offered them a fair contract that came with a stellar reputation, and she'd somehow shown them that his company had a future.

"Can we talk about something else?" Maria muttered, raising her empty wine glass and looking at her husband pointedly.

"Of course, *mi amore*." *My love*. Fabrizio hastily summoned the waiter and business discussion was dropped.

The waiter came to take their orders then and conversation turned to food and other topics. As everyone chatted, Apollo leaned over to whisper in Paige's ear, "You have no idea how much what you just did means to me."

She gave him a quick, confused glance. "Are you sure it wasn't overkill?"

"It was so perfect I could kiss you..." He pressed his lips to the soft spot behind her ear and smiled as she shivered. He was going to enjoy making love to her tonight, and that was all he could think about as the evening wore on.

By the time they'd completed a five course meal, finished several bottles of wine, shared luscious desserts and sat around sipping brandy and cognac, it was clear that Pio and Fabrizio were on board for the deal. As they walked out to their waiting car and driver, Pio shook Apollo's hand.

"It's been a lovely evening. We are looking forward to working with you."

"Thank you." Apollo shook his hand. "I look forward to it as well."

"*Bella*." *Beautiful*. Clara smiled warmly at Paige as she hugged her and whispered in her ear. "Whatever is problem with Apollo —you fix. He is good man; you will have excellent life together." She winked and got in the car.

Apollo shook hands with Fabrizio and Maria, and stood with his arm around Paige as their car disappeared down the busy street.

"You did it!" she whispered happily in his ear.

"*We* did it!" He turned to kiss her soundly on the lips.

"Is it really a done deal?" Her eyes shone with happiness for him. "I mean, is it possible they go home tonight and change their minds?"

He shrugged as they waited for his car to come up. "Anything is possible, but not likely. Pio's been in the industry a long time and is known to be a straight shooter—tough as nails, but honest and fair. I doubt he would give me a handshake with a definitive answer and then jerk me around."

"I'm so excited for you!" she said.

"Baby, it was all you." He bent to kiss her and she moved up against him.

"You've never called me *baby* before," she murmured.

"Don't you like it?"

"I like *koukla* better, but with your accent, *baby* is really sexy."

"Yeah?" His smoldering eyes met hers and he felt the twitch in his slacks that reminded him how badly he wanted her. "So when I make you come tonight, which one do you want me to use?"

Her breath hitched in anticipation but she didn't break his gaze as she whispered, "Both of them."

*H*e drove home on autopilot—although downtown Athens on a Saturday night always required at least a little concentration—thinking about all the different ways she'd made him happy in just two days. She continued to surprise him, and he wasn't sure why. He'd known she was special the moment they met, so his reluctance to admit that she was the one for him had to stem from a subconscious fear that she didn't feel the same. She wanted him—the sexual tension was practically palpable—but she was holding back. She still hadn't even entertained the possibility of staying in Greece, and that's what scared him. He knew two days wasn't nearly enough time to decide to spend the rest of your life with someone, but he couldn't imagine letting her go now that he had her back. Convincing her to stay would be something else entirely, though.

"Did you call Melina?" she asked as they drove. "You promised you'd tell her what happened."

"I sent her a text," he smiled. "And told her I was taking the morning off unless Pio or Fabrizio called."

"Are we sleeping in?" she asked innocently.

"We don't have to sleep," he shrugged. "But you're going to be tired."

"I don't know what you mean," she pretended to look confused. "But I do need to make a phone call when we get home. If you want me to stay a little longer, I have to talk to my boss. I sent an email but he hasn't responded."

"Of course," he replied. "You should take care of that right away."

His plan had been to carry her up the stairs and ravage her, but getting her to stay in Greece longer was more important and he respected her wish to be up front with her boss. He wasn't sure what his plan would be if her boss refused and she tried to leave in two days, but if he had to, he'd get on the flight with her and spend a week or two in Vegas. Once this contract was inked, he'd deserve a week's vacation.

They walked inside and he led her to his office. He booted up his computer and told her to log in to anything she liked before he headed upstairs to give her privacy. He hung up his suit and lounged against the pillows on the bed, pulling out his phone to check messages; three from Melina, one from Tasos, and two from his mother. He would have to talk to his mother soon—he'd been avoiding her since Paige had arrived—but certainly not this late. It was after midnight and the only thing on his mind tonight was Paige. Though he desperately wanted to be inside her and make her scream his name a few times, it wasn't truly about sex. He just wanted to be with her, continue getting to know her and enjoying the little nuances that made her special. Sex would come; of that he was sure.

He heard her steps on the stairs and put down his phone,

surprised to see her dejected face when she came through the door. She kicked off her shoes and threw herself down on the bed, resting on her stomach and folding her arms under her head.

"What's wrong?" he asked. "Weren't you granted any more time?"

She made a face. "My fucking ex! Ugh!" She sat up, sitting back on her haunches and folding her arms across her chest.

"What happened?" He had an uncomfortable feeling in his gut, but didn't want her to see it.

"The way we met was through my job. The first week I started the team had an open house, where we invited local businesses and celebrities to a special evening. The players were all there and they turned on the charm, a total booze fest intended to sell VIP boxes and top-of-the-line season ticket packages. Tom was already a rising star accountant at his firm, and when one of the junior partners couldn't go because one of his kids was sick, Tom took his place. He zoomed in on me the moment he saw me and when I told him I wouldn't go out with him, he said he'd get his firm to sponsor a box in exchange for one date—no sex, no pressure, just that I would give him a chance and get to know him."

Apollo shook his head. "And of course you said yes, because for a brand new employee in the sales department, that kind of sale immediately gave you status."

She nodded. "And he's a genuinely nice guy. I'm not in love with him, but it's not because he's an asshole or anything… I just don't think he's the right guy for me."

"That makes sense." He already hated this Tom guy, but the last thing he wanted to do was behave like a possessive jerk.

"Anyway, apparently Tom is trying that again. He's a junior partner now and he called today to talk to me. When he got my voice mail message stating that I'm on vacation, he called my boss and said that his firm was interested in two sets of premium season tickets—but the catch is that he and his partners want me to go in and *personally* make the presentation."

"*Ksekoliaris*," he muttered under his breath. *Asshole.*

"I don't know what that means, but it's probably not something I should learn this early in my Greek lessons." She tried to smile but couldn't quite manage.

"Just means asshole," he said gently, sitting beside her and reaching for the zipper at the back of the dress. "Come on, get comfortable and we can talk."

"I'm not really in the mood anymore..." she murmured sadly.

"I didn't say anything about sex, did I? I'd have to be an idiot not to know that the mood is ruined for you."

"I'm sorry." She sighed as he unzipped the dress and gently pulled it over her head. Even though she was in nothing but her panties and strapless bra, she barely noticed that she was half-naked in front of him; all she could think about was having to leave him in a few days.

"So what did your boss say?" he asked softly, leaning back against the pillows and bringing her with him so she could rest against his chest.

"That of course my personal and professional life are separate, but that these types of sales make management happy and could mean another nice bonus for me."

He grunted. "How much of a bonus? I'll give you the money to stay!"

"About two thousand dollars."

"That's it?" He shook his head. "You're definitely wasting your talent there, Paige. The way you wowed Pio and Fabrizio tonight, you should be running a marketing department at a big company somewhere."

"I need a few more years of experience under my belt before anyone like that would hire me."

"I'd hire you in a heartbeat."

She smiled wanly. "You want to sleep with me."

"I'd hire anyone who did what you did at dinner tonight."

She just sighed again, nuzzling into his chest. "I don't want him to manipulate me," she whispered. "But I don't want to get fired. Even if everything fell into place and I could stay here forever, I'd want to leave my job like a professional—and a lady."

Pride surged through him as he listened. Damn, she was something else. Though he wanted her to stay with him, he respected her desire to leave her job in good standing; that showed integrity and told him a great deal about who she was on the inside. He'd already sensed that about her, but hearing it made him want her even more.

"So how did you leave it?" he asked after a moment.

"I said that I hadn't used all my vacation last year and wound up losing several days, and that I felt Tom was trying to manipulate me into getting back together with him. He asked if I would consider coming back for the meeting and perhaps returning to Greece later in the summer." She rolled her eyes. "Not that he offered to buy me another ticket!"

"So you're being forced to return on Monday?"

She nodded miserably.

"You know, sometimes you have to fight for yourself," he said slowly. "This morning, Pio and Fabrizio put me through hell. They asked every dumb question in the book and then came up with more ways to waste my time and delay the deal. Finally, I'd had enough and told them so. I explained that I would talk about the contract or answer specific questions about the deal itself, but otherwise the meeting was over. When I did that, Pio laughed, said he liked a man who stood up for himself or some such shit, and the meeting was over. Maybe they're testing you because they can. Is there a higher-up you can contact?"

She frowned. "I have a good relationship with the team's general manager, who's essentially everyone's boss, but I think it'll piss off my immediate supervisor if I go over his head."

"Your boss sounds like a greedy jerk who doesn't see what's happening here. If you and Tom remain broken up, is he going to force you to go out with him once a year so they renew their season tickets? You're setting a bad precedent going forward—and I'm sincere when I say that, Paige. I can easily afford to buy you a ticket to come back later in the summer if you truly want to get back to make this deal. But it feels smarmy to me."

She nodded slowly. "It does to me too." She looked up into his face. "Thank you."

"For what?" He looked surprised.

"Listening. Not judging. Giving me genuine, practical advice that not only shows respect for me, but also for my job. I know you want me to stay, but you didn't try to make me feel bad or tilt the situation in your favor. You're the most amazing man I've ever known." She leaned up so she could touch her lips to his just as he reached down to run his fingers through her hair. Their mouths came together slowly, eyes locked, breath getting shorter as they touched.

"Baby, if you start this, I'm not going to be able to stop," he whispered.

"I don't want you to stop. If I have to leave…we only have 48 hours left to make love and I'm not sure that's long enough."

"I thought you weren't in the mood?"

She flushed prettily. "My husband is such a great guy, I can't seem to help myself."

"My wife is so incredibly sexy I'm not going to be able to keep my hands off her."

When he kissed her again, it was with passion he'd been holding back for the entire three years since they'd last slept together. Now that she'd given him the okay, he was going to make every last second of their time together count, and he wanted most of it to be spent in bed.

$\mathcal{H}$is kiss went through her like a spark igniting a flame, and she was fully prepared to burn. This had been a quietly simmering ember for more than three years and she was ready to turn up the heat. She loved him for respecting her and wanting to be a gentleman, but that ended now. Her frustration with her boss, with Tom, and with the sudden end to her time with Apollo left her aching for something only he could satisfy. This was so much more than sex, so much more than having an orgasm and definitely more than a spring break or summer fling. He was a piece of the puzzle of her life that made her complete. She'd known it the first time she'd met him and she knew it now. It seemed that fate would continue to conspire to keep them apart, but nothing could keep him out of her soul.

She reached down, running her hand along the erection poking out of his boxers and gently squeezed. His mouth was still greedily fastened to hers but she slowly moved away, pressing her lips to his skin and nipping little sections as she moved down his chest. The dark, wiry hair tickled her face but she could only inhale deeply, trying to memorize his scent, his taste, the way his muscles tensed beneath his skin when she touched him. She slid her mouth wetly down his stomach, fascinated by how flat it was and the neatly trimmed curls at his groin.

"Paige, is that something you enjoy?" he asked in a rough voice, his fingers threading into her hair and tugging lightly.

"I do with you," she whispered, gripping the elastic of his boxers and pulling them down when he raised his hips.

"Do you know how beautiful you are with your hand around me like that?" he asked, watching her slowly stroke him.

Her only response was to reach down with her other hand to cup the taut, heavy sacs beneath his throbbing penis. He shuddered against her as she toyed with them, squeezing a little and then running her fingernail lightly across the surface. She waited until he was breathing hard to lick just the tip of his cock, smiling when he trembled ever so slightly. Using both hands now, she stroked him until he was beautifully thick and erect. With patient precision, she traced the vein that ran along the top with her tongue, making him moan. She could feel the muscles in his thighs tightening as she moved over him, sucking gently on each of his balls with unhurried motions until he was shivering against her. When he growled her name, she kissed her way back up to the head and ran her tongue over the slit at the top. Keeping the pressure light, she watched his reaction as she let him slide in a little deeper with each stroke of her mouth. She sensed he liked it when she went faster, so she slid him between her lips with hard, fast bobs of her head. She alternated sucking and gliding her tongue along the soft, velvety skin until he started to tense. With her hands firmly around the base, she kept up a rhythm that made him groan. It seemed like he'd gotten bigger with each passing second and she knew he was straining to hold back.

"Not the first time, *koukla mou*," he growled, pulling out of her mouth and dragging her up across his body so her lips were right against his. "When we do this, I want to be deep inside you, watching your face as we come together."

"That sounds like a wonderful plan," she sighed.

He flipped her onto her back and covered her body with his. Digging both of his hands into the hair on the sides of her head, he pulled it up to meet his heated kisses. Their tongues clashed together, twisting and curling until they couldn't get any closer.

"So beautiful...so sexy...so mine." He panted out the words between kisses, nipping and licking her lips until she was gasping with need. Desperate to feel all of her, he lifted to his knees and used one hand to lift her torso as well. With one flick of his fingers he unsnapped her bra and tossed it aside, looking down at her breasts with sheer pleasure. They were exactly as he remembered; sweet round globes that fit perfectly in his hands, with raspberry nipples that puckered the moment he touched them. He lowered his head to suck one deep into his mouth, chuckling when she gasped and seized a handful of his hair.

"Still sensitive," he murmured, easing back and letting his tongue trace lines around the areola while he pinched the other nipple between two fingers.

"Oh!" Her chest arched up into his mouth and he sucked a little harder.

With each thrust of his tongue and pinch of his fingers, she got more and more sensitive, her breasts turning pink as he moved his hands, mouth and stubble over them. Enjoying the sounds she made as he did it, he took his time, not allowing her to move away or shift positions.

"Are you wet for me, *koukla?*"

"Yes! Please!" Her chest was rising and falling rapidly.

"Soon, baby." He moved away, reaching for the foil packet on his nightstand and quickly sheathing himself. He slid between her parted thighs and ran his hands along the sexy, soft skin. She was bare now, unlike three years ago when she'd had a patch of sweet, light brown curls. He wasn't a fan of bare pussies, finding them reminiscent of girls instead of women, but he had to admit it was sexy as hell on Paige.

"You shaved," he whispered, kissing the crease of her thigh and then licking little patches of skin as he got reacquainted with her body. He'd only had the pleasure of going down on her once before but he remembered everything about it: her taste, her scent, and the exact spot that made her come. He'd save that for next time, though. Tonight, as promised, they would come together.

"You don't like it?" she asked, almost nervously.

"Normally I don't," he admitted, his eyes meeting hers. "But on you...damn, it's hot." He placed a soft kiss right at the top of her sweet mound, careful to keep pressure light and away from her clit. She was dripping with need and he'd been serious about wanting them to climax together, so he merely teased her with his mouth until he was sure she couldn't stand any more.

Without warning, he pushed a finger into her vagina and nearly lost control when she started to pulse around it. She was so ready, he couldn't wait anymore either. He slid up and kissed her, soft and tender, covering her with his body and letting his weight press them tightly together.

"Do you remember the first time?" she whispered hoarsely, her eyes finding his.

"You trembled," he whispered back, nipping at the skin on her neck. "You asked me to go slow because you thought my size might hurt you... Do you remember what it felt like when I started to put a little inside you?" He pressed against her now, closing his eyes against the feel of her tight entrance clamping around him.

"How gentle you were... How slow we went until..."

He was pushing deeper now, a tiny bit at a time, just as he'd done that first time.

"Until?" he prompted.

"Until I was so desperate for more I begged you to give me all of it," she panted.

Without warning, he drove into her with such force her breath left her in a rush. He nearly lost his mind as she opened to take him, her warmth enveloping his cock like a glove. "Still so tight," he ground out. He moved slowly, letting her adjust, moving in a circular motion that allowed him to touch different parts of her. Her hips jerked against him, and when she wrapped those silky legs around his waist he knew he wouldn't be able to hold out very long.

He put his hands under her ass and squeezed, lifting her against his hips as he started to thrust harder and faster, watching her face each time he shifted into a slightly different position. There, he thought, as her eyes squeezed shut and her mouth fell open.

"Oh! Apollo! Apollo..."

She was close. He could feel her clenching around him now, tighter and stronger as he stroked the spot that seemed to be moving her towards release.

"Open your eyes, *koukla mou*," he whispered, working desperately to focus on her pleasure without losing control first.

When those beautiful hazel eyes locked with his, it was all over. He didn't need her pussy to bring him over the edge; he only needed the look in her eyes. It said the words she'd never said aloud, but in that moment he saw it all; her love, her need and her complete devotion to him.

He pumped into her twice more before the world seemed to explode around them both. She was crying out his name, bucking against him, nails digging into his back, all while he crushed her mouth with his. Tangled, sweaty and shuddering with tiny aftershocks, neither of them could move except for a few reflexive jumps each time their joined bodies twitched.

"Just like before," she whispered against his throat. "So different than with anyone else."

"Different?" He pressed light kisses on her temple as he pushed sweaty tendrils out of her face.

"It's so...*boring* with others. I think of other things...work, or what bill I forgot to pay, or some movie star I fantasize about."

"So, it's not boring with me?" he teased, smiling into her face. "You weren't fantasizing about that Thor guy or something?"

"Chris Hemsworth?" she giggled. "Nah. I don't need a Norse god—I have a Greek one."

8

With a satisfied smile, he reluctantly pulled out and slid off the bed to dispose of the condom. She padded after him, following him into the bathroom and waiting until he'd tossed the condom before using the facilities. She seemed oblivious to the fact that he stood in the doorway watching her until she glanced up and caught his stare.

"Am I not supposed to do this in front of you?" she asked curiously.

"It's fine with me," he smiled. "Just most women usually don't."

She got up and washed her hands, glancing back at him. "Do you have a lot of women spend the night here?"

He shook his head. "No. Only one woman who's not related to me has ever been here and she never spent the night—I always drove her home after."

She nodded even though she hated the thought that he'd shared the bed they'd just made love in with someone else.

"Does that bother you?" he asked, following her back to bed.

"How can it?" she countered. "We didn't see or talk to each other for more than three years. I have no right to be jealous."

"But you are." A faint smile tugged at his lips. "I've had my share of boring sex as well, you know?"

She sat on the edge of the bed and wrapped her arms around herself.

"Are you cold, honey?"

She shook her head. "No. Just a little sad and overwhelmed."

"Why are you sad?"

"Because in 48 hours I'll be on a plane going far, far away from you." Tears puddled in her eyes.

"You can come back," he said, dropping to his knees in front of her and moving between her legs. "And in winter, when business is slower, maybe I could come to you for a week or two."

Big tears splashed down her cheeks and he pulled her close, hating to see her cry, especially when he was the cause. "*Signomi,*" he whispered. *I'm sorry.*

"What?" she sniffled.

"That means I'm sorry. I hate that both times we've been together made you cry."

"Not your fault." She nestled against him.

"Come. Let's go to bed." He got to his feet and crawled onto the bed. He held out his hand and after a moment she took it, allowing him to pull her close. "In the morning we'll think of something. I promise."

"You really want me to come back?" she whispered in the darkness as they started to doze off.

"*Koukla mou.* I don't want you to leave."

*A*pollo was sound asleep when something bounced on the bed, startling him awake. He sat up with a start, staring at Paige in shock as she bounced on her knees, her eyes shining.

"I can stay! I can stay!" She gripped his arm. "Did you hear me?!"

"The whole neighborhood probably heard you," he murmured,

pulling her down and into the curve of his arm. "How about you tell me what's going on by whispering softly so I can get my heart rate back to normal."

"*Sig-nomi!*" She giggled and wiggled until she was resting her chin on his chest so she could look at him. "So last night, after I talked to my boss, I was upset and I emailed my friend Becca. She's the head of media relations for the team, but since that's another department, and she's not my boss, we've gotten friendly. I told her what was happening and asked her what she thought I should do." She took a breath. "Well, I guess she went in and told Steve, my boss, what she thought of him. She sent me an email a couple hours later telling me to stay another 10 days! She said she was giving me permission and that she'd handle the deal with Tom's company personally!" She finally stopped talking and looked into his eyes. "I guess she went to our GM and got Steve into trouble—hey! Are you listening? Aren't you happy?"

He took her hand and slowly brought it to his crotch, letting it rest on his erection. "Very, very happy."

Two hours later, after another round of passionate lovemaking and an equally erotic shower together, they were sitting on his balcony drinking espresso and nibbling some pastries he'd bought at a bakery down the street. Her feet were propped up on the rail as she stared out at the water, a smile on her face.

"Is that smile from good sex, good coffee or the sea breeze?" he asked, watching her.

"All three?" she laughed, her hair flowing out behind her as the wind picked up.

"You're a ray of sunshine in my life," he said, leaning over to run his lips across hers.

"It's not causing sunburn, is it?" she asked in amusement.

"Not yet."

Grinning over at him, she couldn't help the happiness that filled her. She had 12 more days with him, and she couldn't express how grateful she was to Becca. She would definitely bring her back a nice gift. In the meantime, she had to remember to call the airlines to change her return flight. Her phone buzzed, indicating she had a text, and she frowned down at it. She was glad Apollo had Wi-Fi at his house but she'd hoped she wouldn't get notifications from work.

Opening the text program she saw several posts from Raegan and groaned.

"What is it?" Apollo asked. "Is it work?"

She shook her head. "It's Raegan. I guess Tom's been calling her…"

Apollo got up and disappeared into the house, coming back a moment later with a cordless phone. "Call her," he said. "I know it's going to bother you until you find out what's going on."

"Are you sure?" She met his gaze worriedly.

"I told you—it's a flat fee. Call her." He kissed her lightly. "I'm going to get dressed."

"Thank you." She watched him go and then dialed the number to her apartment.

Raegan answered on the first ring. "Oh my God, what's going on?!"

"So much," Paige sighed.

"Are you really at Apollo's house?" Raegan had been shocked when she'd gotten a text from Paige last night telling her some of the news about Apollo.

"I really am. I'll text you a picture of the view from his balcony in a minute," she said, grabbing her cell phone as she balanced the cordless house phone on her shoulder. "But tell me what Tom said."

"He called here and left, like, a thousand messages in the last two days," Raegan grumbled. "And since I obviously didn't call him back, he came to work!"

"He went to the casino?" Paige asked in disbelief. "Seriously? Oh my God, Raegan! He didn't get you into trouble, did he? I'm going to talk to him!"

"It's fine, he was very nice, just a little freaked out that you'd gone out of the country by yourself and that you weren't answering your phone."

"I turned off roaming," Paige rolled her eyes. "Geez, it's expensive. But I've got Wi-Fi at Apollo's house and I can check in via email every day."

"Tell me what happened at work," Raegan said excitedly. "And whether or not you got lucky with your Greek stud!"

"Oh, I definitely got lucky, in more ways than one," Paige giggled. She told Raegan about her conversation with Steve and then Becca's subsequent email. "So I'll be here an extra 10 days."

"Do you want me to call your parents?"

Paige grimaced. "No, I'll call my mom tomorrow. I still can't believe Tom actually went to find you at work."

"He's pretty freaked out," Raegan said slowly. "I think you need to sit down with him when you get back and let him know it's really over. I don't think he believes it, like this is another one of your stall tactics."

"I should have ended it after the first time he proposed." She looked up with an appreciative stare as Apollo came back out in a pair of khaki shorts and a polo shirt.

"Well, you're going to have to deal with it now, I guess," Raegan said. "Especially since you're technically married to someone else."

"Yeah." Paige sighed. "Anyway, thanks for holding down the fort for me. I'll email Tom and tell him to knock it off."

"Don't worry about Tom—I'll handle him until you get home— just call back sometime when you can give me details!"

Paige laughed. "I will—promise!"

"Love you! Have a blast!"

"I will! Love you too!" Paige hung up with a grin.

. . .

fter sending an email to Becca and another to Steve, Paige got dressed and they headed into Athens. They were going to the place he'd mentioned before, Monastiraki, where she could do a little shopping and they could eat the big midday meal. She wasn't used to the schedule in Greece but found it interesting that they ate their big meal of the day just a bit later than Americans ate lunch, usually around 2:30 or 3:00. Then, later in the evening, often as late as 10:00 or 11:00, they would have a lighter meal. Apollo said some people ate two large meals, but because he was often up early, he didn't like to eat that much right before bed.

"Last night was a bit of an exception," he explained as they parked in a pay lot and then walked down the winding streets. "If I eat a big meal at 2:30 or so, I like to eat something light around 8:00. If I'm in bed at midnight, I've had time to digest. Otherwise, it can keep me up."

"How does everyone else do it?" she asked curiously.

"Well, the lifestyle here is interesting. Except for small children and the elderly, most of us are up late. We go out at 10 or 11 for coffee or drinks and dancing… You'll see the restaurants and cafes are always packed, no matter what day of the week it is. Especially in the summer."

"On nights when the team is off or out of town, I'm usually in bed by 11," she said. "Kind of boring, I guess."

"Different lifestyle, different culture."

"How did you adjust when you went to the U.S. for college?"

He grinned. "I was 18 and full of piss and vinegar—getting ready for a four-year party! It was great. I loved living in the U.S."

"But you were anxious to get home, too," she said, glancing up at him.

"The whole reason my parents paid for my fancy education was so I could take over the business. Otherwise, I could have gone to the university here in Greece."

"Is the education you got in the U.S. so much better?"

"I went to Yale," he shrugged. "So yes, that's a big deal even here, but besides that, I spent a lot of time making contacts, especially in grad school. My father has always wanted to expand the business and by sending me to school in the U.S., he not only expanded my understanding of the language, he immersed me in the culture so that I could mingle with businessmen from both Europe and North America."

"That's smart." She paused. "Are you still looking to expand the business into America?"

He hesitated, not wanting to mislead her about the chances of him moving to the U.S. They were trying to expand into either Los Angeles or San Francisco, but so far the logistics had been a nightmare and he didn't have a good grip on what was going to happen. "We'd like to, but the expense doesn't seem like a worthwhile risk right now. We have a steady income with what we do now, but I'd have to invest everything we have to open a branch in the U.S. With the economy the way it is here, I'm not sure that would be wise."

"No, probably not." She looked around at the busy streets, trying to ignore the disappointment that washed over her. Athens was bustling with energy all the time—it reminded her a lot of Las Vegas. Except the buildings were a lot older and there was the most gorgeous beach she'd ever seen nearby. Not to mention a green-eyed hunk who rocked her world in more ways than one. A tiny voice inside of her asked why she couldn't live here. She would miss her family but she would have Apollo. Of course, just because he was gorgeous, rich and absolutely everything she'd ever dreamed of in a man, that didn't mean he felt the same way about her. Sure, he was interested and there was this *thing* between them, but this was his country, his home, his family. If she moved here and something went wrong, she'd have no one to turn to, no one she could count on. How could she take a risk like that?

She was startled back to the present when he stopped walking and pointed. "That's the Church of the Pantanassa. I can't remember dates and such, but it's the cathedral from the monastery for which this area got its name. The monastery is gone, but this building remains."

"Built in the tenth century," she giggled. "I looked up *Monastiraki* before we left this morning so I had an idea what I would see in the area."

He leaned over and kissed her. "You don't need me for anything then!"

She reached up to touch his face. "Not true. You've made me so happy in two days, it's a little hard to believe this is just a vacation."

"No matter what happens between us," he said quietly, "this is much more than just a vacation. Now come on—let me play tour guide."

Monastiraki was like an entire neighborhood of flea market shops and stalls. She found everything from jewelry and clothing to souvenirs, gourmet spices and wines. Though she didn't have a lot of spending money, since she wasn't paying for two of the four nights she'd budgeted for at the hotel, she was able to buy gifts for her parents, Nicky, Raegan and Becca. She wandered through shop after shop, lost in everything Greek, completely unaware of how much time had passed.

Apollo followed amiably, watching her delight as he carried her bags, helped her barter with some of the more crotchety shopkeepers, and pointed out historical buildings in their midst. Finally, when the sun was high in the sky and they were both hot and sweaty, he nudged her towards a food court of sorts, filled with restaurant after restaurant.

"We can come back another day," he said firmly. "But I'm dying of thirst and starving."

She grinned. "Me too! And everything around here smells yummy!"

They chose a place where Apollo knew the owner and Paige discovered the joy of *souvlaki*. She tried both lamb and chicken, plucking the grilled, savory meat off the skewers and dipping them in tzatziki, which had become one of her favorite things. Afterwards, they walked back through the shops and she stopped in front of one selling hand-painted canvases of different images of Greece. There was one in particular that she loved—a sunset view of the Temple of Poseidon, so realistic she felt like she was there. It was too big for her suitcase, though, and she fretted over how she would get it home.

"I own a shipping company," Apollo whispered in her ear. "I could probably stick it in a crate somewhere and get it to you."

She bit her lip. She wanted it desperately, but it was expensive as well as difficult to transport.

"Let me buy it for you," he said softly. "You haven't let me buy you anything all day. What if it's a belated wedding present?"

She smiled. "I want to say no, but I can't—I want to look at this painting forever."

"Consider it yours." He spoke to the artist in Greek and within minutes they were moving back down the street, the painting securely wrapped in foam and ready for transport.

"Thank you!" She threw her arms around his neck happily. "This has been the second-best day ever!"

"I know you're going to tell me *last night* was the best day ever, right?" he joked, laughing with her.

"Last night was the very best *sex* ever," she amended, "but the best day ever is still watching the sun set while we were in Sounion."

He kissed her forehead. "Well, tonight we watch the sun set at the Acropolis. Let's take a cab back to the car to drop all this stuff off and then we can walk up there."

"Okay." She followed along, a little bit tired but having too much fun to care. She'd dreamed of seeing the Acropolis in person most of her life and now she was going to climb right up and touch it, walk on the same grounds as the ancient Greeks had more than 2,000 years ago. It was a little surreal and when they got to the gates, where Apollo paid the entrance fee, she felt somewhat awed.

"How many times have you climbed up here?" she asked as they set out on the path.

"Dozens," he said. "And though I don't go out of my way to come anymore, I still find it very inspirational to see what they accomplished so long ago, with no modern tools or conveniences."

"I can't even stand it," she said, staring up towards the top where the Parthenon stood in all its majesty.

"Come on, sweet dreamer… Let's get today's adventure under way."

"Wasn't the whole day part of the adventure?" she asked.

"That was shopping," he chuckled. "*This* is adventure!"

Laughing, they walked the rest of the way up, pausing to sit in the seats of the Odeon of Herodes Atticus, located on the southern slope of the Acropolis. It was magnificent, and though she knew it had been restored sometime in the last hundred years, enough of its original beauty was still intact to add authenticity.

As Paige leaned back on one of the hard stone seats, Apollo pulled out his phone and took her picture. She was sunburned and sweaty, but he'd never seen her look so alive. Her eyes flashed with excitement—almost as sexy as they'd been last night when she'd come undone beneath him—and her skin glowed from both the sun and the fresh air. Tonight he wanted to make love to her on the balcony of his house, long after the neighbors were asleep. With the lights out and a blanket to partially cover them, no one would be the wiser and there would be nothing but their bodies, the wind, and the sound of the sea in the background.

"The sun is going down soon!" Paige called to him. "And they'll close! Come on!"

Laughing, he followed, caught up in her excitement.

. . .

They'd just gotten back to the house when he got a series of texts from Melina. She seemed a little frantic, telling him he had to call her immediately and he reluctantly dialed her number.

"Where have you been?!" she cried.

"Lena, come on—that's a dumb question."

"*Baba* was in the office today!" she whispered. "*Working.*"

"What?" He froze. He'd taken over his father's office but the old man still had a key. He didn't have business secrets from him, but the divorce papers were probably still sitting right where he'd left them on the edge of his desk. Shit!

"And Mr. Carozo came in! They were in your office for over an hour."

"Are you serious?" Apollo felt annoyance crawl through his gut, leaving him a little out of sorts. If it hadn't been for the divorce papers left on the desk, he wouldn't give a shit, but based on Melina's panicked voice, he was guessing they'd been found. "So he saw the papers?"

"Oh, yes." Melina was still whispering; she lived with their parents, so it was hard to have privacy.

"And?"

"Be prepared. They're having a meeting now—Mama, *Baba,* *Yaya*, Sophia and Giorgios."

"Like it's any of his business!" he muttered. He wasn't fond of his brother-in-law and avoided him as much as he could.

"There's a little good news, though."

"Thank God."

"The Italians signed all the contracts—the deal is done and you've made *Baba* very happy."

"I'm not sure any amount of money will make Mama get over my being married for three years without telling her. To an American, no less."

"Well, that's the other thing—Mr. Carozo adores Paige. I mean, he went on and on about her for at least 30 minutes, telling *Baba* all about how she put Mrs. Romano in her place and how she would be such a great addition to the business—and the family."

"Oh, shit." He groaned. "He said all that?"

"Yes!" Her voice dropped. "I have to go—Mama's calling for me!" She disconnected.

"What's going on?" Paige had been watching Apollo intently and though she didn't understand more than one or two words of Greek, his facial expressions and body language said it all.

"As you Americans say—the cat is out of the bag."

Her eyes widened. "About…us?"

"I left the divorce papers on my desk and my father went in to meet with Mr. Carozo today."

"Oh, shit."

"It'll be okay." He pulled her close. "Thanks to you, we just closed a deal worth millions. Even if they're upset with me, they won't be upset with you. Apparently, Pio Carozo is a big fan of yours."

She flushed. "Maybe I should go home and come back in a month or so, after you've had time to talk to them and—"

"No." He kissed her. "I'll handle my family. Once they meet you—"

"Meet me?!" She shook her head vehemently. "That wasn't part of the deal. Your sister was one thing, but no way! Apollo, that's just asking for trouble! No matter what, the outcome goes against us!"

"How?" he demanded.

"If they like me, and we can't find a way to make this work, everyone will be hurt and it'll make it even harder for us to split. If we decide to try to stay together but they *don't* like me, it's going to make it that much harder for me to stay. And, of course, if they don't like me *and* things don't work out between us, you're going to hear *I told you so* forever!"

He grunted. "That last scenario is the least of my concerns, but you have a decision to make. Now that they know about us, either I sign the papers immediately and put you on a plane home, or you stay like we planned and meet the family. There are no other options. I mean, you could stay anyway, but they would find us. Athens is a big city, but unless we went to an island or something, people know me and if my mother started making calls, they'd find us. Not to mention, my mother has a key to my house."

She sighed. "You know, maybe this is a sign that this is just too complicated."

His eyes darkened and a scowl covered his features. "Really? After all we've shared the last few days, you're willing to walk away?"

"What choice do we have?" she asked in a helpless voice. "I'm not ready to decide to move to Greece, and you can't move to the U.S. We were supposed to have two weeks to see if we even wanted to work that hard, but now that your family is involved..."

"So you've already made your decision? Were you going to tell me?!" He glared at her.

She narrowed her eyes. "Don't put words in my mouth! I haven't made any decisions but you already hurt me once—even though I was equally responsible for how dumb we were! But now? After last night? What do you think it's going to do to me to go home knowing I'll never see you again? I don't know how to make this work but I'm staying because I can't imagine living with the knowledge that I didn't even try! Dammit, I love you, Apollo!"

9

The words had come out in a rush and she blanched as soon as she said them, taking an inadvertent step back and closing her eyes. "Shit." She blew out a breath and practically ran towards the stairs; she had to get away from him quickly.

"Paige." His voice was quiet but held a command she couldn't ignore.

She stopped, though she didn't turn around.

"Why are you walking away from me?"

"What else am I supposed to do when I just committed the cardinal sin of relationships?"

"Paige. Turn around, please."

She hesitated, warring with the humiliation burning through her.

"Please turn around, *koukla mou*."

She swallowed and slowly turned to face him. His face was emotionless, but his green eyes burned with so much intensity she was rooted in place as she watched him struggle to say whatever was on his mind.

"I love you, too." He hadn't known that's what he would say until the words came out, but once they did, it felt right. Raised as a strong, proud Greek man, showing this kind of intimacy and vulnerability was unheard of, but he didn't care. He was secure in both his manhood and his feelings for her; showing her the way he felt didn't make him less of a man in his mind.

"Three days!" she whispered, tears pooling in her eyes. "Three days together, then three years apart, and today marks the second time we've spent three days together—how can we feel like this?! It's…it's…it's stupid!"

"Is it?" He approached her slowly, reaching out to wipe the tears that were spilling down her cheeks. "Why is it stupid?"

"No foundation! No history! We still don't even know each other!"

"Sure we do." He smiled. "You have a degree in marketing, speak Spanish in addition to English, and work for a professional hockey team. I know what your parents do for a living, that you have one sister and that you love Greek food. You're 24 and were born and raised in Las Vegas. Your best friend is Raegan, your ex-boyfriend is Tom Malone, your sister is Nicky, and this is your first trip to Europe." He paused, running tender fingers along her cheek. "You're smart, classy and independent. You like to giggle and you snore very softly." He moved closer so their bodies were touching. "When you make love, your skin turns a flushed pink color, and when you come, you dig your nails into whatever part of my body you happen to grab on to." He rubbed his lips very gently along hers. "And you're very fond of adventures. Now tell me what you know about me."

"What?" She was blinking at him in confusion.

"What do you know about me?"

"I, um…" She looked up and for a moment couldn't remember anything. Then his green eyes locked on hers and everything fell into place. "You're 25 and were born here in Athens. You went to Yale and got both your bachelor's and master's degrees. You speak three languages—Greek, English and Spanish. You have two sisters, Sophia and Melina, and you're very close to Melina but almost never mention Sophia."

He smiled. "Correct. What else?"

"You run your family's shipping business because your father had a stroke and it's very important that you make it a success. You love your country, especially the beach, and you're very knowledgeable about your heritage. You don't like onions—"

"How do you know that?" he demanded, laughing in surprise.

"You picked them out of the salad the other day and again with the *souvlaki* we had."

He nodded. "What else, *koukla?*"

"You're generous, caring and thoughtful. You're passionate when you make love, but also very gentle, which tells me who you are as a man. And although you're too busy most of the time, you seem to like adventures too."

"What's your favorite color?" he asked.

"Um, pink. *Hot* pink."

"Mine is azure—the color of the Mediterranean." He squinted slightly. "I love American hot dogs, especially Hebrew National, and the band Nickelback. I want children, but not quite yet, and visiting Japan is at the top of my bucket list."

She was still looking into his mesmerizing green eyes. "I, um… I love cheesecake and my favorite bands are Rise Against and Nickelback. I want children too, but they scare the crap out of me, and visiting Australia is at the top of my bucket list."

"Do you like sushi?"

"No."

"Good. Me either." He cocked his head. "What else is there, baby? I think that covers the important stuff."

"Apollo?" She was on the verge of tears again, overwhelmed by everything she was feeling and how fast things were moving.

"You said you loved me and the feeling is mutual. Can we please go upstairs and make love?"

"It's not that simple!"

"But it is." He scooped her up in his arms and carried her to bed.

*a*pollo was sitting on the balcony with a cup of coffee when his phone rang just after seven. He'd let Paige sleep —they'd made love until late in the night—but he'd needed to mentally prepare himself for the day. His father would be the first obstacle, but with the deal with the Italians finalized, he wasn't too worried about it. His mother and Sophia would be another story, but luckily, it was his father who was calling now.

"Kalimera." Good morning.

"Apollo!"

His father's voice held a booming passion Apollo hadn't heard in months, and it made him happy, though he didn't say anything about it. "I hear you were in the office yesterday meeting with the Italians," was what he said instead.

"With Pio, not Fabrizio."

"Did you not trust me to handle it?"

Dimitri Lakkas laughed, long and deep.

"I'm glad you're amused," Apollo said dryly.

"Apollo. I was involved in every aspect of this deal—did you really think I would leave something this big to chance?"

Apollo frowned, his heart rate picking up as he tried to read between the lines. "Wait a minute—was this fake? Did you set this deal up as a test?"

"It wasn't fake! Don't be ridiculous! But yes, this was a test of sorts."

"A test." Apollo clenched the phone in one hand and made a fist in the other. "So it wasn't really a deal."

"Yes, yes, it was a deal! You just solidified a multimillion-dollar contract for us! You've done an incredible job. I'm proud of you."

"What the hell are you talking about?" It took all his self-control not to yell, but even though he was angry, he hadn't raised his voice to his father since the stroke and he wouldn't start now.

"The deal was already in the works before I got sick. Pio had a heart attack just two weeks after my stroke and things fell to the wayside. We spoke about six months ago, out of genuine concern for each other, and discovered that each other's companies had been taken over by family members. We decided we would set up a little test to see how they worked when the stakes were high. You passed with flying colors. With a little help from your pretty friend."

Apollo snorted. "I've been busting my ass seven days a week, 12-hour days most of the time, and you thought I needed to be tested?!" His voice got a little louder.

"Son, I trust you with my life, but not everyone loves you as I do and—"

"And you made a fucking fool out of me!"

"Apollo." Dimitri's voice dropped. "That's not true. You need to—"

"I don't need to do shit. I can't talk to you right now. I'm sorry, *Baba*, I have to go." He disconnected and realized his hand was shaking. "Sonofabitch!" He threw the phone across the balcony where it bounced against the wall and a piece of the protective casing snapped off.

"Good thing you have a cover," Paige said softly, kneeling beside him. "What happened, babe? You sounded so upset."

He took a deep breath and repeated the discussion with his father.

"Damn, I'm sorry." She lifted to her feet and settled on his lap, wrapping her arms around his neck. "I can't imagine how much this hurt you."

"If he wanted to be part of this deal, because it was so big, I would have understood, but to set me up? Damn." He ran a hand through his hair and then rested his head on her shoulder.

"Did you hang up on him?"

"Kind of. I said I had to go and *then* hung up—I'm a lot gentler with him since the stroke, you know? Greeks yell a lot, but watching him almost die changed that some."

"I can imagine."

They didn't speak for a long time, as the sun rose higher in the sky and it got warmer. Finally, Paige stirred, getting to her feet and holding out her hands.

"Where are we going?" he asked.

"Shower." She smiled. "You're all sweaty and we smell like sex."

He chuckled. "I wonder why."

They padded into the shower and Paige gently pushed him under the spray. When he was wet, she turned him so his back was to her and nudged him towards the wall.

"Put your hands on the wall," she said softly.

He did as she asked, letting his head hang down as she lathered up a washcloth. She washed his back with slow, firm strokes and then moved down over his well-shaped ass and thighs. Adding more soap, she did his arms and then slid beneath them so she could move around and wash his chest. His eyes were closed, his breathing steady, and she could almost feel the pain radiating from him.

"Let it out," she said softly. "Yell, cry, hit something…it's okay. I'll be right here."

He reached out and wrapped his arms around her, squeezing so tight she almost couldn't breathe. He buried his face in her hair, his body shaking slightly as he tried to hold back the powerful emotions raging through his veins. Men like him didn't cry, but this was the first time in his life as an adult he wanted to. The lack of trust from his father hurt like nothing else ever had, and he couldn't understand the need to dupe him. Two old men playing games with the younger generation. He'd sacrificed a lot to make sure the family was taken care of while his father had been so sick they didn't know if he would recover. And this was the thanks he got.

The water had cooled and he felt Paige shiver in his arms. He quickly reached over to turn off the spray and grabbed a big towel to wrap her in. "I'm sorry," he whispered. "I didn't realize the water had gotten cold."

"It's okay." She frowned suddenly. "What's that noise?"

He paused and then a groan escaped him. "Fuck. They're not going to let this go. Get dressed—it's time to meet the family. I'm not sure *which* of the family, but someone is here."

She nodded. "What do you want me to do?"

He leaned over and kissed her. "Not a damn thing. Just be yourself. I don't care what they think." He dressed more quickly than she did and reached for her hand as she combed the knots out of her wet hair. "Come down when you're ready. I meant what I said last night—I love you and they're going to have to get over the fact that we eloped three years ago. This new development with the business has shown me that I've sacrificed too much, and I'm definitely not going to sacrifice you."

She squeezed his hand. "I'll be down in a few minutes. Go make up with your father. No matter what, he did what he thought was right and I know how much you love him. Staying angry doesn't help anything."

"Maybe not, but it makes me feel better." He turned to go.

"Apollo?"

He paused, glancing over his shoulder at her. "Yes?"

"I love you too."

*H*e headed downstairs with a faint smile on his face. Hearing those four words made up for a lot of what had happened this morning, and now he knew exactly how he was going to face it. He'd been prepared for a fight when his parents found out he'd been secretly married to a *ksena—foreigner* —for three years, but now he had leverage. Though he was still pissed at his father, a part of him understood the older man's reluctance to leave something this big to his somewhat inexperienced son. However, he now had the opportunity to use it to his advantage. For his father to be here this early in the morning, he most likely felt guilty—despite this hiccup, Apollo and his father were close, so Dimitri would know his lack of trust had hurt his son.

As he'd predicted, his father stood in the mostly empty living room with Melina. Father and son faced off and she made a hasty exit, heading upstairs to find Paige after pressing a quick kiss to her brother's cheek.

"It's early," Apollo said dryly. "You couldn't wait for me to get to the office?"

"I figured there would be words," his father responded, equally droll. "Better we exchange them in private."

Apollo shrugged. "Don't bullshit me—you wanted to catch Paige and me off guard. Admit it."

His father smiled. "You know me well."

"Not as well as I thought." Apollo folded his arms across his chest and waited. His father was a ruthless businessman, but a softie when it came to his kids.

"You have to understand why I did what I did."

"I don't and I never will. You could have told me. You could have given me the respect I've always given you. You should have —because my reputation has been irreparably damaged. The staff will never respect me now."

"Apollo! This is ridiculous! They know nothing!"

"They know that right after I supposedly landed a multimillion-dollar contract, my father came in and closed the deal. It doesn't matter what was said or how it was said—you effectively erased every bit of respect I'd earned in the last year. You'll have my resignation by the end of the day."

"Apollo!" Dimitri's face flushed red. "This is nonsense! This was Pio's game and I played along because he asked it of me! He didn't trust Fabrizio, and I didn't think it would be a big deal to make it seem as though I had the same issue with you, but this was never my—"

"Again, if you truly trusted me, you would have told me and we could have done things differently. By going in there yesterday to handle the actual signing of the paperwork, you undermined everything I'd done. Since you obviously want to be back at work, it's the perfect time for me to spread my wings, perhaps take my skills elsewhere."

"Apollo, enough!" Dimitri's voice was loud but controlled. "I apologize for going behind your back, but it was not you whom we were testing. I was having a little fun, but not because of distrust or because I thought you couldn't do it."

"It amounts to the same damn thing!" Apollo yelled, throwing up his hands. "Even if you walked in there today and had a meeting with the staff to tell them exactly what happened and that this was a little game you and Pio played, the seeds of doubt are planted. And if I'm not capable of running the business, there's no point in my being the CEO. You might as well come back to work, *Baba*."

Dimitri pursed his lips. "You're overreacting because your mind is on the pretty American—something else we have to discuss."

"There's nothing to discuss." Apollo met his father's eyes defiantly. He'd planned to draw this out a little, make his father grovel, but he was madder now than he'd been when he first found out.

"*Kali-mera*." Paige tried to keep her voice steady as she stepped into the room with her hand outstretched to Dimitri. "I'm Paige."

"*Kalimera*, Paige." Dimitri smiled at the young woman in surprise. Pio had told him she was very attractive, but he hadn't expected her to be wholesome as well. Apollo's taste in women over the years had leaned towards less sophisticated, wilder and a bit on the trashy side. He understood that those women had been chosen for one specific reason, without substance or interest in a relationship, but Paige didn't even come close to what he'd thought was Apollo's type and he was pleasantly surprised.

"Let's have some coffee," Apollo said.

"I'll make it." Melina had come in behind Paige and turned around again.

"It would be helpful if you had a place for people to sit," Dimitri muttered in Greek, looking around.

"I'll get chairs from the kitchen," Paige said.

"I'll get them." Apollo put a hand on her arm. Though he wouldn't throw her to the wolves, he knew his father wouldn't be unkind if he left them alone. Even if he didn't like her or approve of their relationship, he wouldn't use his first opportunity with her to say or do something hurtful. His mother might be a different story, but not his father. He left the room after putting a soft kiss on her cheek.

"Do you speak English?" Paige said quietly.

"Enough," he nodded. "I speak less, understand more."

She nodded. "I'm sorry we're getting off on the wrong foot. Apollo and I did something foolish, but we really care for each other. We were young and..." She held up her hands, palms up as she shrugged. "I can't explain why we did it."

"Love," he said simply, a twinkle in his eyes. "Sometimes this is not easy to explain."

She knew her cheeks turned pink, but she didn't avert her gaze. "We just wanted a little time to be together...to see if we still feel the same. Does that make sense?"

He nodded. "Of course. This is smart. The situation with the business—" He said something in Greek she didn't understand and paused at her frown, scratching his head. "Bad timing?"

She smiled. "Yes. An added complication."

Apollo came in with four folding chairs and set them down, opening each and motioning for his father to sit. He walked with a cane even though he didn't need it most of the time. It was simply a little extra protection for when he occasionally lost his balance, and Apollo didn't like the thought of him getting overtired.

"I'm going to get the table too," he said, going back to the stairs.

Dimitri sat down and looked up at Paige. "You will sit also? You are too tall."

She smiled and sat beside him.

"Apollo is angry," he said after a moment. "I did not wish this."

"He's hurt," she corrected mildly. "He thinks you don't trust him—and he's worked very hard to earn your trust. It means a lot to him to know you're proud of him."

The older man's eyes grew cloudy. "Very proud!" he whispered hoarsely. "He is…" He launched into a torrent of Greek that she didn't understand, but it wasn't hard to get the gist of it: how much he loved his son.

Standing just outside the doorway listening, Apollo felt a moment of shame at his earlier behavior but he had to stand his ground. The older generation often tried to micromanage everything and had a hard time letting go. He didn't begrudge his father coming back to work, but undermining a deal he'd worked so hard to make happen was humiliating. He couldn't let this be a precedent; hopefully, there would be a way to work past this because despite his waning anger, he knew the guys at the office would be looking to his father now instead of him. It was the way things worked in a small company like theirs, and he hadn't put in this many hours and given up so much to go backwards.

Walking into the room, he pulled out the legs of the card table and set it in front of Paige and his father. Melina came in with a tray of coffee and some kind of sweets that she'd obviously brought with her since he didn't have any in the house.

"You'll have to translate," Dimitri said. "I cannot carry on a quality conversation in English."

"I know." Apollo nodded, sitting next to Paige and reaching for her hand. She squeezed his fingers and he was surprised to see how clammy hers were; she was putting on a brave front despite her nervousness.

"I would like to know your plans," Dimitri looked from Paige to Apollo. He'd said this in English though he didn't think the rest of the things on his mind could be spoken as easily in a foreign tongue.

"We don't know," Apollo admitted, responding in English since his father understood the language better than he spoke it. "She's staying for another 10 days and we're going to try to figure it out."

"Your mother is extremely unhappy with you," Dimitri switched to Greek. "This will be complicated for both of you."

"I know." Apollo responded in kind. "But I can't help that now. We've been married for three years and we don't have a lot of time to make a decision."

"It seems to me your hearts have already made the decision. It's just the details that have to be worked out."

"The details include jobs that are 7,000 miles apart," he said dryly. "Although it appears that I may have to start looking at other options now."

"Ridiculous!" Dimitri grunted. "The men in the office will do as they're told or they will find themselves unemployed!"

"That's just it," Apollo sighed. "We can force them to do as I say, but we can't force them to respect me. You know I'm right, *Baba*. I understand why you did it—I really do—but you've hurt me both personally and professionally. I can forgive you the personal hurt, because I know what was in your heart, but I don't know what to do about the professional situation."

Dimitri sighed, shaking his head as he sipped the strong espresso Melina had made. "This is something we must discuss, but for today, you have much bigger problems."

"Mama?"

The two men locked gazes and Dimitri nodded.

Paige didn't understand the words but she could tell something had just happened that brought them together. She'd gotten used to hearing the pronunciation of *Baba* and *Mama*—with the emphasis on the second "a" and a "b" sound instead of a "p" sound for the Greek version of *dad*—but when Apollo said *mama* this time, it was filled with trepidation.

"What about your mother?" she asked worriedly.

He met her eyes. "It's not going to be fun."

"The good news," Melina said after a moment, "is that you're going to love *Yaya*." *Yaya* was also pronounced with emphasis on the second "a."

"And Sophia?" Apollo asked.

Melina grimaced. "Well, maybe a present would help soften her up."

Apollo groaned. "Look, she's my wife. If we decide to end it, that's our business, but I'll be damned if it's going to be because Mama and Sophia don't like her or try to run her off. I'm serious —if they try to make me choose sides, I'll be on the next flight to America."

Melina's eyes widened but Dimitri merely nodded. "I will attempt to talk to your mother, but you know how she is."

"Mama is expecting you for dinner. 2:30." Melina looked nervous.

"Could we tell Sophia not to bring Giorgios?" Apollo muttered.

Melina snorted.

Dimitri shook his head. "This is probably not the best day for that."

---

aige merely watched, wondering how she fit in here. She understood why they kept switching back to Greek, but not knowing what they were saying made her uncomfortable. They were undoubtedly talking about her, whether it was intentional or not, and she hated being left out. This was what she was afraid of if she somehow decided to stay with him—her heart had already made a decision but she knew she had to listen to her head as well.

"Paige?"

She started, glancing up guiltily. "Sorry, I let my mind wander."

"We're going to dinner with my family at 2:30," Apollo said. "But I was thinking we'd go to the beach for a couple hours. It will give us a chance to talk."

She nodded. "Sure. Whatever you want."

"You okay, honey?" He looked at her closely.

"Just a little nervous. I'll be fine."

He made a strange face but nodded and rose to gather coffee cups.

. . .

*M*elina and Dimitri left a few minutes later and Paige went upstairs to slip on her bathing suit and put her hair up. Going to the beach sounded like a great idea; a place she could relax, think, and prepare herself to meet his family. Things had gotten far more complicated than she'd anticipated when she'd agreed to stay, and part of her desperately wanted to go home. If only that didn't mean leaving Apollo. It was crazy, but loving him felt natural and as she'd sat there listening to him and his father, she'd realized just how connected they were. Marriage, in the legal sense of the word, was nothing more than a piece of paper. One signature on those papers at his office would terminate it and technically it would be like nothing had changed in her life. Except being with Apollo again had essentially changed *everything* in her life.

Going back to her life in Las Vegas seemed so foreign after just four days in Greece, and she couldn't explain it. The idea of going out with Tom ever again was laughable. Even though she enjoyed her job, it didn't tug her to go home. She wanted to give notice and leave in good standing, but if the choice was between her job and Apollo, there was no question which she would pick. Her family and friends were another story, though. She was close to her parents and sister, and she couldn't even imagine living 7,000 miles away from Raegan. Not to mention learning a new language, new customs, and a whole new city to find her way around. Would she work? Stay home? Would being with him compensate for so many potential problems? She wanted to say yes, but her brain told her to slow down; this was such a big decision to make for a man she'd technically known less than a week.

"What were you thinking with such a serious face?" he asked her when they were finally settled on two chairs on the beach.

"About this. Us."

"Which part?" he chuckled.

She smiled wanly. "How we can possibly be together."

"Is it so difficult for you to think about living here? With me?" He didn't look at her, his heart pounding as he waited for her answer.

"No more difficult than it would be for you to think about living in Las Vegas with me. Remember, I have a family too. Friends. A job. Granted, I don't make the money you do and I don't own my own business, but I have a life there."

"I know." He squeezed her hand. "But for us to be together, one of us would have to make that sacrifice."

"And it would most likely have to be me because you make a lot more money."

"It might be difficult for me to make the kind of living I make here over there."

"I know."

"But the other side to this is that my father has hurt me professionally here in Greece. I might actually have to think about working in the U.S."

"That would work for me, but I don't think it will for you," she said slowly. "You have a bigger family and, despite what's happened with this deal, this is still your family business and your legacy. Your father will eventually pass away and it will be up to you to take over."

"That might not be for 30 or 40 more years," he pointed out. "My father is only 48."

"It's just so complicated."

"After what we've shared in just a few days, do you believe you'll be able to simply walk away from what we have?" he asked. "Because I'm having a hard time imagining my life without you in it now that you're here."

"Me, too." She looked up and shook her head. "Is this real, Apollo? Are we really trying to decide if we want to stay together?"

"I don't know what you're doing," he said levelly, still not looking at her for fear she would see the vulnerability in his eyes that he hoped was hidden in his voice. "But I've regretted walking away from you for more than three years and I plan to do everything in my power to convince you to stay with me."

"What happens if things don't work out?" she asked, realizing she needed to be honest. Their relationship was still new and their time together limited; she couldn't keep things to herself because the clock was ticking.

"What do you mean?"

"I mean, if I uproot my life to stay here with you and you find someone else or a year down the road you figure out that you're not happy…or something. I'm afraid, Apollo."

Their eyes met and he gripped her hand so he could bring her fingers to his lips. "If you're concerned that things might not work out between us, leaving you stranded in a foreign country, that's a fair concern. I can't think of any reason you would ever be in a situation like that—we're married, which means you would have access to everything I own. My home, my bank accounts, almost everything. If we decided to separate at some point, I couldn't give you part of the business—Lakkas, International belongs solely to my parents until they're both gone—but you would have your own money and half of everything we bought together."

"It's not about money," she protested. "It's about a safety net. If you and I have a fight, who can I talk to? I would only have you. If your mother hates me, every meal, every holiday, everything will be about me being stressed and dreading it, with nowhere to go."

"We'll argue," he said softly. "But we'll never *fight*. There's a difference and I make that promise to you now."

"My friend Nina in high school was Greek and her parents fought all the time, with everyone—each other, the kids, the rest of the family, neighbors. One time I got so uncomfortable her mother pulled me aside and told me it's a Greek thing—they fight as passionately as they love, it's just their way. Is your family different?"

He paused. "Yes and no. We don't fight like that regularly. We did a lot more before my father's stroke, but since then we've had to learn to stay calmer and talk more, instead of yelling. Sophia and her husband do a lot of yelling, but I think that's more because they shouldn't be together. He's a prick. I can't stand him and neither can Melina or my father. My mother tolerates him because his family has money and she thinks that's important, that Sophia be taken care of, especially in these difficult economic times.

"Personally, I was never a big yeller. Yeah, sometimes—I guess it is in my blood to some extent," he chuckled. "But not in an ugly way. And living in the U.S. for five years showed me a lot. I didn't come home at Christmas; I went home with my best friend and roommate, Mick. His family showed me that you don't have to yell all the time, that you can get your point across with class and well-chosen words. Don't get me wrong, my family isn't like some Greek families who scream and yell and hit each other. Greek men have been known to smack their wives around, but my father never did and I certainly never would..." His voice trailed off. "I guess what I'm trying to say is that our marriage—our relationship—would be a mixture of both cultures.

"I love being Greek. We're a strong, proud people with history and passion and, to be honest, the best food in the world."

She chuckled. "I will absolutely agree with that."

"But I also loved living in the U.S. There's so much of everything, and the idea of the American Dream is still alive and well. Some of the people I met are still what I consider friends for life; Mick is as close to me now as he was when we lived together. Texts, email, the occasional video chat—hell, we still bet on football games every Sunday! So there is nothing keeping me from potentially living in the U.S. It's just..." He sighed.

"The business is here, and no matter how angry or hurt you are now, or how much you bluster at your dad—you still want it to be yours."

He looked away. "Sort of. I also think that maybe a few years away would make a difference. Maybe I could get a job in a similar industry in the U.S. and learn from someone else. Someone who isn't my father. You know? Maybe this is a sign that it's time for me to make changes."

Their fingers were still linked between them and she used her thumb to stroke his forefinger. "I would love having you come to Vegas with me, but you probably wouldn't find a job in the shipping industry there."

He shook his head. "No. Most likely I would need to be in L.A., San Francisco or New York."

"Lots of sports teams in those cities," she reasoned. "I'm sure I could get a job. Those are really expensive places to live, though. Like 10 times more expensive than Vegas."

"Let's not get ahead of ourselves. Let's just focus on us right now, okay? We have to be sure that we want to be together before we upset both of our lives. If you move here, it's going to be a huge change for you, and even though I've lived in the U.S. before, it would be totally different this time. Finding a job, getting a green card, and both of us in a new city. I'm sure moving away from Vegas would be stressful for you no matter where you go."

She nodded. "Probably. But being with you...well, I think it would be a lot easier."

He smiled, leaning back in the chair and closing his eyes. "Honey, I did the pros and cons in my head last night and the pros definitely outweigh the cons. We just have to make a decision, but I think it's too soon for that. Let's enjoy the morning and I'll try to prepare you for meeting my family."

She groaned. "There went my relaxing morning at the beach."

"Lena's on our side and my father promised he would try to get my mother on board, at least to give you a chance."

"I guess that's all I can hope for."

. . .

"Are you sure it's okay to wear this dress?" Paige asked Apollo three hours later as she got dressed.

"It's beautiful," he said, pressing a light kiss on her bare shoulder. She was wearing the same white dress she'd worn the day she'd first come to the office to see him, and he loved it. She was much darker now that they'd spent almost every day outdoors, and the stark contrast of her darker skin against the white of the dress was stunning. "You're beautiful."

She smiled. "I don't know if I'll ever get used to hearing that."

He frowned. "Didn't Tom ever tell you he thought you were beautiful?"

She shook her head. "Pretty, cute—he'd call me sexy when we were in bed, but it seemed forced, as though he *had* to say that because we were having sex."

He scowled. "He sounds like a douche—I don't care who you are or who the woman is, when you give a compliment, especially during sex, mean it. Beauty is subjective, so if I say it, it's because I think you're absolutely gorgeous. And frankly, I don't give a damn if anyone agrees with me, because you're mine and I'm the only one who has to think so."

This time her smile lit up her whole face as she stepped into sandals and held out her hand to him. "So, are we ready?"

"Honestly—no." He laughed, wrapping his arms around her. "But it's going to be okay. I promise."

She arched a brow. "You have absolutely no way of promising me any such thing!"

He lightly kissed her. "I can do my damnedest, though!"

They drove to his parents' house in a neighborhood not far from his own. They'd bought it only 10 years ago, upgrading from the tiny home he'd grown up in. Though it had been clean and functional, it was small, just two bedrooms and one bathroom for two adults and three children. It had been close to the beach, though, and his parents had gotten good money for it. Then they'd bought this house, which cost a fortune and wasn't quite as close to the beach, but still just a ten-minute walk there. It was big, with three bedrooms and two and a half bathrooms. Everything was modern and sleek, with beautiful floor-to-ceiling windows in the main room and a balcony that wrapped all the way around the second floor, so each bedroom had access to it. He and Sophia had moved out, of course, so with his parents in one bedroom and Melina in the other, they now had a room for his grandmother, though she was always willing to give it up for guests and would sleep on the couch no matter how much anyone protested.

Pulling into the small driveway, he glanced at Paige who seemed pale suddenly. "You okay?" he asked, going around to open her door for her.

"Kinda." She made a face. "I might be a little nauseous."

"We'll just tell my mother you're pregnant and the thought of grandchildren will make her forget all about how we got married."

She snorted. "You're not helping!"

"Sorry." He kissed her, his lips claiming hers gently but insistently. "I'm really sorry I have to put you through this, but this is my family, you know? I don't care if my mother gets mad about how we did things; as long as you make an effort, that's enough for me."

"I will," she whispered. "I just...what do I say when they ask if I'm moving to Greece? You know they're going to try and separate us today so they can size me up."

He nodded. "You tell them we're trying to figure it out but that you're open to it. That'll hold them off until we make our decision."

"Okay." She gripped his hand tighter than she intended but he didn't protest, guiding her through a pretty garden filled with roses and up to an ornate front door.

Apollo threw open the door and pulled her inside as he called out to his mother. "Mama? *Pou ise?*" *Where are you?*

"*Etho!*" *Here.*

Paige took a deep breath as they continued through what appeared to be a small den of some kind into a big open room at the back of the house. A large table was set in the center of the room, and there was a man sitting at it eating a piece of bread. He looked up and narrowed his eyes, nodding at Apollo and sliding his eyes up and down Paige's body without even trying to hide it. She felt the heat of embarrassment warm her cheeks at his blatant perusal of her chest but Apollo slid an arm around her waist and tugged her against his side.

"Paige, that's my brother-in-law, Giorgios. Giorgios, this is Paige. My *wife.*" He emphasized the word as the other man gave her a smarmy smile.

"Hi." Paige's voice was almost a squeak and she quickly averted her eyes, searching for anyone else she could focus on. She suddenly understood why Apollo didn't like his brother-in-law; he was a creep. Why on earth was Sophia married to someone like him?

"Apollo." His mother came out of the kitchen with a smile for her son, ignoring Paige entirely.

"Mama." Apollo kissed her on each cheek and then pulled Paige forward. "This is Paige. Be nice or we're leaving."

His mother scowled at him. "When have I ever been not nice to a guest?" She turned to Paige and switched to English. "Hello, Paige! I am Maria Lakkas—welcome to our home."

"Thank you. What I've seen so far is lovely." Paige hoped she didn't sound like an idiot, but she felt like one right now.

"This is my daughter Sophia," Maria turned to someone who'd come in behind her and the surly-faced young woman arched a brow.

"I've heard so much about you," Paige said, holding out her hand.

Sophia ignored her gesture. "I wish I could say the same."

"Sophia." Apollo's voice was barely a whisper but laced with an edge that got his sister's attention.

"What?" she asked, shrugging. "I don't know her."

"That's why she's here. Behave or we'll leave."

"Makes no difference to me," Sophia chuckled.

"It makes a difference to me!" Maria snapped in Greek, smacking her daughter in the arm. "Go get the salad."

Sophia left the room after rolling her eyes and Maria held out a hand to Paige. "Come. Don't pay attention to Sophia—she is having the hormones." She said something to Apollo, who scowled, but turned to Paige.

"She's been unable to get pregnant again so she's taking all kinds of drugs to see if they'll help."

"They can wreak havoc on your body," Paige said sympathetically.

"Yes, it has been difficult for her." Maria had a deep accent but seemed to have a better command of English than her husband did.

"Where is her little boy?"

"Mihalis is with his other grandparents for today—we thought it better not to have him running around while we talked."

They moved towards the table.

"How do you like Greece?" Maria asked as she motioned for Paige to sit.

"I love it!" Paige smiled. "Especially the food."

"Be careful or you will be fat," Giorgios drawled, his eyes meeting hers.

"I keep busy," Paige replied lightly. She could feel Apollo stiffen beside her so she simply kept smiling. "With all the walking I've been doing, I think I'll be okay."

Giorgios appeared as though he was going to say something else but the sliding glass doors opened and a tiny woman in black appeared with a broad smile on her face. She had short, curly gray hair, a time-weathered face and a fantastic tan. She wore a shabby black dress that fell below her knees, covering most of her skin, and it was her eyes that captivated Paige; emerald green like her son, grandson and younger granddaughter. Sophia, she'd noticed, had dark eyes like Maria.

"This is my grandmother," Apollo said, getting up and hugging the older woman, laughing as she pinched both his cheeks and then slapped one of them lightly. Whatever she said to him made him laugh harder and he took her arm as he presented her to Paige. "This is Thespina Lakkas, my father's mother and the world's greatest grandmother."

"Yes, I am special!" she laughed, reaching out to hug Paige and kiss both cheeks. Then she went off in Greek and Paige looked at Apollo helplessly.

"She said you're gorgeous and that we're going to have beautiful babies."

Paige turned red but laughed too. "*Efharisto!*" she said, nodding at the older woman.

"Oh, please tell me you're not really trying to impress anyone with your Greek!" Sophia rolled her eyes, setting a huge bowl filled with Greek salad on the table with a thump.

"You don't have to be nice to *her*," Apollo stage-whispered to Paige.

Paige simply turned, fixing a look on Sophia. "Two wrongs don't make a right, and anyway, I totally understand how she feels. If my sister married some guy and then brought him home three years later, I'd be a little put out too."

Apollo gave her a small smile as they sat back down. His grandmother sat across from him and Paige, smiling and asking questions that Apollo had to translate. He didn't mind. He adored his grandmother and they were close. He didn't see her a lot these days, but she'd helped raise him and his sisters while his mother did everything she could to help Dimitri get the shipping company off the ground. They'd been young, just 18 when they married, 19 when Sophia was born, 21 when Melina came along and only 23 when Apollo was born. Three kids under the age of five had been a handful for Maria, so Thespina had stepped in and taken over, allowing Maria and Dimitri to work.

As he explained what it had been like growing up with his grandmother, Paige and his *yaya* exchanged smiles and looks that seemed to have more meaning than words and Apollo mentally thanked his grandmother for stepping in when he needed her. She always had, of course, but as the kids had gotten older, Maria had become more and more jealous, and when Apollo was 13 Thespina had left and gone to live with another one of her children, who lived a few hours north of Athens. She'd gotten sick while Apollo was away at Yale and Dimitri had put his foot down, bringing his mother back. She and Maria seemed to have made their peace, but it was obvious that *Yaya* still liked to make mischief, from the way she was happily accepting of Paige.

Maria and Sophia took turns asking Paige questions about her parents, her job and her life in Las Vegas. Yaya asked questions about what she'd seen while she'd been here in Greece. Giorgios essentially shoveled food in his mouth, his eyes drifting to Paige's chest every so often until Sophia would snap at him. Dimitri was mostly silent, watching his family alternately bicker and laugh, but refraining from joining in. Only Melina seemed relaxed, talking with Paige and Apollo as if they'd always been a couple and ignoring her mother, sister and brother-in-law completely. The meal was strained but polite until they were just about finished eating.

"Look, I don't know why we're dancing around the subject," Sophia said, putting down her fork and looking around the table. "That's the whole reason she's here, right? To find out what's going on?" She was speaking in English and looked right at Apollo. "So, tell us, little brother—what are you doing with her? She came here with divorce papers so she obviously has another man back in the U.S. Are you truly going to allow her to make you her final fling, or whatever she's doing, until she goes back to some other guy?"

"Sophia!" Apollo slapped his hand down on the table so hard the dishes rattled and Melina jumped, her hand flying to her heart.

"Don't raise your voice to my wife!" Giorgios growled in Greek.

Apollo cut him a look. "Really? Because you never do?" He turned back to Sophia. "If I have to be nice to your asshole of a husband, you sure as hell will at least be respectful to my wife."

"My husband and I are actually married!" she spat. "Living together, building a future! You and Paige didn't even bother to stay in touch and she came here to get a divorce! Do you not see what she's doing?!"

"We were two scared kids who did something impulsive and then didn't know what to do about it!" he snapped. "She came here to see me in person before we signed those papers—otherwise she could have sent them by FedEx and been done with it."

"So are you moving to Greece?" Sophia turned to Paige, switching back to English. "I mean, seriously, are you going to give up your life and move here to be with him?"

"Maybe." Paige lifted her chin and knitted her brows together. "We're still sorting through the details, but it's definitely on the table."

"Oh please!" Sophia rolled her eyes. "Girls like you don't pick up and move to another country! You're going to jerk my brother around so you can enjoy a little Greek cock, and then go on your merry way!"

"Sophia!" Maria felt snapped to attention, her dark eyes blazing. "*Skase!*"

"Am I the only one worried about Apollo?!" Sophia protested, glaring at her mother. "Women don't just leave their whole lives behind and move halfway across the world for a guy they've known a week! And it's obvious he's crazy about her so he'll do anything she wants!"

"Just because *you* chose the guy who was comfortable instead of a guy you were in love with," Melina interjected softly, "doesn't mean all women would."

11

A shocked silence filled the room as Sophia gasped, then got up and ran out, the door slamming behind her. Maria waited a beat, looked at Giorgios—who suddenly seemed interested in another helping of *pastitsio*—before going after her daughter.

"What just happened?" Paige whispered to Apollo.

"I'll tell you later," he whispered back.

Thespina said something to Apollo and he nodded. "*Yaya* wants to show you her garden... Would you walk with her? I'm going to try to calm everyone down."

"Of course." Paige got up and the older woman took her arm, leading her outside.

They walked in silence and then Thespina began to speak. "My English, not so good, but I understand everything. You understand?"

Paige smiled and nodded. "You speak quite well!"

The old woman waved a hand. "Not good, but when children are small, they learn English and *Yaya* must help with studies. I learn because they are talking all the time. I do not speak, just listen, but now I try."

"It's okay, I don't mind if we don't talk."

"Talk is good, no?"

"Oh, yes!"

Thespina knelt in front of a bed of roses and said something in Greek before snipping a beautiful white rose and handing it to Paige. "Beautiful flower, yes?"

"Yes, thank you." Paige held it to her nose and inhaled deeply, enjoying the fragrant aroma.

"You like Greece?" Thespina tended to her roses, not looking up, but Paige sensed an underlying meaning.

"I love Greece," she said slowly. "I just don't know if Apollo and I can make this work."

Thespina paused and looked up at her, squinting. "Make work. Like marriage?" She chuckled. "All marriage work! Just needs love and respect."

"Love and respect…" Paige smiled at the older woman. "We have a lot of that, I think."

"You love Apollo?" Thespina straightened up and looked at Paige curiously. There was no censure or accusation in her eyes, only a genuine desire to know the answer to her question.

"Yes." Paige sighed, twirling the rose between her fingers. "He's…wonderful. Smart and handsome and so sweet. I don't know what to do."

"Is easy." Thespina headed around to the back of the house, opening a door that led to some sort of basement. "Come." She led her down a short flight of stairs into a cool, dark room filled with boxes, trunks and what appeared to be random pieces of furniture. She dug through a few boxes and pulled out what looked like books. She held them against her chest before settling into an old rocking chair. "Sit." She motioned to Paige.

Paige sank onto a stool next to her, looking at the contents in her lap curiously.

"Family," Thespina said softly. "My husband—he die long time."

"Apollo said before he was born."

She nodded. "Yes, many year." She opened the largest book and it turned out to be more of a photo album. "This is Apollo—my *husband*."

Paige's eyes widened; it was almost eerie how much Apollo looked like his grandfather. They had the same broad-shouldered build, dark hair and chiseled features. And Thespina had been fair-haired as a young woman, similar to Paige. Seeing Thespina and the elder Apollo together in the old pictures brought a wave of nostalgia over her that she couldn't quite identify. This wasn't her family or her heritage, but looking at them was like looking into a mirror. Their wedding picture was similar to many of the era; two unsmiling faces wearing simple wedding attire. Yet the twinkle in Thespina's green eyes was unmistakable, even in a faded, black-and-white picture.

"We do not love yet," she said, pointing to the picture. "We are..." She squinted, trying to think of the word. "My father and Apollo father decide we are to marry—we do not love."

"Oh, an arranged marriage?"

Thespina nodded. "Yes. This. Apollo is angry, love another woman—not good. I am happy. My father is mean, I want to leave. We get married and I tell Apollo he can be with other woman—I want only to be safe." She murmured something in Greek. "Is hard to explain...my father not good man. You understand?"

Paige nodded.

"Apollo still loves other woman...but she is not happy with me. She wants marriage, and she tell my father I am not good wife, that I shame my family. My father come to take me—he hits me very much, takes me home, says I have failed." Her eyes were far away suddenly, lost in the past.

"I'm so sorry," Paige whispered.

Thespina snapped back to the present, her eyes twinkling now. "Is not bad. My Apollo is good man. When he comes home and finds things broken—no wife—he understands something is bad. He goes to my father house, sees me with blood…" She motioned to her face, indicating swelling. "He is angry, fights with my father, says I am the best wife, *his* wife, he will take home." She smiled. "He tells me he is sorry, he will not see this woman again, that he sees that my father is very bad man and he will take care of me. And I am having baby."

"You were pregnant?" Paige's eyes rounded.

Thespina giggled like a teenager. "We have bed, yes? No love, but…" She frowned, struggling to find the word she wanted in English.

"Sex?" Paige supplied, blushing but unable to resist helping her find the right word.

"Yes! Sex!" Thespina laughed loudly, slapping her thigh. "Much sex for wedding—I know man wants this and we are married, so I do! Other woman has no brain…she lose my Apollo because she should not go to my father. Very bad!"

Paige nodded. "Yes, that was terrible!"

"Then Apollo love me." Her eyes sparkled as she talked about him. "We are close, love comes quickly, and then children…was good life. He die soon." She sighed. "But memories…" She flipped the pages of the photo album, showing one of her and her husband probably in their 30s. They were laughing, staring into each other's eyes, their love all but wafting off the page.

"Apollo looks like him," Paige whispered, fingering one of the pictures.

"You take." The older woman pried the picture off the page, handing it to her.

"No! You should give that to Melina or Sophia!"

She rolled her eyes. "Melina good girl, but has no luck. Sophia…" She made a motion with her hand that Paige assumed was disparaging, but didn't say anything else. "You will take, so you will remember."

"I'll always remember you!" Paige smiled. She pulled out her phone and held it up. "Selfie?"

Thespina narrowed her eyes. "This is phone?"

"Camera," Paige said with a smile. "Look." She leaned against her and hit the button to switch to the front camera, taking a picture of them. Then she showed it to her.

Thespina frowned. "No! Is ugly! Outside, with sun! Come!" Like a child, she put down the photo album and tugged Paige's hand until they were outside. "Now!" She grinned.

Paige took several more pictures of them, laughing as Thespina made funny faces in all but one. Then she pulled her own phone from her skirt pocket and held it out. "Picture?"

"Let me see." Paige turned it on and studied the symbols. Almost everything was in Greek but she recognized the camera icon and touched it. It wasn't a fancy phone, but it seemed to have all the basic features so she played with it until she realized there was no selfie function. "We can't," she said sadly. "But I can send you this one."

Thespina cocked her head. "No self-eeee?"

"It only takes pictures out…" She pointed and took a picture of the rose garden. "See?" She held it out for Thespina to see.

"Bad phone!" Thespina muttered.

"What are you two up to?" Apollo came around the corner smiling at them.

"I showed her how to take a selfie on my phone," Paige explained. "But she seems annoyed that she can't do it on hers."

"I can take a picture of the two of you," he said in Greek to his grandmother, taking the phone from Paige. He grinned as Thespina hugged her tightly, and snapped the picture. When he showed her she grinned back at him.

"Beautiful!" she said in English. She looked up at him and switched to Greek. "You must not let her go, Apollo."

He nodded. "I'm trying, *Yaya*, but Sophia didn't help the situation and it's not easy for her to just quit her job and move here."

"If you let her go, you will always regret it," she said gently. "Like Sophia. And Melina."

"Melina?" he frowned. "Did she leave someone back in America?"

Thespina just smiled, taking Paige's hand and leading her inside. "Come. We will have sweet now."

"Dessert," Apollo corrected her.

"That wasn't a hard one to figure out," Paige smiled at him. He leaned over and kissed her, his lips smacking hers soundly. "What was that for?" she asked.

"'Cause whatever you and my grandmother did, you made her smile and laugh, which makes me happy."

"She's delightful," Paige said. "We didn't do anything special!"

"Every day is special, no?" Thespina asked.

They walked back into the house and found Dimitri, Maria, Giorgios and Melina having coffee. Sophia wasn't there and Maria looked up as if nothing had happened.

"Did you and Thespina have a nice walk?" she asked, getting up and greeting Paige.

"Yes. Her roses are beautiful. I wish things would grow like that in Las Vegas, but it's hard to have that kind of garden in the desert."

"Is it very hot?" Maria asked. "More than now in Greece?"

"Well, there's no ocean, and that makes a difference."

Without Sophia, the rest of the afternoon was pleasant. They had a table full of desserts and then strong Greek coffee. As Dimitri, Giorgios and Thespina dozed in different chairs, Paige and Melina helped Maria put away the food in the kitchen. Apollo had disappeared to return a phone call to a client so Paige had no choice but to follow the ladies.

"You must not be angry with Sophia," Maria said after a moment. "She is angry. The baby..." She glanced at Melina.

"They don't know why she can't get pregnant again," Melina

said. "There's nothing wrong with her, but it's been three years since Mihalis was born and nothing. Not even a miscarriage."

"Has Giorgios been tested?" Paige asked reasonably.

Mother and daughter exchanged looks. "That's not a thing here," Melina said quietly. "He says nothing is wrong, and won't get checked out."

Paige frowned. "Well, if there's nothing wrong with her…"

Maria nodded. "Yes, difficult situation. But Greek men are very proud—not like in America."

"I don't think a medical condition has anything to do with pride," Paige said. "But I may not understand the culture."

"Do you think you will be happy in Greece?" Maria asked, wiping her hands on a towel and looking directly at her.

Paige was starting to get used to these abrupt changes in conversation, but she wasn't sure what to say. "I think I could be, but it's scary. Apollo is…amazing. I just don't know how we would do it. I don't speak Greek, I wouldn't be able to work—I don't know what I would do. He works long hours and I would be alone. No friends, no family—"

"You have family!" Maria said firmly. "We are family now."

"But you don't know me," Paige said quietly. "I can't explain why, Mrs. Lakkas, but I love your son. We did something foolish three years ago, but now that we're together again, I know exactly why we did it: he's wonderful and I guess he thinks I am too."

"I absolutely do," Apollo said, coming in behind her and wrapping his arms around her. "You're not trying to talk her into leaving, are you?"

"We try to talk her into staying," Maria said gently. "But I don't think she's ready. And I don't think you are either, Apollo." She looked from one to the other. "I would like very much to see one of my children happily married…and I can see that you and Paige are very much in love. The trouble is that she's American and you're Greek. Very American and very Greek. This is not simple, to change your whole life and move to another country."

"Mama, after what *Baba* did, maybe it's time for me to spread my wings. Find a job in America and—"

"Apollo!" Maria's eyes widened. "You cannot!"

"Listen to me," he said gently, gripping her hands in his. "Not forever. But a job for a major shipping company in the U.S. might be good for me. I could learn how other, bigger companies do things, build my résumé and come back to Greece when the time is right."

"If you go, you will not come back," Maria said sadly.

"That's not true," he said, glancing at Paige. "If I spent five years in the U.S., working in the shipping industry, would you be willing to give it a try here in Greece?"

"It would give us time to be really sure this is going to work," she said softly. "But I don't want you to do that unless you really want to."

"It wasn't the plan," he admitted, "but after what happened with this deal, I feel like maybe the universe is trying to tell me something. *Baba* is ready to come back to work and I think Lena could do a lot more. She didn't go to college in the U.S. to work in a clothing store! She could help until I'm ready to come back."

Paige was watching him intently. "Apollo…"

"I know," he said quickly, looking at her. "I *know*. But as I watched things play out yesterday and today, I truly feel like it might be time to do something different. Mick could help me get my résumé together and—"

"Is Mick still in San Francisco?" Melina asked quietly.

Apollo glanced at her. "Technically, yes. How did you know that?"

"We're friends on Facebook," she shrugged. "But I haven't seen him on lately."

"He's been in Japan working on a big project for his firm," he said absently. "You should send him a message. I'm sure he'd love to hear from you."

"Maybe." She shrugged.

"Your father will be upset," Maria said.

"I'll talk to him, but deep down, I think he'll agree that the experience I'd get could be invaluable," Apollo said. "And honestly, I can't lose her again." He glanced at Paige.

Paige moved into his arms, burying her face in his chest. She didn't know why he'd suddenly decided to come to the U.S. after spending the last week trying to convince her to stay in Greece, but it made her happier than anything ever had in her life. She couldn't imagine losing him either, and this seemed to be an excellent compromise. If things worked out, she would definitely be open to moving to Greece. It would give her time to learn the language and for them to build a foundation they didn't have now. It seemed like the best possible plan; she just couldn't quite believe it was happening.

It was late in the day before they got home. As expected, Dimitri wasn't happy about Apollo's plan to move to the U.S. and Paige had sat by helplessly as they argued in Greek, leaving her to her thoughts and worries. Apollo seemed to have made up his mind, sticking to his guns without ever raising his voice and spending a lot of time talking with his father. Eventually, they'd said their goodbyes and headed home. With the exception of Sophia, everyone had been friendly and kind, even Maria, which appeared to have surprised Apollo.

"My father must have threatened my mother within an inch of her life," he laughed when they got back to his house. "I've never seen her so polite in a situation she obviously had issues with."

"Maybe she realized that being already married is different than, 'hey, we're getting married,' or, 'hey, she's pregnant and we have to be together,' or something like that."

He laughed. "I suppose there is that."

"Apollo, you changed your mind really quick," she said softly. "Are you sure you want to move to the States? I think it's a knee-jerk reaction to your father hurting your feelings, combined with my hesitation to moving here."

"Maybe," he acknowledged. "But it's not a bad idea and I think I could learn a lot. It would give you time to feel more comfortable about us, you know?"

"What about you?" she asked. "Don't you feel as hesitant as I do?"

"It's not as extreme of a change for me," he said gently. "I lived in the States for five years and I have friends. I know the language, know my way around some, and have my own money. Even if I don't work for my father anymore, I have money put aside and dividends that come to me no matter what. You don't have that, so I understand why you're reluctant. I really do."

"Your family is going to hate me for stealing you away," she said softly.

He shook his head. "Just as yours would hate me for the same reason."

"It's different for girls," she said. "No matter how much we claim to be strong, modern women, most of us still let a man be the main breadwinner. Many of us can survive on our own, whether we're secretaries or pharmaceutical reps or teachers, but I can only think of one of my girlfriends who makes the kind of salary that would support a family. Maybe that's just my corner of the world, but my parents would be happy I found a man who could take care of me. As long as I was happy and could come to visit once a year or so, they wouldn't be nearly as emotional about it as your family."

"I think I need to put out some feelers—I'm going to talk to some buddies from college and my friend Mick—while we enjoy the time you have left in Greece. I don't know that I can come until I've got some job opportunities, or at least some interviews. You'd still have to move, though. You know that I can't work in the shipping industry from Vegas?"

"I know."

"So you'll have to leave your friends and family—and your job, which I know you love."

"I love you more," she whispered, meeting his eyes.

"Music to my ears." He scooped her up and carried her to bed.

The next night they went out in a big group. Though Apollo loved having her to himself, it was becoming clear that they were going to try to stay together and that meant becoming immersed in each other's lives. Paige already got along well with Melina and now he wanted her to meet some other important people in his life. His closest friend in Greece, Xristos, wanted to meet her, as well as a handful of other friends. He wished Sophia wasn't being such a bitch, but after Melina spilled the beans about her ex-boyfriend yesterday, she'd kept her distance. Even without Sophia and Giorgios, though, they were a big, noisy group that settled across several tables at George's Steak House in Glyfada.

"We eat family style here," Apollo whispered in Paige's ear as Dimitri began to order.

"It sounds like he ordered enough to feed an army," Paige whispered back, chuckling when Thespina ordered a beer.

"He did." Apollo chuckled too. "And wait till she gets tipsy—it's a hoot."

Paige had been a little nervous about being with a large group of Apollo's friends and family, especially since most of the conversation was in Greek, but when the waiter brought an order of something called *saganaki,* she forgot all about that. It was a kind of cheese that was melted and fried, and when the waiter poured some kind of alcohol on it, setting it on fire, she was enthralled.

"Oh my God!" she whispered. "That looks amazing!"

"You have no idea." Apollo cut a section off the seared cheese and put it on her plate. "Go on—take a bite."

Paige did and had to close her eyes as the flavor sent her taste buds into culinary nirvana. This took the idea of mozzarella sticks to a whole new level and she let out a slow moan of delight.

"That's almost how you look when I make you come," Apollo murmured in her ear.

She glanced at him with a grin. "And it's almost that good— damn, it's probably a good thing you're coming to the U.S. instead of me living here… I'm going to weigh a thousand pounds by the time I get home!"

"Nah." He nibbled her neck. "We'll work off those calories in the bedroom."

She flushed, but it was a happy feeling, and she settled in with the group, suddenly feeling like she belonged. Maria and Dimitri laughed and joked, behaving much differently than they had the other day at dinner. Tonight they were relaxed and very much a couple, holding hands and occasionally whispering as they looked into each other's eyes. Melina and Xristos were obviously good friends, enjoying casual banter and switching back and forth from Greek to English. Thespina was by far the life of the party, keeping everyone in stitches as she told stories half in English, half in Greek.

Then the food arrived. From the most basic—French fries—to the meatballs Apollo had told her about, she couldn't seem to try everything fast enough. It was the meatballs that did her in, though. She couldn't even describe the flavor—garlic and onions and meat so tender she wanted to moan. They were bigger than Italian-style meatballs and oval shaped; she'd never seen or tasted anything like it. Though she protested when Apollo dropped five on her plate, she ate every crumb. Along with Greek salad, more *saganaki*, French fries sprinkled with cheese and some kind of fried eggplant that made her mouth water. There was bread, pita and *tzatziki*, along with beer, wine and soda. She ate until she could barely move and then looked at Apollo apologetically.

"I'm pretty sure I'm not going to be able to get naked tonight," she whispered in his ear. "I think I'm going to explode."

He chuckled, brushing his lips across hers. "That's okay, *koukla*. We can wait till morning."

When the waiter brought out complimentary watermelon, she took a bite, surprised at how refreshing it was. "This is the best food ever," she sighed. "I may have to move here just for that."

"You like the food better than you like me?" he pretended to pout.

"Not a chance—but it's close!" She laughed as he nuzzled her cheek.

"You two are pretty disgusting," Melina said with a smile.

"I don't think I've ever seen you quite so enthralled with a woman," Xristos said in Greek.

Apollo shrugged. "Well, it was time, eh?"

"Speak English!" Melina nudged Xristos. "You speak just fine!"

"My accent—is bad!" He shook his head.

"If *Yaya* can speak English," Apollo pointed out, "you can too!"

"English!" Thespina held up her beer and laughed, letting out a loud burp as she did.

"Maybe it's time to go home and leave the young people to have fun," Maria said with a wry smile at her mother-in-law's antics.

"Yes, is time," Dimitri nodded, getting to his feet.

Maria, Dimitri and Thespina left and Melina leaned back with a grin. "Let's take her to Lake Vouliagmeni—it's beautiful at night and we can have a drink or a coffee."

"I don't think I can eat or drink anything," Paige moaned.

"It's beautiful and romantic," Melina winked. "It's actually the remnants of a cave after the roof collapsed. The waters are supposedly therapeutic and during the day it's part of a spa. In the evening, they light up the walls of the rock on the opposite side of the lake—it's stunning."

"I'd forgotten about that place," Apollo admitted.

"'Cause your wife was thousands of kilometers away," Xristos chuckled.

"There is that!" Apollo laughed. He looked at Paige. "You want to go?"

"Sure." She nodded. "It sounds wonderful!"

Paige and Apollo left on his motorcycle while Melina took Xristos and Thanos, one of her and Apollo's cousins, with her. Paige wrapped her arms around Apollo's waist tightly, turning her head to the side so she could rest it against his back as they rode alongside the darkened beaches. It was eerie but beautiful at the same time and she realized that as frightening as it was to think about moving to Greece, she was going to miss this. There would be no motorcycle rides like this, no amazing Greek food, and definitely none of the carefree summer nights. Though she knew realistically winter had to be different even if they stayed here, she couldn't imagine being anywhere else, with anyone else, doing something that wasn't *this*. She was so immersed in Apollo and this life they'd somehow built in just over a week, she didn't know how she would leave him.

"You okay?" he asked as he pulled to a stop at a red light, glancing back at her.

"I'm wonderful!" she whispered, holding him tighter.

"Me too." He closed one hand over one of hers that was clenched around his waist.

They got to a large but somewhat dark parking area and Apollo locked up their helmets in the trunk on the back. Then he grabbed her and pulled her against him, finding her lips with his. It was both tender and animalistic, his mouth somehow doing things to hers that left her feeling exhilarated, frustrated and aroused beyond belief. She was panting, her fingers digging into the leather jacket he wore as she tried to pull him closer.

He had no idea what had her so turned on tonight, but her eyes had been brighter than usual at dinner and on the way here she'd clung to him as if she would never let go. Now she was kissing him with unbridled heat, her tongue so deep in his mouth he could barely keep up with her.

With his cock shifting into high gear, the sound of another car pulling into the gravelly lot made him pull back even though he didn't want to. Her whimper of distress told him she didn't either, but there was no help for that now. He put a hand on her cheek, looking down into her eyes, and whispered, "A couple of hours, baby, and then I'm going to make this up to you."

"I don't know what came over me," she flushed, looking up almost guiltily.

"Me either," he grinned, "but I hope you keep it up!"

She glanced down at the erection poking through his jeans. "Me too!"

They laughed softly, and he paused to adjust his zipper before draping an arm across her shoulders and moving towards Melina, Xristos and Thanos. Joking and laughing, they made their way inside, finding a table near the water. Paige was once again mesmerized, staring at the beautifully lit scene before her. There was a lake she could barely see, but on the other side, the remnants of the cave resembled a mountain with colored lights illuminating it from the bottom. The dock and deck area seemed to make a semicircle, giving the lake shape and allowing visitors to feel immersed in the lake and the caves, even though it was completely open.

As they settled into chairs around a table, she was once again overwhelmed with the thought that she would have to leave soon. No matter how many times she tried to tell herself she was jumping into this, her entire being rebelled against it. She was meant to be with Apollo; it didn't make sense, but sometimes things didn't. That didn't make them wrong. In fact, in her mind, it made them better. Her life with Apollo had started three years ago and they'd foolishly almost lost it. This time, she had to do better. She didn't know how, but she refused to let this fall apart without doing everything she could to make it work.

Staring across the table as Melina and Xristos laughed and told jokes, she suddenly felt part of something real. This might have started out as an adventure, but it had become much, much deeper than a holiday fling; this was her husband and these people were going to be her family. She could feel it right down to her bones and for the first time since she'd discovered they were legally married, she was ready to accept it. She had a thousand questions, a hundred concerns and probably a dozen issues to resolve, but the moment she looked at Apollo's relaxed, happy face, she couldn't imagine doing anything differently.

"So I got a message from Mick today," Apollo was saying, snapping Paige back to the present. "He's going to come to Athens for a few weeks before he starts a new project in Santorini."

"Mick's coming to Athens?" Melina blinked, looking slightly startled.

Apollo cocked his head. "Yeah—you guys always got along, didn't you?"

"Yes, of course, I just…haven't seen him in ages." She took a sip of her coffee.

"He and I were roommates at Yale for four years," Apollo explained. "He's still one of my closest friends—like the brother I never had."

"He's a lot of fun," Melina said with a smile. "I went down there a few times for Apollo's birthday and other special events and that boy can drink!"

"I seem to recall you getting pretty shit-faced as well," Apollo chuckled.

She flushed. "Well, we were in college—what was I supposed to do?"

He laughed. "It'll be good to see him."

"Where does he live?" Paige asked.

"Technically, San Francisco, but he's been in Prague and Tokyo the last couple of years, and now he'll be starting a project in Santorini. He only gets home during the holidays. He loves his work and has moved up the corporate ladder quickly."

"What does he do?"

"Architect," Apollo said.

"Good one," Melina said lightly, glancing at Paige. "I've followed his work online and he's really talented."

"I look forward to meeting him," Paige said, wondering why Melina looked so strange. It was the first time she'd ever seen her sister-in-law look out of sorts and she couldn't help but wonder if Apollo's sister had a crush on his best friend; it wouldn't be the first time something like that had happened. Apollo seemed oblivious, moving on to other subjects while Melina stared off into space.

"So you're really going to move to the U.S.?" Xristos asked him when Paige and Melina went to the ladies' room.

"Why not?" Apollo asked, leaning back in his chair. "She's amazing and I love her. It might be a little crazy, but we only have one life to live—why not have as many adventures as possible?"

"Are you sure about her?" Thanos asked quietly.

Apollo frowned. "You mean, am I sure she's not after my money or that she won't slice my throat while I sleep?"

Thanos chuckled. "Perhaps. I just meant, are you sure she, and the U.S., are what you want?"

"I want her, no doubt about that."

"And the U.S.?"

Apollo sighed. "My father did something really unnecessary and although I think I could work past it, it feels like this was a sign that it's time for me to do something new. Paige is nervous about moving here, and I understand that. She's a woman and she would be here all alone. No job, no money of her own, and she doesn't even speak the language. I not only speak English, I have degrees from a prestigious university I have my own money, and friends I could turn to in case anything ever happened. It's a lot scarier for her. If we can do this in the U.S. for a couple of years, it will give me time to boost my professional résumé and reputation, teach her some Greek, and give her time to truly trust me. I think it's a fair trade."

Thanos nodded. "You're right—I hadn't thought about it from her perspective. If it was my sister, I'd be dead set against it."

"Exactly." Apollo took a sip of coffee. "I'm going to miss you guys, though. My family…the beach."

"You never see the beach," Xristos said dryly. "All you do is work. Maybe America will be good for you."

"You'll work even more in America," Thanos interjected. "They don't get much vacation there, not like we do here."

"I haven't had more than a few weeks' vacation in two years," Apollo shrugged. "We own the company and my father hasn't been able to work so there was no way for me to leave."

"Just make sure she's the one," Thanos said quietly. "She seems lovely—beautiful, educated, smart, and very sweet. But is that enough?"

"Is there anything else?" Apollo asked curiously.

"Compatibility beyond the bedroom?"

Apollo just smiled. "I think I've got this under control."

*I*t was late when they got home and even later when they finished making love, but Paige couldn't sleep. Her mind raced with thoughts about leaving Las Vegas, actually living life as a married woman—as Apollo's wife, no less—and moving him thousands of miles from his family. Intellectually, she knew one of them had to make the move but she couldn't help the guilt she felt that it would be him. Technically, he had the better job, owned a home and had more money, but she would be taking the bigger risk. However, the latest development with his father had changed the plan and it was eating at her.

Sliding out of bed, she slipped from the room and down to his office. It was 3:30 here, which meant it was 5:30 in the afternoon in Las Vegas and her mother would most likely be home getting dinner ready. She walked out onto the balcony and sank into one of the chairs as the phone rang.

"Hello?" Her mother's cheerful voice made her smile.

"Hi, Mom."

"Paige!" Angela Carter sounded pleased to hear from her older daughter. "Goodness, I've been a little worried! You went off to Greece and then said you were staying longer… Are you okay?"

"I'm fine." Paige sighed, closing her eyes as she leaned back. "I have so much to tell you, Mom."

"You met a man." Her mother's voice practically crackled with amusement.

"I met him three years ago. He's the reason I came to Greece."

"Really." Her mother sound perfectly calm.

"Why don't you sound surprised?" Paige asked suspiciously.

"Because although I didn't know when, where or who, I had a feeling the reason you could never truly get excited about Tom was because there was someone else."

"I couldn't get excited about Tom because he's not exciting," Paige grunted. "And he doesn't understand adventure."

"I didn't realize you were so adventurous."

"It's not that simple." Paige paused, took a deep breath and told her mother everything. When she finished, she was exhausted and ready to sleep, but she had to answer her mother's questions.

"I have to admit this is not what I was expecting to hear," she said gently. "You've been married for three years and too afraid to find out for sure? Paige, that's so unlike you! And this young man —Apollo? Are you sure, Paige? I mean, really sure?"

"Surer than I've ever been about anything, to be honest."

"Well." Angela hesitated. "It seems to me I'd like to meet this husband of yours."

Paige smiled. "But what do I do, Mom? He's been trying to convince me to move here and that makes the most sense—financially anyway. But now he's willing to come to the States with me and it feels…wrong."

"In what way?"

"He makes the money—what if he can't in the U.S. and blames me for making him go or ruining his career or—"

"You aren't making him do anything. The change in plan was because of what happened between him and his father. He can't put that on you, no matter what happens."

"You don't sound upset," Paige said hesitantly. "Like you wouldn't mind either way."

"I want you to be happy and every time you say his name, your voice changes…you sound like a woman who's found her place in the world. I don't know how else to explain it."

"But won't you miss me?"

"Of course!" Her mother burst out laughing. "But there are planes—in both directions—and what makes me happy is seeing you and your sister happy. Let's be honest, Paige—your entry-level corporate job in the sales department is nice but it doesn't make you happy. You should be doing something else, something that allows your brilliant mind and enormous heart to shine!"

"Mom, if I move to Greece I'll be a stay-at-home wife—not even a mom 'cause we're not ready for that yet!"

"If you move to Greece you're going to find a way to help Apollo with the shipping company, just like you did the other night. Didn't you say you helped him close that deal?"

"That deal was going to close no matter what, so my presence was superfluous."

"Nonsense. His father set up a test and not only did he pass with flying colors, you did too, even though no one expected you to be part of the equation."

"If he moves to the U.S. we'll have to move to L.A. or San Francisco and I'll probably get another entry-level position, which won't be any fun."

"It sounds to me like you want to move to Greece," Angela said lightly.

"I do but…"

"But what, sweetheart?"

"I'm kind of afraid."

"Your dad and I are always just a phone call away. There is nothing that would stop us from either sending you the money to leave or coming to get you. No matter how far away you are, you'll never be alone, Paige. We're always here for you."

Paige felt tears sting her eyes. "I know. I just… As much as I love him, I still feel kind of dumb, like I'm lost in this spring break fantasy and trying to recapture something that should've ended more than three years ago."

"Then why are you still there? Why did you extend your trip, all but move in with him, risk your job by asking for more vacation time, and already form a bond with one of his sisters and his grandmother? This sounds very real to me, sweetie. You just have to find the courage to do the right thing."

"How do I know what the right thing is?" Paige asked softly. "For me to move here or for him to come to the U.S.?"

"That's between you and him." Angela paused. "But trust your gut. You're a smart girl and if you really love each other, you'll figure this out."

"I love you, Mom."

"I love you, too."

1 3

The next week was uneventful, with Apollo going in to the office each morning while Paige slept in and caught up on work emails. Then they would get on his motorcycle and ride to a different beach, baking in the sun until they were exhausted, hungry or both, before going home to make love and shower. They spent one evening with Maria, Dimitri and Thespina, and another with Melina, Xristos and Thanos again, sitting up talking until late in the night. Apollo and his father had done a lot of talking as well and seemed to have come to an understanding, but Paige got the feeling neither of them were happy about it.

"I've booked a seat on your flight," Apollo said as they lay in bed that night.

"What?" She turned onto her side, staring at him. "I'm leaving in two days—you can't possibly pack up your life in such a short time!"

He smiled. "I'll have to come back to do that, but for now, I thought I'd come home with you, meet your family, start putting out feelers for jobs. Once it's set I can come back and handle all of this."

"Apollo?" She rested her chin on his chest and let her eyes find his in the moonlit room.

"Yeah, babe?"

"I'm worried… I don't think you're going to be happy working for someone else. You're used to being the boss."

He smiled. "The thing that makes this different is that I'm not starving or in desperate need of work—I can quit if it's not working out. I can always come home. And the same goes for you. If you wind up getting a job you hate, you can quit and either find something else or you can stay home. I don't plan to take a job that doesn't pay enough to support us."

She nestled against him. "You make everything sound so easy."

"It won't be easy, but we've decided it will be worth the struggle." He paused. "Right?"

She nodded against his warm chest. "Oh yeah. It just seems like it was all about convincing me to move here and then suddenly you switched gears. I know what happened with your dad upset you, but I think you're going to wake up in six months and want to come home."

"In six months, maybe you'll be ready to give Greece a try."

She lifted her head to meet his gaze. "I think it'll make a big difference once you meet my family and friends."

"What about Tom?" he asked dryly.

She giggled. "You want to meet Tom? It'll be a pretty boring event."

He snickered. "I don't want to, but I think it'd be a good lesson for him—understanding that you can be a responsible adult, be in love and still have *adventures*."

She laughed, nestling even closer against him. "And that's why I love you."

"It's going to work out, *koukla mou*. Trust me. I'm not letting you go again."

"You'd better not."

. . .

*P*aige woke up alone the next morning and stretched lazily. Apollo had gone to the office early to get his father up to speed on any deals that hadn't been solidified or were in the early stages. His friend Mick was arriving today, so he also wanted to make sure he was done relatively early so they could go to dinner after Mick got settled at the house. Apollo had offered to put Mick up at a hotel, but Paige had said that was ridiculous and she didn't need the spare room just for her clothes and makeup. Besides, he would only be there two days before heading to Santorini, which would be right around the same time she and Apollo left for Las Vegas. Apollo wouldn't have a lot of time with his friend and Paige could sense how close they were.

It was still early, but she wanted to get to Apollo's office so she could use the computers there. His personal computer was good, but the ones at the office were faster and she needed to send artwork to a client for an ad and the file was too big to send from here. She showered and did her hair, putting on minimal makeup since it was so hot outside. It was only June and it was almost as hot as Vegas, but with a sea breeze, she found she didn't mind the heat. She pulled on a pair of shorts and a sleeveless top, grabbing her phone off the nightstand. She was about to drop the phone in her purse when she noticed she'd gotten several texts. She opened them and was surprised to see Tom's name pop up over and over.

Are you there?

I need to talk to you. It's about Raegan.

Raegan's been in a car accident—where are you?

I don't know if you have internet but I'm also going to email you. Your phone isn't working and you're not answering texts. It's bad, Paige. I need you to call me ASAP.

With her heart pounding in her chest, Paige ran downstairs to get on the landline in Apollo's office. She called Tom with her heart in her throat, pacing as she waited for him to answer.

"It's about time!" he growled as an answer.

"What happened?" she demanded, ignoring his outburst.

"They think she fell asleep at the wheel," he said, his voice quieter. "She's in surgery now. We won't know anything else until she gets out."

"Oh, my God." She took a deep breath. "I'll get on the first flight I can find."

"I can buy you a new ticket—"

"No, that's okay, I got it. Thank you." She disconnected and ran back to Apollo's room, yanking her suitcase out of the closet and throwing her clothes into it haphazardly. She left Melina's fancy red dress and matching shoes in the closet, along with the bathing suit Apollo had bought her and the pretty white dress she'd been wearing when she'd gone to see him her first day in Greece. She would get them next time she came or he could bring them with him when he met her in Vegas.

Working on autopilot, she finished packing as she used the phone to call the airlines. Since she could call the U.S. without long-distance charges, she called them directly, tearfully explaining the situation to the ticket agent who answered. There was a flight leaving at 1:00, just under four hours from now, and for a fee she could get on the flight. She quickly agreed, giving the woman her credit card number and throwing the last of her things into her carry-on bag.

Pulling her suitcase and carry-on to the street, she was grateful to see a taxi at the corner and gestured wildly until he saw her. She got in and told him where to go. She had to explain to Apollo what had happened and let him know she was leaving; after their abrupt parting three years ago, she didn't want there to be any misunderstandings. She was upset, though. The idea that Raegan had fallen asleep at the wheel bothered her. She knew her friend worked too many hours but nothing like this had ever happened before. She wondered if something had changed, if Raegan had run into trouble financially. Raegan was the best friend a girl could ask for, but she was terrible with money. Paige had finally gotten her to a point where rent and groceries became a priority. Paige forced Raegan to give her money every night she worked so that her share of the rent would be covered, and for a while things had gone well. Paige had been distracted the last few months, though, and with her being gone for two weeks, she could only imagine what Raegan had been spending.

The cab slowed to a stop in front of Lakkas, International, and Paige asked him to wait, just in case Apollo was too busy to take her to the airport. Between meetings with his father and the staff, and Mick's arrival, she didn't want to interrupt his day. She would see him in two days, after all, when he got to Vegas.

She walked in and smiled at the staff who recognized her now and called out greetings.

"Is Apollo in his office?" she asked Melina, who was working today.

"Yes, he's—" Melina didn't even finish talking before Paige disappeared down the hall. She hated being rude but she had no time today.

Paige heard muffled voices as she approached the office and paused when she heard Apollo saying, "...and I had to do something."

"So you never planned to live in the States?"

"Not really." Apollo's sigh was barely audible.

Paige's hand flew to her mouth and she froze, unsure whether to walk in or keep listening.

"Dude, if you love her—"

"Of course I love her—that's why I don't want to lose her!"

"And you think starting your marriage on a lie is the best way to *not* lose her?"

Paige's thoughts were reeling and she felt a little sick, but she couldn't do this now. Raegan needed her and there was only so much she could sacrifice for Apollo; if he truly loved her, he would understand. Whatever he was discussing with Mick would have to be dealt with after she was sure Raegan was okay. If she confronted him now, it could turn into a long, heated discussion and she would barely make this flight as it was, even if she left right this minute.

Frustrated, she turned and hurried back to the front, calling out to Melina as she breezed through the door. "I have an emergency at home—my roommate was in a bad car accident. I'm on the next flight so I have to go! Tell Apollo to call me!"

"Paige!" Melina stood up in alarm. "Wait! How are you—"

"Taxi!" Paige called out, rushing out the door. She glanced back at her sister-in-law and gave her a soft smile. "Thanks for being my friend through all of this—you're a wonderful sister-in-law. I really hope I see you again." Then she was gone.

For a moment, Melina was too confused to move. By the time she got to the front of the building, all she could see was the back of the cab and she stared for a moment. Then she turned and hurried back to Apollo's office. She didn't want to spend any more time with Mick than necessary, but something had obviously happened for Paige not to talk to Apollo and run to the airport in a cab.

She stalked into her brother's office scowling. "What did you do?!" she hissed, putting her hands on her hips.

Apollo paused mid-sentence, his mouth opening slightly as he knitted his brows together. "Lena, what are you talking about?"

"Paige was just here. She came running back to see you and then turned around and ran back out, yelling that someone back home had been in an accident and that she was taking a taxi to the airport. What were you two talking about that would have made her do that?"

Apollo groaned and Mick grimaced.

"I told you lying wasn't good." Mick shook his head.

"What did you lie about?"

"Nothing!" Apollo got up. "Shit, did she say what flight she's on?"

"No, and there are probably a couple leaving in the next two hours or so."

"Is she going to make it?" Mick asked dryly. "I mean, it's an hour to the airport."

"She'll make it," Apollo grunted. "Dammit, I can't even go after her until the day after tomorrow when—"

"Day after tomorrow?" Melina stared at him. "Have you lost your mind? Do you love her?"

"I feel like I've spent the last week answering that question!" he grunted. "Yes, I love her! What did we say? Anything she heard was out of context! I have a lot of different things going on and I'm trying to figure out which one will allow me to make the most money, eventually wind up in Greece and have her too!" He looked completely bewildered.

"You're a dumbass!" Melina rolled her eyes. "You better be on the first flight to the U.S. tomorrow. I don't know exactly what you said or what she heard, but instead of telling you her plans, she hauled ass out of here—which can only mean you've done something that hurt her!" She turned on her heel and went back up front, shaking her head. Her brother could be so stupid sometimes, and he was spectacularly stupid when he was with Mick; the two of them were terrible influences on each other when it came to women. It wasn't that Mick was a bad guy, but when he and Apollo were together, they were a train wreck. They'd broken hearts all over Yale and then—she stopped, shaking her head. No way was she going down that road. Her history with Mick was nothing she wanted to think about ever again. She'd let him break her heart once; she would never let him get that close to her now that she'd already experienced it. He'd ruined her for all men anyway; she was damned if she'd let him hurt her again too.

· · ·

*P*aige went straight to the hospital when she got off the flight, grateful she'd left her car parked at the airport. It was just after 8:00 in the evening and she was exhausted, but all she could think about was Raegan. She'd texted Raegan's mother, Nora, when she'd landed and found out the room number, so she was headed there now. Nora had said she would wait for her in the lobby outside the elevator on the fourth floor since visiting hours were ending soon, but instead of Nora, Tom was there. Paige frowned when she saw him, awkwardly patting his shoulder and turning her face when he tried to kiss her.

"Welcome home," he said quietly.

"Where's Nora?" she asked abruptly.

"I offered to wait."

"Tom, I don't have time for this right now—I just want to see Raegan."

"I thought maybe you'd missed me," he said after a moment.

"Honestly, I didn't." She bit her lip as she looked at him. "I'm sorry, but you're the one who said you didn't know if we would see each other again, and the truth is that I *am* married. I'm sorry —I can't do anything until I sort that out."

"But you're going to divorce him, right?"

Paige felt a wave of discomfort as Mick and Apollo's conversation flashed through her mind: *So you never planned to live in the States? Not really.*

What kind of game had he been playing? Had he really been leading her on? She couldn't think about it, though, and she met Tom's worried gaze. "I don't know yet. We're working on things."

"You're working on things?" His eyes widened and he looked truly baffled. "Are you kidding me? I didn't waste the last two years with you so you could run off to Greece!"

"You didn't *waste* the last two years!" she shot back angrily. "We had a relationship that was lovely most of the time. It just happens that it's not meant to be—I'm sorry you find that a waste of your time! I learned a lot from our time together, and I don't regret it at all."

"Probably because you needed someone to keep you warm while you waited for your husband to decide whether or not he wanted you!" he snapped, his eyes blazing with anger.

Paige had never hit anyone in her life, but her hand seemed to move of its own volition when she reached out and slapped him. "You need to leave!" she hissed. "This is why I couldn't marry you. You're all pretty and polished on the outside but petty and mean on the inside. Please don't ever contact me again." She turned on her heel and hurried down the hall, so angry she was shaking. But then she saw Nora and waved.

"Paige! Oh, thank goodness you're here!" Nora hugged her tightly. Paige and Raegan had been friends since they were 17 and knew each other's families well.

"Is she okay?" Paige's eyes filled with tears.

"She's not out of the woods, but she's resting and stable." Nora sighed, rubbing her eyes. "She fell asleep at the wheel. She's been working two jobs—did you know that?"

"Two jobs?" Paige frowned. "No! She was taking extra shifts at the casino but I didn't know about anything else."

Nora nodded sadly. "She took a job…stripping."

"Stripping?" Paige couldn't stop her mouth from falling open. "Are you sure? I mean, really?"

"Yes." She looked away. "I know she's never been great with money, but she's been doing so well since you two graduated… I told her she should wait on her MBA, but she didn't want to."

"But how…" Paige tried to wrap her mind around it. "I don't understand!"

"The only reason we know is because she was driving another one of the girls home and she wasn't hurt very badly…just Raegan."

"How bad?" Paige met her eyes.

"Her leg is broken—they put her in a cast for that, but they had to operate to remove her spleen and repair a punctured lung. She broke several ribs and one of them punctured the lung, which collapsed, so she was in surgery for hours. She was asleep when I came down to meet you but she's slept on and off all day, so she'll probably be awake again soon."

"Damn." Paige sighed, trying to imagine how Raegan would get up the stairs to their apartment.

"The car was totaled, but I haven't told her yet. She's asked several times—I know she's thinking about work—but I told her we didn't know."

"She's going to be upset," Paige said quietly. "What can I do?"

"I think she just needs her best friend right now. She's freaked out and scared, thinking about everything except getting better. You're going to have to convince her to come home, Paige. She can't stay here in Vegas."

"She doesn't want to go back to Phoenix," Paige said softly.

"I know that, but her father and I can't afford to pay her expenses while she's healing. I'm so sorry to say this, but it looks like you're going to have to find another roommate."

"I'm not worried about me," Paige said quickly. "I just want her to be okay."

"I'm going to go get some coffee—do you want some?"

"Yes, thank you. I'll go see how she is."

Paige walked into Raegan's room and sighed when she saw her friend. One leg was in a cast and she looked terrible. There was a bandage on her forehead and bruises on her arms and what she could see of her chest.

"I can't leave you alone for five minutes," she said softly, trying to force a teasing lilt to her voice.

"Oh, God, Paige, what am I gonna do?" Raegan looked defeated and Paige hurried to her side.

"Don't worry—I'll figure something out!"

"I can't go home!"

"I know!"

"My mom doesn't—"

"I know. Don't worry. You're not going home. I'll figure something out."

"If you go to Greece, I won't have any choice." Raegan's blue eyes filled with tears.

"Why didn't you tell me you were in trouble?!" Paige demanded. "I might have been frustrated with you, but I could have helped!"

"It's not what you think!" Raegan whispered. "It was the car. Over a thousand dollars in repairs and then I didn't have the money for the books for my next class!"

"Oh, Raegan." Paige sighed, but reached out to stroke her friend's hair.

"I know."

"Let me think about it. It'll be okay." Paige sank into the chair next to her friend's bed and tried to focus. So many things had happened in such a short time, she was overwhelmed. She couldn't even start to worry about Apollo right now; her first priority was Raegan. Technically, they could move in with Paige's parents. It would be a huge inconvenience and miserable for everyone, but that was the safest place they could afford. Paige could swing the rent at their apartment for a couple of months but the logistics of getting Raegan up and down the stairs would be a nightmare.

Where's Apollo when I need him, she thought miserably. The thought came out of nowhere and she realized how much she'd come to rely on his quiet strength and stability. She refused to jump to conclusions about what she'd heard, but she'd needed to get to Raegan and she had to have faith that he loved her. His only motivation for maliciously leading her on would be sex, and that was ridiculous. A guy like him could have a different woman in his bed every night, so luring Paige into bed seemed unnecessary; she would have slept with him even if he'd signed those divorce papers and they both knew it. She regretted not talking with him, but aside from her panic about getting to Raegan, she'd also been a little shell-shocked. What had she heard? Why had he felt it necessary to lie about anything? Moving to the U.S. had been *his* idea, so she didn't understand any of it.

She'd have to think about it later, she realized. Right now she had to take control of Raegan's situation. Nora was bipolar, and although she loved her daughter, she was oblivious to things that had gone on while Raegan was growing up. She was finally correctly medicated, but still had bad days and Raegan's father took care of her; no one could say anything negative about him to Nora so they didn't even try anymore. However, Paige would take out a personal loan rather than let Raegan back in that house.

Apollo could help. The thought flashed through her mind and she glanced at her phone longingly. She was desperate to call him, but part of her wanted him to come after her. She hadn't done that on purpose—her only thought had been getting on that flight —but now it felt like it was his chance to make it up to her for whatever he'd been lying about. Lies were rarely black and white, as she'd learned through this experience. She hadn't *lied* about being married while dating Tom; she'd simply chosen to bury her head in the sand because she was afraid. Since Apollo had done the same thing, it was clear that they'd been young and foolish, despite having genuine feelings. They just hadn't been able to figure out what to do about them. Because of all that, she would give him the benefit of the doubt. He had to be the one to reach out, though. Otherwise, whatever he was hiding would sit between them and fester into something ugly. Something that would force her to ask for those divorce papers... She sighed.

"Paige?" Raegan was staring at her worriedly. "I have to tell you something."

"Don't worry, I'll call my mom," Paige said abruptly. "You can move into my old room. Our lease is up in August, so I'll manage the bills until then and move out as soon as I can. It's only about eight weeks."

"Aren't you moving to Greece?"

Paige shook her head. "I have no idea, to be honest. I left Greece like a bat out of hell and Apollo and I had a little bit of a misunderstanding…but no matter what happens with him and me, I'm not leaving until you're on your feet again."

"What kind of misunderstanding?" Raegan frowned.

"It doesn't—"

"Hi, honey!" Nora came in with two large coffee cups, handing one to Paige absently.

"Thanks." Paige glanced up at her. "You look tired. Why don't you go get some rest?"

"Oh, I'm fine. You're the one who's been on a plane for hours and hours!"

Paige nodded. "I'm okay, I slept on the plane. I just want to stay with Raegan."

"I could use a little nap," Nora said, yawning.

"Why don't you go to our apartment and sleep?" Paige asked softly.

"I suppose I could do that." Nora looked uncertain. "Are you sure?"

"Of course." Paige pulled out her keys and took the key to the apartment off her keychain. "Go relax. I'll stay with Raegan tonight and go home to shower and change in the morning."

"Thank you—you're a good girl." Nora hugged Paige, kissed Raegan and left.

"She's going to fight us on this," Raegan whispered, glancing at her friend.

"Don't worry about anything except getting better," Paige said, squeezing her hand. "Really. I'll take care of your mom."

"I'm sorry," Raegan said after a moment. "This isn't your responsibility."

Paige cocked her head. "Responsibility? You're my bestie—like my sister—this is what we do."

"This is an epic fail, even for me. I can't work with a broken leg, Paige—what am I going to do?"

"You're going to get some short-term disability and then find a job you can do sitting down."

Raegan just sighed, her tear-filled eyes meeting Paige's. "We really have to talk about—"

"We don't have to talk about anything tonight. You look exhausted, so just relax, okay?" Paige held on to her hand tightly. "I'll be right here."

"You're, like, the best bestie in the world."

"I know." Paige grinned at her.

14

Apollo couldn't believe the turn things had taken with Paige. One minute, everything was fine and they were getting ready to leave for Las Vegas and begin their life together; the next she was gone and he was struggling to figure out what she'd overheard. He was an idiot, trying to act so nonchalant about everything, as if Mick couldn't see right through him. He loved Paige and didn't want to lose her; it was that simple. His father's game with Pio had given him an easy way to get what he wanted, which was Paige. If she was nervous about moving to Greece, he could kill two birds with one stone by moving to the U.S. for her and teaching his father a lesson at the same time. Instead, it was all starting to backfire. Mick had shaken his head, telling him how stupid he was and both Melina and his mother were pissed.

"We just started to like her and now you did something to make her leave?!" his mother had reprimanded him. *"Hazos ise?!" Are you stupid?!*

"She left because her friend was in an accident," Apollo had replied with a sigh.

One of his and Mick's friends from Yale was now a detective

in Henderson, Nevada, and Mick had reached out to him to find out what was going on. He'd confirmed that a young woman named Raegan Warner had fallen asleep at the wheel—no drugs or alcohol found in her system—and drove head-on into a concrete crash barrier. Her passenger came away with a few cuts and bruises but Raegan had required surgery for a multitude of injuries, as well as a broken leg. According to the police report, Raegan had simply been exhausted from working multiple jobs and going to school.

Knowing Paige hadn't lied, that she'd truly had an emergency that made her leave Greece without even saying goodbye, made him feel better but he didn't know what to do now. His flight to the U.S. left in the morning and he wanted to be on it, but part of him was as reluctant to leave Greece as she'd been to stay here permanently. That was the hard part; he didn't want to lose her, but he didn't want to leave his family, the company he loved or his lifestyle. He'd enjoyed living in the States—and wouldn't mind visiting a couple of times a year—but in the summer he wanted to be in Greece. The beaches, fun evenings at outdoor restaurants and cafés, and the overall long, lazy days were things he wasn't sure he could live without. And Paige enjoyed them too. If only he could convince her that everything would be okay if she stayed— he wouldn't let anything happen to her if things didn't work out between them romantically. He'd put money in her name only, or give it to her parents—whatever she needed to feel secure.

He heard the bell downstairs, indicating someone was at the door, and he frowned. It was 3:30, siesta time here in Greece, and he wasn't expecting anyone. He was headed down the stairs when he heard the door opening and he sighed, knowing it had to be his parents or one of his sisters. Instead, his grandmother was standing in his useless kitchen, a frown on her face.

"What is this? No wonder your wife left! How is she supposed to do something with this mess?"

"She was here on vacation, *Yaya*," he said with a smile, leaning down to kiss her cheeks. "If she'd moved here, the kitchen would have been a priority."

"What did you do?" she asked softly. "Tell me the truth."

He sighed. "I was talking with Mick…" He told her everything he could remember as they settled into the two folding chairs left in the room.

"You'll go tomorrow, yes?"

"I don't know." He looked at her helplessly. "I want to go after her, but it hurts that she didn't even give me a chance to explain."

"Her friend was badly injured and she had very little time to get to the airport."

"Then why hasn't she called?"

"Why haven't you?" His grandmother cocked her head. "Be the man, Apollo. Don't expect her to chase you—you have to chase *her*. She needs to know you want her enough to fight for her. Especially since you walked away from her three years ago. Yes, you were both responsible, but you were the man. She was a scared girl who did something very foolish; it wasn't her job to hunt you down. And it's not her job now, either."

"But *Yaya*, what do I say? How do I explain it?"

"You tell her the truth—you love her and are willing to do whatever is necessary to keep her. And you'll see…it might take a little while, maybe even a year or two, but she wants to come to Greece. I could see it in her eyes. She's afraid, and I don't blame her. What young bride wants to go to a foreign country with a man she's only truly known a few weeks?"

He closed his eyes, nodding. "You're right. I know you're right."

"Here." She pulled the gold chain from inside her blouse and unhooked it. Taking her wedding ring off the chain, she handed it to him. "Give this to her. I know you'll want something nicer, more modern, but for now, give this to her as a promise. Tell her it's hers, even if things don't work out between you. She brought so much love and joy to my heart in the time we spent together, I want her to have it."

"But Sophia and Melina—"

"Neither of them want it. Sophia would never lower herself to wear something so small and cheap, and while Melina would wear it to please me, she's not truly sentimental. Paige—Paige would wear it with love. Eventually, maybe on a chain around her neck, but for now, it's the only ring you have."

"Thank you, *Yaya*." He leaned over to hug her.

"Now, go. Pack, get ready. You have a very long trip and an even longer journey to winning over your wife. Don't come back without her, Apollo."

He smiled. "I'll do my best."

Between Nora's incessant nagging that Raegan move home to Phoenix, jet lag and lack of sleep, Paige was in a horrible mood. She'd left Greece a little more than 48 hours ago and she'd only managed about five hours of sleep on the flight and five more in an uncomfortable chair at the hospital. In addition, Tom had been texting her repeatedly, under the guise of concern about Raegan. When she questioned Raegan about it, Raegan admitted he'd been visiting her at work and giving her big tips to get information about Paige. Although Raegan hadn't told him anything about Apollo, Paige had a feeling he was planning to use those big tips as a way of manipulating Raegan into helping him win Paige back.

"Great," Paige muttered as they talked about it. "Now he's blowing up my phone and threatening to come visit! Raegan, you need to cut him off. I know the money he was throwing at you was great, but I'm going to be the one taking care of you and I can't have him up my ass all the time."

"I know. I'm sorry. I won't respond to his messages anymore." Raegan looked down.

"Raegan?" Paige knew her friend well enough to know she was hiding something.

"Have you talked to your mom?" Raegan asked after a moment.

"Yeah. We'll figure it out. I'll sleep on the couch and you can have the futon in my old room. My mom turned it into a sewing room, so the double bed is gone, but that's no big deal."

"Oh, hell, Paige, I'm sorry." Her blue eyes filled with tears and Paige shook her head.

"Stop apologizing—it's okay. My mom is worried about you going home and Nicky could probably stay with friends on weekends so I can sleep in her bed. It's going to work out."

"But you have to go to work and you need your rest and—"

"Would you shut up?" Paige scowled at her. "If roles were reversed, you'd be taking care of me, so just let it go! I want you to rest and get better."

"Can you bring me my laptop—I need to let my professor know what's going on. I have a paper due next week that isn't done."

"Should I write it for you?" Paige asked dryly.

Raegan chuckled. "That would be nice, but no, I'll get an extension." She sighed. "Damn, I've got so many bills and no money coming in. I'm really in deep shit, Paige."

"Didn't I tell you—" Paige broke off abruptly as a huge bouquet of flowers came in, completely covering the identity of the person bringing them.

"Surprise!" Tom peered around the massive bouquet. "I thought these might cheer you up."

"Oh! They're so pretty." Raegan's eyes lit up but Paige had to resist rolling her eyes.

"How are you feeling, kiddo?" Tom put them on the table and then went to stand by Paige, though he was talking to Raegan.

"Tired, sore...you know."

"When are they letting you out of here?"

"Not sure yet." Raegan shook her head. "They want to watch the lung a little longer."

"I was thinking about that—and your leg," he said slowly.

"There's no way you can get up and down the stairs at your apartment, so why don't you come stay with me? I can set you up in the downstairs guest room and Paige could even stay with you so—"

"Tom." Paige clenched her jaw as she spoke in a tight voice. "I need to talk to you. In the hallway."

He glanced at her. "Paige, I know you're still upset with me but this is about what Raegan needs."

She took a breath. "Outside. Now."

He sighed. "Fine." He turned and walked out.

Paige gave Raegan a look before following him and Raegan gave her an apologetic shrug.

Out in the hallway, Paige walked until they got to the lobby by the elevators, wanting to make sure they had a little privacy.

"What's this about, Paige?" he asked, leaning against the wall and raising his eyebrows.

"I don't know what you think you're doing, but bribing my best friend isn't going to work."

"I don't know what you're talking about."

She rolled her eyes. "Are you planning to buy her loyalty or her love or what?" she asked quietly.

He narrowed his eyes. "What the fuck does that mean?"

"Why were you hanging out with her at the casino while I was away? You two were never best friends before. Suddenly you were spending all your time with her? To what end, Tom? Big tips to bribe her into getting info about me? To get her on your side so she could help change my mind?"

"You're kind of full of yourself," he said with a huff. "You think you're the only woman in the world who might go out with me? You think I'm going to wait for you forever? What do you think we've been doing these two weeks since you've been gone?"

Paige raised her eyebrows. "What, exactly, were you doing, Tom? Sleeping together?"

"Yes. Exactly." He gave a little smile of satisfaction. "And now she knows what you're giving up."

Paige felt a moment of revulsion—both at him and at Raegan —but managed to keep her disgust at bay. "All I'm giving up is a boring guy who doesn't know how to have fun."

He slowly moved towards her, squinting his eyes slightly as he leaned forward. "She's smart enough to know that *money* is all you need to make life fun. Something you seem to forget as you max out your credit cards in some stupid search for adventure—whatever the fuck that means. She knows now that money can make everything better…I was willing to compromise for you, you know. All you had to do was tell me what you wanted. Instead, you lied and cheated—"

"I never lied or cheated on you!" she hissed, glaring at him.

"No, but you cheated on your *husband* with me." He smirked. "Is he broke like you?"

The elevator doors opened and Paige clamped her lips together, waiting for the nurses to walk past them. "I didn't know if we were actually married," she ground out. "We did a dumb thing during spring break and I was too afraid to go find out one way or the other, but that's not the same as cheating and you know it!"

"All I know is I was willing to give you the world, and you threw me away for what? Some hot, sweaty sex on a beach in Greece? Was your hubby as fun as you remembered or did you come home with a little Greek bun in your oven and a broken heart to boot?"

Paige took a step back and forced herself to breathe. "Believe it or not, having fun doesn't mean being an irresponsible fool. I made one reckless decision three years ago—and honestly, I can't call it a mistake because he's a great guy."

"Then why are you back here?"

She rolled her eyes. "Because my best friend was in a terrible car accident?"

"And where is he?"

"In Greece, running his family's business."

"What do they do? Are they olive farmers? No, wait—fisher-men?" He was grinning at her, condescension all over his face.

She shook her head. "Does it make a difference, Tom? You want Raegan? You can have her, but she won't be interested in your little McMansion and weekend golf outings once she's back on her feet. Remember the girl with the pink hair and tattoos? Not exactly the country club debutante you have in mind."

He snorted. "She'll do it because she wants the money, the prestige—and she'll do anything to stay away from her daddy."

Paige stiffened, unable to believe Raegan had told him about that. "Well, that's between you and her, I guess, but I don't want anything to do with you."

"No?" He walked towards her again, pausing right in front of her, making her uncomfortable with his proximity. "Not even a little bit jealous, honey?"

"Not a single iota." She turned her face away, taking a step back as he leaned forward. "Besides, if you want Raegan, why do you care what I think?"

He chuckled. "Men like me? We don't like to lose..." His voice dropped to a whisper. "You wasted nearly two years of my life and now I have to start over with Raegan, who's going to need a lot of training to learn how to behave, how to dress, how to act appropriately in front of my colleagues—time I don't have. I'm up for a promotion in January and I need a fiancée before then."

"If you think that's going to be Raegan," she laughed, "give it your best shot. She won't give up her piercings and tattoos for anyone—much less you."

"She gave it all up when she was in my bed last weekend," he shot back. "And I have pictures to prove it."

She couldn't help but chuckle. "You know Raegan collects sex videos, right? Like, she has them of pretty much every guy she's slept with. It's her idea of porn."

He growled, advancing on her until she was up against the

wall. "You really fucked me over, Paige. Now I'm scraping the bottom of the barrel because I'm out of time."

Paige felt a moment of concern but reminded herself she was in a public place and he was a big baby anyway. She remembered a time he'd hurt his ankle golfing. It wasn't even a sprain but he spent two days on the couch, moaning and whining like he'd broken a bone. Despite his bullish stance, she wasn't afraid of him; she was too ticked off.

"Leave me alone, Tom," she said in a tired voice, wondering why she'd put up with him for so long. "If you think Raegan is the woman you can mold into what you need, go for it. Take her home and take care of her and pay all her bills—she has a ton, by the way."

He grunted. "She'll pay me back. One way or another."

"Really?" Though she just wanted to get away from him, part of her was angry that not only was he willing to replace her with her best friend, but that he was taking advantage of Raegan's precarious situation in the process. If she'd told him about her father, he knew Raegan would do almost anything not to have to go home to Phoenix. Which left her at his mercy.

"What's the matter, Paige?" He reached out to rub his knuckles across her cheek. "You starting to see what you'll be missing?"

Paige was vaguely aware of the elevator door opening again but she was squirming to move away from his disgusting touch and nauseating closeness. "Get away from me!" she hissed. "I don't miss anything about you!"

"How are you going to pay your rent without Raegan's share, hmm?" He chuckled. "You'll be on your knees, begging me to take you back—probably in about two months. And that's where I'm going to make you stay—on your knees."

"Go to hell!" Paige moved to the side, trying to get away, but he closed fingers around her wrist painfully. "I'd rather be homeless on the street than living with you!"

"You're too proud for that and you know it! Maybe if you drop to your knees right now, and give me a little head, I'd consider—"

"The only thing you should consider is taking your hands off my wife." Apollo's deep, resonating growl made both of them jump, but Paige reacted first, practically vaulting herself into her husband's arms.

15

"Apollo!" She buried her face in his chest as one of his arms closed around her waist and held her tight.

"Who the fuck are you?!" Tom spat out.

"I just told you—I'm her husband. And if I ever see your hands on her again, I'll tear you apart."

"You and what army?" Tom snarled, suddenly full of bravado.

Someone moved from behind Apollo, a tall guy with a bald head and the biggest hands Paige had ever seen. She blinked, lifting her head slightly to stare.

"The name's Michael Laughlin," the big man said to Paige, winking and smiling down at her. He glanced at Tom. "Also known as the army that's going to kick your punk-ass if you don't get the hell out of here."

Tom's face was red and he was sputtering, but he moved into the open elevator doors. "You'll be sorry, Paige! You and Raegan both will be sorry! Mark my words—when these Neanderthals leave you high and dry, don't come running to me!"

"I won't," she whispered, shaking her head. "Believe me."

As the elevator doors closed, she sagged against Apollo in relief.

"Hi," he said gently, looking down at her.

"Hi." She blinked away tears. "You…you're here."

He smiled. "Wasn't that the plan?"

"I don't…how did you know where to find me?"

"I knew Raegan's name, and figured she could only be at a handful of hospitals. I made calls before I left and we came straight here from the airport."

Tears started to fall as she buried her face in his chest. "I don't know what's wrong with him," she sobbed. "He was just boring—he was never mean or crazy like this! He was a nice guy, just not you—when did he change? What just happened?"

"Guys do dumb things when their hearts are broken," Mick spoke quietly.

"I'm sorry." Paige struggled to wipe her face and Mick presented her with a handkerchief.

She blinked, staring at it. "You have a handkerchief?"

He laughed. "Yeah, I know. Weird, right? Something my grandfather instilled in me."

"And he's been getting laid because of it since college!" Apollo grunted. "So keep your sex-fueled hanky away from my wife."

Paige gave a half-hearted giggle, snatching it from Mick's hand while nodding shyly. "Thank you."

"You're welcome." He winked.

"Are you okay, *koukla mou*?" Apollo asked after she'd wiped her face and blown her nose, holding her close to him.

"I am now that you're here," she admitted. "I don't know what's wrong with Tom—he's never behaved like that before."

"It doesn't matter. I'll make sure he doesn't come near you again."

She swallowed hard. "I'm really glad you're here, but we have to talk," she said softly.

"Yes." He kissed the top of her head. "But we'll do it later, when we're alone. Right now, we should go check on Raegan and see what we can do for her."

"You don't have to do anything!" she protested. "That's my responsibility and—"

"Anything that's your responsibility is also my responsibility." He wrapped his fingers around hers, his green eyes boring into hers intently. "We have to talk, absolutely, but everything can wait until we've settled things with Raegan. Tell me how she is."

Paige updated him on her friend's condition and he nodded. "So she'll need care."

"Yeah, but…" She sighed. "It's a long, complicated story."

"Then you'll catch me up later. Let's go talk to Raegan and then I desperately need some sleep."

"Crap—Raegan's mom is staying at our apartment!"

"I can get a hotel," Mick said immediately, nodding. "Don't worry about me."

"We're married," Apollo reminded Paige when she hesitated. "And I'll be damned if I sleep at a hotel a few miles away from my wife. Raegan's mom is going to have to get over it."

She nodded quickly. "You're right, of course. I'm being silly. Come on." She slid her hand into his and tugged him towards Raegan's room. She was still reeling at the fact that he was here and she felt like there was so much they needed to say. She also had a lot to say to Raegan and now she was a little overwhelmed. When she glanced at Apollo, he just gave her a reassuring smile and leaned over to kiss her cheek.

"Whatever's going on, don't worry—we'll handle it together."

She smiled, a slight flush turning her cheeks pink. "I feel bad about the way I left, but you…"

"We'll talk later," he repeated firmly.

They walked into Raegan's room and she was sitting up, her eyes wide as she looked at Paige. "What's going on?! I just got the craziest text from Tom."

"You slept with him?" Paige demanded, shaking her head.

"I tried to tell you…"

"When?"

"Before! But you kept interrupting and telling me to rest and my mom was here and the pain meds and…" She burst into tears.

"Oh, Raegan."

"Who did she sleep with?" Mick asked, confused since he'd come in a few seconds behind them.

Apollo shot him a look but Raegan's eyes widened and she swiped at her face. "Who are they?" she finally whispered.

Paige smiled and pulled Apollo forward. "Don't you remember Apollo? From spring break?"

Raegan managed a faint smile. "You've filled out."

He arched a brow. "That's good, right?"

"Yeah."

"This is my closest friend in the world. Three years ago he decided to go to the Bahamas for spring break and I came here." Apollo glanced at his friend. "So, Mick, this is Paige and Raegan. Ladies, this is the one and only Michael Laughlin…otherwise known as Mick."

Mick shook both of their hands and smiled, his blue eyes twinkling with what could easily be construed as perpetual mischief. "So…who'd you sleep with?" he asked Raegan, cocking his head.

Apollo bit back a laugh but Raegan merely sighed, closing her eyes. "Tom—but it was a moment of weakness," she whispered.

"Yeah, but—why?" Paige looked baffled. "He's boring and…I've told you he wasn't very good."

"He wasn't bad," Raegan bit her lip. "He just doesn't have any imagination—about anything."

"You still didn't tell me *why.*"

"Because you called me from Greece and said you were falling in love with your husband, thinking about staying—which meant that I was going to be here alone and he was there. With a house and money and the answer to all my problems."

"I told you I wouldn't leave you high and dry!" Paige protested.

"And do you really want to sell your soul to Tom for some money?"

"It's not just money," Raegan said quietly. "It's security. I've never had that, Paige. Remember how I grew up—I've never had safety, security, money or even love. My mother loves me as much as she's able with her mental health issues, but my father is an evil man. Something that guarantees I never have to ask him for anything is worth selling my soul for."

"So that's what you're going to do?" Paige asked, frowning. "You're going to start dating Tom? Do you know what he just said to me? I mean, he showed a side I've never seen before."

"He was pretty aggressive," Apollo said. "I know this is really none of my business, but I would think twice about getting involved with a guy like him. I'm glad we showed up when we did."

"He asked me to suck him off, right there in the elevator bay," Paige told her. "Is that what you have to look forward to?"

"I don't know," Raegan said sadly. "But I can't work, Paige. I can't pay my share of the rent. My credit cards are maxed out and—"

"We'd paid all but one of them off!" Paige said in exasperation. "Did you seriously max them out in two weeks?"

"The transmission blew on the car!" Raegan said. "And the brakes were gone. It was over a thousand dollars!"

"And the other four thousand?" Paige asked dryly.

"You know I don't cook, so I was eating out every night. I got the other job and needed new shoes—really sexy but comfortable enough for me to dance in. And new clothes."

Paige made a face. "Yeah, we need to talk about your new job."

"I didn't want you to have to bail me out again so I got a job dancing, just two nights a week. They said I could make 300-400 a night on weekends and I worked the rest of the week at the casino. I figured I could pay off the credit card in a couple of months and stop working there but now..."

"Now you have to decide what you want," Paige said firmly. "I'm willing to do whatever's necessary to help you, but if you choose Tom…"

"I would never choose Tom over you!" she cried. "But this is a huge burden for you. You've been taking care of me—one way or another—since we met. It might be time for me to take care of myself."

"Letting Tom buy you is how you take care of yourself?" Paige shook her head.

"Can we talk alone for a minute?" Raegan asked softly. She glanced at Apollo and Mick apologetically. "I'm sorry, but I need a few minutes. Some of this is personal and I can't…I don't really know you guys."

"No problem." Apollo leaned over to kiss Paige's cheek. "We'll go get a cup of coffee and give you guys about 20 minutes, okay?"

"Thank you." Paige felt an overwhelming urge to run after him and ask him to stay; the last thing she wanted was for him to run screaming from so much drama. He hadn't come 7,000 miles to run away, though; she knew him well enough to know that. She was torn in several directions right now and wanted to handle all of them at once. Since that wasn't possible, she decided to take care of Raegan first. They'd been there for each other since they were 17—but Raegan had a decision to make.

"I can't believe you slept with Tom!" was all she managed to say once they were alone.

Raegan looked away. "Me either."

"Wasn't it spectacularly disappointing?"

Raegan nodded sadly. "Kinda. And then I felt guilty, like I was cheating on you."

Paige burst out laughing. "I don't think it works that way."

Raegan smiled wanly. "I know. I was drowning, Paige. And now I'm basically underwater. I don't know how you're going to help me. Especially now that Apollo's here. It's obvious he loves you and you're going to—"

"If he loves me, he'll want to help you too. But you have to decide, girlfriend. Really. I hate being the kind of person who demands you take sides, but after the way he behaved earlier, I don't want anything to do with him."

"I don't want to be with him either. After we went out a couple of times, I realized what you were talking about—he's really self-absorbed and boring. All he talks about is work, his house and golf. The sex was okay…it wasn't terrible, but there was no chemistry. I was really dumb. Please don't be mad at me."

"I'm not mad—I'm just worried about you. Your judgement lately, your issues with money, your relationship with your mom…at some point, Raegan, you have to take control of your life."

"I know." She looked down sadly. "I just don't know how."

"Look, I really, really need to talk to Apollo. I left without a word—I just told his sister to tell him I had an emergency and left. I overheard something that made me doubt our future, and we have to talk it out or this is never gonna work. Can you promise me you won't say or do anything until I come back in the morning?"

"Can we ask the nurses to keep Tom out of here?" Raegan looked like a scared little girl. "Whenever I'm around him, he's like a whirlwind. Money, solutions to everything, even the sex—it's like he mesmerizes me with his plans until I can't think straight."

"I'll talk to them. All you have to do is rest, okay?"

"Okay."

"If Tom shows up, text me. Is your phone charged?"

"Yes."

"Can you handle your mother if she gets here before I get back in the morning?"

"I think so. Yes."

"I'm going to find Apollo, so we can talk. Then I'm going to get some sleep and I'll be back in the morning. If Tom bothers you at all, though, text or call me."

"Okay."

"Promise?"

"Promise."

Paige hugged her, gathered her things and headed out to find Apollo. Luckily, he was just stepping off the elevator and she walked right into his arms. Burying her face in his chest she whispered, "I'm sorry."

"For?"

"Leaving like that. It was a shitty thing to do but I was so worried about Raegan and then I heard you…"

"That's my cue!" Mick leaned over to kiss Paige's cheek. "I'm glad we got to meet but I'm going to get some sleep. I assume you two have a lot to discuss and, to be honest, I've been on too many planes, in too many time zones, in too short of a time!" He slapped Apollo on the back, got in the elevator and disappeared.

"He seems like a good guy," she said when they were alone.

"The best." He looked down into her eyes. "You look exhausted."

"You too." She slid her arms up and around his neck.

"I'm actually hungrier than I am tired," he admitted. "Can we go eat?"

"Sure. What do you feel like?"

His eyes crinkled into a deep smile. "A burger. A thick, juicy American burger with cheddar and bacon and BBQ sauce."

She raised her eyebrows. "No cheddar, bacon or BBQ sauce in Greece, huh?"

"Not even close."

"Let's go." She moved against him as they stepped into the elevator.

*T*here was a local restaurant nearby that had great burgers so she drove them there, hands linked between them on the center console of her car. They didn't talk, somehow content to just be together. They got out of the car, clasping hands again immediately, and sat on the same side of the table when the hostess led them to a booth. Finally, after they'd ordered and had drinks, Apollo shifted next to her and used his hand to cup her cheek.

"I don't know what you heard or how much of a mess I made of things, but let me tell you this before anything else: I love you. I'm *in love* with you. My chest was so tight when Melina told me you'd left, I thought I might get sick. The thought of losing you again…it was more than I could stand."

"It'll take a lot more than a muffled conversation that I over-heard by accident for you to lose me this time," she said softly. "I heard you talking about sort of lying to me about moving to the U.S. and I couldn't deal with it right that second. I was scared for Raegan and trying to get on that next flight… I knew if I stopped to find out what you were talking about I'd probably miss the flight and I couldn't. And maybe…" She bit her lip.

"Maybe what?" His green eyes bore into hers.

"Maybe I wanted you to chase me." She couldn't break their gaze. "You walked away last time and never even gave me your number—just a business card. This time, I think subconsciously I didn't want to make it that easy…you needed to want this as much as I do."

"I do." He pressed his cheek to hers and pulled her against him. "God, I do. If you want me to come to the U.S., like we talked about, I will. I can do everything we talked about—put out feelers, get a job, work in the shipping industry a few years. I just don't know if I could live here forever."

"I love the States and I was starting to really love Greece too." She moved her head so her lips were just millimeters from his. "But I love you more than both. I love you more than *anything*. I'd follow you to the ends of the earth. I'm scared to move to another country, but the idea of being without you is a hell of a lot scarier."

He crushed his mouth to hers, kissing her with three years'

worth of pent-up frustration, longing and passion. Yes, they'd had a lot of sex in Greece, but hearing her say she would follow him anywhere brought sex to a whole other level.

"If my stomach wasn't literally growling and making me a bit nauseous," he rumbled against her lips, "I would skip the burger and take you home."

She chuckled. "I'm kind of hungry too—food at the hospital has been less than satisfying. Especially after the food in Greece."

"Now that we've settled our feelings, let me explain what Mick and I were talking about." He paused, though he kept her close to his side. "When I was in college I loved living here. By the time I got to my senior year, I didn't want to leave. I was trying to convince my father that I needed my MBA too, and I'd applied for a job as a teaching assistant to offset the cost. That's when you and I met—spring break of my senior year and my father still hadn't agreed to let me stay. I was in a hurry to get back to school so I could make sure I got that TA position to use as leverage. My parents were coming for graduation and then..." He paused. "Look, there's a whole lot of family drama in this part of the story, but let's skip that for now and just focus on us."

"Okay."

"At graduation, my father was still on the fence about letting me stay because Sophia had had a baby during the school year and she and Giorgios were getting married."

"Wait—what?" Paige looked confused.

He nodded. "I know, that's the family drama I mentioned, but right now, I just want to talk about us."

"She was still here in the U.S.? But she's...like four years older than you, isn't she? Wouldn't she have been done with college by the time you were a senior?"

"My parents didn't want her coming to the U.S. alone, so she did some classes online while she waited for Melina to graduate high school. They came together, got an apartment, all that." He gave her a brief history. "Anyway, I was being pulled in a bunch of directions at that point… Sophia's wedding, a new nephew, Lena suddenly keeping her distance. I didn't know what to do, but it felt like my family needed me. So we compromised. I stayed through the summer and took a full course load, worked as a TA and got my master's in just over a year. I had two classes left at the end of the next school year and purposely left the ones I could take online so I could take them from Greece.

"There just wasn't any way for me to see you again, to figure out if things could work between us and at that point I knew I couldn't stay in the U.S. It didn't make sense that you would come to Greece after spending three days together, and to be honest, I let it go because it was easier. Had things in the family not gone crazy, I might have looked you up, maybe made plans to spend more time together, but I didn't have control of my life and you were just another casualty of me having to leave my life in the U.S. behind."

"What does this have to do with what I overheard?" she asked softly.

He sighed. "It's been three years but I still waffle between loving the States and loving Greece. When my father pissed me off with that deal, it was like everything fell into place. I'd get back at him and teach him a lesson. I'd get to come back to the U.S., something I'd wanted to do since before I left college. And I'd get you."

"But you already—"

He put a finger over her lips. "You weren't there yet. You were scared and apprehensive, and I get it. It seemed like the stars were aligning for me for once."

"But?" She squinted slightly, looking into his troubled face.

"But I'm not a 22-year-old college student anymore. I'll be 26 this fall and I love Lakkas, International. I've spent the last two years truly making it mine, in spite of my father's meddling. I love Greece six months of the year and like it a lot the other six months. My family is big and crazy, but really close and loving and fun. My grandmother is getting older and I hate the thought of something happening to her while I'm living far away…"

"So you don't really want to leave," she said softly.

"Not completely." He swallowed. "But if the choice is you or Greece, I pick you. I'd love for you to give Greece a chance, but it doesn't matter. If it takes a year, or five years, or never, I still choose you."

She felt emotion coursing through her veins, a wave of love mingled with pain that made her a little light-headed. She rested her head on his shoulder and tried to breathe, struggling to articulate the disparate thoughts racing through her mind. She wanted to go with him, but she was unsure. Staying married wasn't optional, but how could she force him to choose? It was too much to process, making her a little nauseous. The indecision was overwhelming and she suddenly just squeezed her eyes shut as tightly as she could before whispering, "You don't have to move here for me."

"Oh, but I do." He kissed the top of her head, noting she was shivering. "Just thinking about the situation is making you shake —hey, look at me." He tilted her chin up so their eyes locked. "I was telling Mick about all these things going on in my head, the same ones you seem to be struggling with right now, and how I didn't know what to do. He's my closest friend and he was helping me talk it out, probably the way you and Raegan do, except in guy language. I didn't actually lie to you, or even purposely mislead you—I was just trying to figure out how to have it all. But once you left, there wasn't any doubt about what I had to do."

"I don't want you to give anything up for me."

"Isn't that what love is, though?" He frowned, fingers trailing her damp cheek. "Aw, baby, don't cry."

"It just seems like you'd have to give up so much more than I would," she whispered. "I don't know why it feels that way— because I love my family and my friends—but I want you to be okay with whatever we decide."

"I'm here, aren't I?" He brushed his lips across hers. "I love you. That's all there is. We'll figure out the details."

"Really?" Her breath sped up a little, still surprised at the way a simple touch from him affected her.

"Really." He was leaning in to kiss her just as their food arrived and he reluctantly pulled away. "But right now, the only detail on my mind is this burger—you mind sharing me for a few minutes?"

She grinned. "Just this once."

He picked up the burger and took a big bite, moaning with satisfaction. "As soon as I'm done, I'm going to show you how grateful I am."

16

An hour later she used the spare key she kept in the glove compartment of her car to let them in to her apartment. They felt like naughty teenagers who'd stayed out past curfew, trying not to giggle. They were exhausted but their need for each other far outweighed the need to sleep. Quietly, so as not to disturb Nora, they kissed hungrily as they made their way towards her bedroom.

"Nora's asleep," she reminded him, tugging his hand and pulling him into the bathroom. She locked the door behind them and smiled.

"Shower," he murmured, leaning over to turn on the water as he yanked off his shirt. "Brilliant."

Watching him get undressed made her heart start beating faster and she dropped her own clothes in anticipation of what was to come; just these few days apart left her yearning for him.

"Damn, I like watching you take your clothes off," he said softly. "But I love your bare body even more."

Strong but gentle fingers fondled her breasts, and she slowly backed against the wall because the pleasure made it hard to think, much less concentrate on standing still. He was cupping

193

one of them now, rubbing the nipple with his thumb and watching as her eyes got heavy. "How does it feel to know you're really mine?" he whispered.

"Wonderful," she breathed. "Like it's the best thing that has ever happened to me."

"Does the idea of being mine forever arouse you?" He was toying with her, playing with her breasts, circling her nipples as they tightened with need.

"Y-yes." She gasped as he pinched one nipple harder than before and then bent his head to soothe the burn with his tongue.

"My wife," he growled under his breath. "You have no idea how much I'm going to enjoy making love to my wife."

"Who did you make love to before?" she panted, fire running through her at his touch.

"A woman who didn't realize she was mine."

"You're a little possessive," she grunted as he moved his hand down her torso, abandoning her breasts, which resulted in an immediate sense of loss. One hand cupped her backside while the fingers of his other hand spread the lips between her legs and began to explore.

"You have a problem with that?" He slid a finger into her and could feel the urgency, her frantic need for him, escalate. She'd become so incredibly wet, so quickly, it excited him to think he had that effect on her.

"No." She could barely talk as he rolled his finger from side to side, finding her already engorged clit and teasing it until it was so stiff and hard she could feel the pressure as he moved over it. She wanted him inside of her and pressed against him, lifting one leg and wrapping it around his legs.

Their mouths locked together feverishly, and he plunged his tongue in and out in a motion similar to what he was going to do with his cock shortly. The whimpers escaping her made him harder than ever and he roughly pulled up her other leg so she was completely off the ground and her wetness rubbed onto his skin. He turned and set her beautiful bare ass on the counter, spread her thighs and used his hand to put the head of his penis against her pulsing entrance. They'd talked about dispensing with the use of condoms when they were still in Greece and he was damned if he was going to worry about it now that she was going to remain his wife, so he drove into her, sheathing himself completely.

"Damn, you feel good," he sighed, closing his eyes against the pleasure. This wasn't just good, it was beyond his wildest dreams. She was so slick the sensations were almost overwhelming when she rocked up her hips in a frantic attempt to bring him deeper, hold him closer.

"Don't ever stop," she moaned, arms around his neck, her lips seeking his greedily.

"Never." He surged deeper, going faster and harder as he felt himself swelling, trying to keep from coming too soon. He reached down to find her clit again, stroking through the tender folds that were now afire for him. She was so ready, he could feel her clenching him, legs tightening around his waist, sweat starting to trickle between her breasts.

He caught her lips in a sweet but scorching kiss just as she broke apart, jerking against him, her scream swallowed in his mouth until he followed suit, his orgasm hard and seemingly endless as they continued to move together. Their torsos remained pressed tightly against one another as if they couldn't bear even the tiniest separation of skin. She was still shaking, her breath coming in little hiccups of need, eyes still closed. In that moment, he became aware that this was exactly what he'd wanted, what he'd been waiting for—the only thing missing in his life. Now that he had her—really had her—he was never letting her go. Whatever it took, she was his and he was hers. Nothing else made any sense.

· · ·

They woke up late in the morning. After a long night of talking and lovemaking that had them up until nearly dawn, it was almost noon before they stirred. Nudging him with her elbow, Paige sat up and smiled down at him.

"I'm hungry!" she announced. "And there is no food in the apartment, so get up!"

Though he barely opened his eyes, he arched a brow. "I live alone, without a kitchen, and there was always coffee at *my* house."

She poked him with her toe. "I've been gone for three weeks! Normally I have coffee *and* bagels!"

He opened his eyes. "Yeah? I'm gonna like that."

"Get up!" she repeated, laughing. "We need to take a shower!" She grabbed her phone to see if she'd missed any calls and found a line of green dots, showing five missed calls and 11 texts. All were from Raegan except one, from Tom:

Stopping by at noon to pack Raegan's things.

Her eyes widened and she jumped to her feet. "Shit!" She called Raegan back immediately but there was no answer.

"What's wrong?" Apollo asked, following her into the bathroom.

"Something is going on with Raegan—get dressed!"

He didn't answer but by the time she'd used the bathroom, washed her face and brushed her teeth, he was wearing shorts and a T-shirt and traded places with her so she could get dressed as well.

Her phone rang just as she pulled a tank top over her head and she grabbed it. "Raegan!"

"Oh my God—where have you been?"

"We were asleep! What's going on?"

"Tom and my mom talked the doctor into getting me released into his care and when I tried to say no they said I couldn't leave without someone to care for me and you didn't pick up and my insurance won't pay for another day unless—"

"Fuck!" Paige slid her feet into a pair of sandals. "Where are you? Tom texted that he's on his way over here to get your things!"

"He took my keys so he'll be there any minute! Stop him, Paige, please! I was asleep and he and my mom had breakfast! I wasn't aware of what was going on until about an hour ago."

"Hang tight, I won't let him get your stuff."

"Someone's coming!"

Raegan disconnected abruptly and Paige turned to Apollo just as they heard a key in the lock. "She doesn't want him to take her stuff!" she whispered urgently. "What do we do?"

He just smiled and pulled something out of his pocket. "I meant for this to happen in a more romantic setting, but I want you to wear it. So put it on now and we'll have a do-over when we're alone." He showed her Thespina's ring.

"Is that…?"

"*Yaya's* wedding ring—she wanted you to wear it until we bought something else, so it would feel more official."

She smiled and pressed her lips to his as he slid the simple band on the ring finger of her left hand. Amazingly, it was a perfect fit and they broke apart long enough to grin just as Tom opened the door. He scowled at them.

"I guess I should have knocked," he said sarcastically.

"You should have." Paige levelled a look at him.

"I'm getting Raegan's things—she's moving in with me."

"She's not." Paige shook her head. "I don't know what you and her mother are trying to do, but she doesn't want to move in with you, Tom."

"That's not what she told me." He smirked as he folded his arms across his chest.

"I think you need to leave." Apollo spoke quietly, but his voice was intense.

"I think you need to make me."

Paige rolled her eyes. "Tom, you haven't been in a fistfight since Robby Carlson punched you in the nose in the second grade! So knock it off. Look, Raegan is terrified of her father and—"

"Her mom told me you would say that," he snapped. "So just let me get her things."

"No. The only way you're getting her things is if she tells me herself. Go ahead and call her, Tom."

Tom gave her a dirty look but pulled out his phone and dialed. He tapped his foot impatiently and then his face morphed into a smile. "Hey, Raegan... No, I'm here at the apartment and—what do you mean?" His smile tightened and he turned his back, as though doing so would keep Paige and Apollo from hearing what he was saying. "We talked about this... No, it's not. Dammit, Raegan, we made a deal!" His free hand clenched into a fist and he stalked out of the apartment, still talking.

"We should get to the hospital," Paige said to Apollo. "I'm afraid he's on his way there to strong-arm her!"

Apollo nodded, following her. "I just want to point out, for what it's worth, that we never had any of this kind of drama when we were in Greece."

She turned, a faint smile playing on her lips. "Sophia and Giorgios seem to have all kinds of drama, but I promise, once we get Raegan settled, there won't be anything else like this. In all the years we've been friends, the only drama has been her being broke!"

He just nodded again, taking the keys from her hand. "Do you mind if I drive? Your hands are shaking."

Paige glanced down and realized he was right. "I guess he rattles me after last night..."

"I know, *koukla mou*." He leaned over to press his lips to hers and let them linger. "But you're always safe with me."

. . .

ick met them at the hospital and was waiting in the lobby when they got there, hurrying over to them.

"That Tom dickhead just went up in the elevator."

"Shit!" Paige turned and ran towards the stairs, disappearing behind the door.

"Are you taking the stairs?" Mick asked Apollo.

Apollo chuckled. "No. I'm taking the elevator because I'm sure Tom won't be taking the stairs, so I'll head him off at the elevator bay if necessary."

"Just in case, I'll go up the stairs," Mick said, a grin lighting his blue eyes. "Dude, I gotta tell you—this is the most fun I've had since college. You didn't tell me meeting the little woman would be this much of an adventure." He headed to the stairs, still chuckling.

Apollo hit the UP button, shaking his head. There was that word again. *Adventure.* She'd only wanted to experience some of life's adventures before settling down and Tom hadn't been willing to give that to her. Except he was unwittingly doing it now, even though the idiot had no idea what that truly meant. It wasn't what Apollo had in mind, either, but he knew if something like this was happening to Mick, nothing would stop him from helping, so he didn't begrudge her taking care of her friend. He just hoped they could handle this once and for all right now; they had a lot of other things to do. There was also something he hadn't told her, but it didn't seem like the middle of a crisis was the right time.

He stepped out of the elevator just as Tom was storming out of Raegan's room. Mick was leaning against the wall, his large body relaxed and amused, his lips twitching as he fought laughter.

"You can have the crazy little whore!" Tom spat at Apollo as he whipped past him.

Without missing a beat, Apollo reached out and shoved Tom

against the wall, his left hand gripping Tom's forearm as Apollo's right forearm pressed against Tom's sternum. "Did you just call my wife a whore?" he hissed under his breath.

"What would you call a woman who was screwing someone else while married?"

"Someone who was separated," he said in a quiet but deadly tone. "Apologize."

"Fuck you." Tom grunted as Apollo dug his elbow into his chest.

"I said apologize."

"I'd do it if I were you." Mick ambled by, his six foot five inch frame dwarfing both Apollo's and Tom's as he leaned over. "He's been in love with her since the first time he laid eyes on her—he might get grumpy if you don't apologize and then we'll all wind up in jail 'cause I'll say you hit him first."

Tom narrowed his eyes.

"Paige said you're up for a promotion," Mick continued, a toothpick appearing in his mouth as though he didn't have a care in the world. "Getting arrested would be bad."

"Damn you!" Tom hissed, meeting Apollo's eyes heatedly.

"For fuck's sake, say you're sorry!" Mick rolled his eyes.

"I'm sorry!" Tom huffed. "Jesus, did it ever occur to you that I loved her? That finding out she was already married might have hurt me?"

"Is that why you're determined to fuck her best friend?" Apollo groused, releasing him abruptly.

"Yeah! Aside from the fact that Raegan's hot, I wanted to hurt Paige the way she hurt me." He suddenly sighed. "But I guess that backfired."

"Look, man." Mick was still chewing his toothpick. "Let it go. Paige and Apollo—I didn't hear about anything else until he left to go back to Greece. They were stupid back then, but there's obviously something special between them and after three years apart, they need to work it out. None of this is Raegan's fault, so why drag her into it? This car accident was really bad—she could have died—and she doesn't need the drama. If you want to be her friend, maybe make some phone calls to help her with the police reports and insurance or something. Maybe send over a meal when she gets settled."

"I don't even know where she's going!" Tom protested, suddenly defeated as he leaned against the wall. "They wouldn't tell me."

"If you'd behave like a gentleman, that might change." Mick patted him on the shoulder. "Go on home, man, and do something helpful for Raegan. Then send her a text and apologize for trying to manipulate her and tell her what nice thing you've done—with no talk about sex or moving in with you. Come on, you're a good-looking guy with money—the chicks have to be crawling out of the woodwork."

Tom looked away. "I guess. They're just kind of boring."

Apollo narrowed his eyes. "Paige isn't boring at all. She would've been willing to meet you halfway but she said you wouldn't compromise."

"I didn't realize what I had," he admitted in a gruff voice. "I didn't know how boring other women were until Paige went to Greece. I went out on two dates and after the second one was so bad I couldn't wait to get away from her, I wound up at the casino talking with Raegan and realized she was a lot like Paige—funny and quirky, but real smart and hard-working. A little bit more of a mess than Paige, but she had that...*something*. I didn't realize how much I enjoyed it until after she was gone."

"Paige is mine," Apollo said quietly. "And she loves me too, but there are lots of smart, quirky women out there that are strong and professional, but still want to live a little before having kids and all that."

"I guess so." Tom seemed sad.

"You'll find someone," Mick said. "Stop pushing so hard."

Tom paused and glanced back over his shoulder as he started walking away. "Are you taking her on adventures?"

"You bet your ass I am." Apollo grinned.

"What kind?" Tom's eyes were guileless, genuinely confused.

"I don't know yet." Apollo didn't know why, but he felt a moment of sympathy for the guy; he was obviously genuinely confused about what that meant. "I mean—here's an example. The day she came to see me in Greece I asked her why she didn't mail me the papers and she said even though it was something done in a drunken haze, it didn't seem fair to end a marriage without a conversation. So I took her to lunch. Once we started talking, I realized that no matter what we decided about the marriage, I wanted her to think back kindly on our time together. I drove us down to Cape Sounion and watched the sun set over the Temple of Poseidon. It was romantic and scenic, a little mini-hike up to the temple, and the most gorgeous view… She said it was her first adventure in Greece. That's when I knew what she needed."

Tom still seemed a little confused, but he nodded. "I, I guess I get that. I, uh, I appreciate your honesty. I have a lot to think about."

"Good luck." Apollo watched him disappear into the elevator and then glanced at Mick. "You're starving, aren't you?"

"Do you know how many awesome breakfast places there are here?!" he demanded.

"You didn't care about any of that stuff you said—you just didn't want to wind up in a fight or in jail!"

Mick laughed, deep and rumbling, shaking his head. "Naw, man, I meant it—I was just using it to my advantage."

"Dude, we're moving Raegan out of here. There's no time for breakfast."

"Yeah, there is." Mick winked. "Come on." He headed back towards her room.

Apollo followed in confusion, but was glad that the situation had been diffused and that he really hadn't wound up in jail. That could get him kicked out of the country, which was not in the plan.

Raegan was wearing shorts and a T-shirt, her hair pulled back in a ponytail as she sat up in bed. The woman in tears beside her had to be her mother, Nora, and Apollo caught Paige's impatient stance as she stood between them.

"I just don't understand what's happening," Nora was sniffling. "Raegan, you're my light and my love, but I don't understand these things you keep saying about your father! You know they're not true and—"

"Mom." Raegan gripped her hands tightly. "I love you. You were the best mom you could possibly be with your issues but—"

"I don't have issues!" Nora was crying harder now.

"Mom!" Raegan squeezed her hands and forced her to look at her. "Please, Mom, listen to me. You have bipolar disorder. You know this. I don't know why you stopped taking your meds but..."

"I had to! I feel like I'm underwater all the time. The only time I feel okay is when I wake up in the morning, but the minute I start taking them, I just float around in a cloud, like I don't feel anything. It's terrible, Raegan."

"Mom—those are the meds that keep you from having suicidal thoughts. Remember? Remember when you tried to kill yourself?"

Nora's tears dripped down her face. "But that stuff about your father—"

"Is true. I don't blame you. You weren't medicated, you could barely take care of yourself, much less me, but I can't ever be alone with him. I won't visit you in Phoenix ever again. Please trust me. Please let me handle this."

"I just don't... How could he?!" Her eyes filled with tears and she sank into the nearest chair.

"That's why he keeps talking you out of taking your medication," Paige added gently. "He knows when you're lucid, even if you don't feel right, the memories can come drifting back."

"But I can't leave him," Nora looked up sadly. "I can't work, I can't…do anything."

"Let me get better," Raegan said quietly. "Then we'll figure out what you can do. Promise me you'll go back on the meds, Mom?"

"Okay." Nora was sniffling so Paige handed her a tissue.

"So, what's the plan?" Apollo asked softly.

"I'm taking Raegan to my mom's until we can find an apartment with an elevator or something else…" She glanced at Apollo. "Can we get her settled and meet my parents and then take care of our stuff?"

"Of course." He looked around. "What do we need to do?"

"Please, someone mention food," Mick murmured.

Raegan smiled. "I like him."

The next 24 hours were a whirlwind. Bringing Apollo to her parents' house and introducing him as her husband had been almost surreal, with what felt like a million questions and endless doubts. Apollo was a rock, though, answering patiently and reassuring her parents that he would take care of her. It seemed to take forever, and while she understood her parents' concerns, she had so many other things on her mind. She still hadn't gone back to work, she was going to pick up Raegan and get her settled in the guest room in a few hours, and she and Apollo still didn't have a plan for the immediate future.

"Holy hot as hell!" her sister, Nicky, murmured as Paige got the sofa bed in the guest room ready while Apollo talked with her father. "I can't believe you're married to him!"

Paige managed to smile. "Get drunk during spring break and you, too, can accidentally marry a Greek god."

"Seems to me he's a lot more than an accidental husband."

"He's pretty amazing," Paige admitted, hugging the pillow to her chest as she paused from putting the pillowcase on. "I just don't know what we're going to do. He doesn't want to live here, but he'd do it for me and…"

"Why don't you want to move to Greece? Are you afraid he would do something to you?"

"Not something terrible," Paige said quickly. "I just think I would be lonely. No friends, with a whole new lifestyle and culture—and I don't know the language. What would I do all day while he worked?"

"Learn the language? Wander the streets and get to know the area? Go to the beach until it's too cold? Spend time with his family? You have a whole country at your disposal."

"I know." Paige finished setting up the bed and was surprised to see that Nicky had gone and Apollo was leaning against the doorjamb watching her.

"Ready to go get Raegan?" he asked.

"Yes." Paige nodded.

"You really need to relax." He pulled her against him and kissed the tip of her nose. "You weren't like this in Greece."

"I had nothing going on in Greece!" she protested mildly. "All I had to think about was you."

"Seems to me you were happier in Greece," he said mildly.

"I was," she admitted. "I really was. The idea of going back to work tomorrow…ugh. I can't even think about it."

"So don't." He put his hand around the back of her neck and held her close as he stared into her face. "I want to take care of you—your crazy friends too. I've been watching you run around like a chicken with your head cut off for two days now and I hate it. What can I do to make this better, *koukla mou?*"

"I don't know."

"In a perfect world, what do you want?"

She looked up at him and bit her lip. "You."

"Here or there?"

"Anywhere," she admitted. "But I… If we have to move to San

Francisco or L.A. or some other crazy place, I think I'd rather be in Greece."

"I'll find a way to make it work here in the States," he said softly. "I only want you in Greece if you feel safe with me."

"I do feel safe with you—I'm more afraid I'm going to be lonely. You work all the time and I don't want your sister to be my best friend out of pity."

"Lena adores you, but you won't be alone that much. I'm going to cut back on the hours because my father is going to be working a little more."

"You really want to do this? With me?"

"I sure as hell don't want to do it with anyone else." He brought her fingers to his lips and kissed them softly, one at a time. "I'm going to put five thousand dollars in an account in your dad's name, here in the U.S. He'll set you up with a debit card and I won't have access to that money. If you ever feel like you need to leave Greece because of me, the money will be there. You'll also have access to all my accounts and your own money. I won't ever let you feel as though you have to ask me for anything you need. Everything that's mine is now half yours."

Tears puddled in her eyes. "That's kind of overwhelming."

"In a good way?"

"Yeah." She nuzzled against his chest. "But how do I tell my family?"

"They already know, *koukla*."

"They do?" She raised tear-filled eyes. "How do they know?"

"Because they already figured out that both of us were willing to make the sacrifice for the other, but in the end, your dad and I had a talk and he reminded me that he expects me to take care of you both emotionally and financially. He knows for sure that I can do that in Greece. Here in the U.S., it's a gamble, and he wants you to be happy and secure more than he wants you to be close by. I'm sure in a perfect world he'd like both, but when he put it out there in black and white, I realized he's right. We talked about what it would take to make sure you weren't just safe, but felt confident and independent in such new surroundings too. So money that I can't touch, perhaps a safety deposit box where you can keep—"

"Wait, stop!" She put a finger on his lips and shook her head, frowning. "I'm worried about things like loneliness and lacking my own money for things like shoes and makeup—not running away from you in the middle of the night! Goodness, I'm not afraid of you, Apollo. I'm nervous about such a huge lifestyle change and not having anyone to talk to the first time we have a fight… I'm thinking ahead to having our first baby and wondering what the hospitals are like. I already know that in the off-chance you beat me or some other horrible thing, my father would either be on the first plane or he'd buy me the ticket to get away. I just don't want to get caught up in life—your work and kids and all that, and find myself alone with no purpose, no job, no life outside of you."

"Honey, you can get a job if you want to. Or you can come work with me at the company—we desperately need a marketing specialist and you've already shown an interest in that." He ran his hands down her back and gently squeezed the soft, round globes of her behind. "But I was thinking about all those adventures you want to have."

"You were?"

"Well, yeah." He grinned. "I'm planning to take a little time off now because you'll need to take care of Raegan and pack up your whole life if you're going to move to Greece. In the meantime, I thought we'd have some local mini-adventures like going to the Grand Canyon and Sedona, things like that."

"God, I love you." She leaned up and kissed him, hard, her eyes glittering with tears.

"That's good," he murmured. "Because I was also thinking we should have a wedding."

She paused, cocking her head. "You're kidding, right?"

"No." He grinned. "I don't think it's right that neither of us remember getting married, and honestly, my mother won't rest until she meets your family. How about we plan a small ceremony here in Vegas and then go on a honeymoon. Would you like that?"

"Yes! Oh my gosh, yes!" She jumped into his arms, wrapping her legs around his waist and hugging him tightly.

"I love you, baby. All I want is to make you happy."

"You have. You are. I am!" She giggled at how flustered she was.

With Raegan settled at Paige's parents' house, Nora back in Phoenix and a wedding three weeks away, Paige gave her notice at work. They were sad to see her go but Paige was moving on and had a million things to do to get ready to leave the country. Although she'd given two weeks' notice, her boss told her not to come back and gave her two weeks' pay anyway—he said he felt bad about all the vacation she hadn't been able to take, as well as the incident with Tom. She was a little sad about leaving so abruptly, but it was exciting too.

Now that they had some free time, she and Apollo spent a few days exploring the Grand Canyon, Hoover Dam and Antelope Canyon. They'd decided they would spend their honeymoon driving from San Diego to San Francisco, taking the scenic route along the coast and stopping for a couple of days in different places along the way. From there, they would go back to Las Vegas and say goodbye to Paige's family and friends before permanently leaving for Greece.

They'd done a lot, throwing out everything in the refrigerator, packing for the trip to Greece, packing for the honeymoon and even packing for the future. Since she wasn't bringing anything large, they'd decided to split up her things so that they could be sent home with Apollo's family. Everyone was coming for the wedding except Giorgios, so they would all have a little room for her clothes, shoes and other necessary items. She'd already arranged for a local charity to come pick up all the things Raegan didn't want, and she, Apollo, her mother and Nicky packed up the rest of Raegan's things. Raegan didn't know what she was going to do but the Carters had told her she could stay until she was on her feet again. Paige would always worry about her, but she knew it was time for Raegan to figure out what she was going to do with her life; she couldn't be the one to rescue her anymore.

"I'm getting kind of tired of never being alone with you," Apollo was saying, forcing her back to the present as they put the last of Raegan's things in her parents' garage.

"I'm sorry?" Her eyes crinkled as she laughed.

"You're not sorry!" he laughed too. "But we pick up my family in about an hour and then I won't be alone with you again until after the wedding."

She laughed. "Adds a little romance and excitement, no?"

"Do you know how horny I am?"

She just grinned. "No hornier than I am!"

They left for the airport an hour later and the days leading up to the wedding were both chaotic and exciting. Even Raegan, who'd been moping about her dire situation, had perked up, and when Mick returned after going to see his family in California for a few days, he took over carting her around so she could participate in all the events.

"This isn't what I pictured for a wedding dress," Paige sighed, staring in the mirror. She'd bought three dresses that would do the trick, but they were all basically glorified cocktail dresses and none of them made her feel bride-like.

"I think we have a solution," Melina said, peeking in. She slipped into Nicky's room, where Paige had been trying on the dresses, and pulled Thespina in behind her. The older woman had a package in her hands and she handed it to Paige.

"For you. Is not—" She said something in Greek and turned to Melina in frustration.

Melina smiled. "Modern."

"Is not…mod-ern…but we fix."

"We took it to a seamstress to clean it, along with one of your regular dresses so that it could be altered, and added a few contemporary touches." Melina handed it to Paige, who was gaping.

"Is this…your wedding dress?" Paige gasped out.

"Yes, yes, you try!"

"Oh my gosh…" Raegan breathed as Paige pulled out the lacy bundle of material.

"Wow." Paige's eyes were round with wonder as she stared at Thespina.

"It was a little small—*Yaya* was tiny when she got married— but the seamstress was able to take out all the seams, design a simple off-white silk sheath to wear underneath and then make the original dress a sort of overlay. You should put it on."

"Yes." Paige nodded as tears puddled in her eyes. "Where's Mom?" she asked Nicky.

"I'll get her!" Nicky bounced off the bed and out of the room as Paige pulled on the sheath and then the soft, lacy cover that retained its original design but no longer contained a modest turtleneck-type top and had been cut at the bottom so that it fell to mid-calf.

"Here." Melina grabbed a clip from the counter and loosely pulled Paige's hair up so that it was off her shoulders, revealing her slender neck and tanned skin.

"*Koukla!*" Thespina said with a smile.

"It's so beautiful," Paige breathed. "Thank you!" She hugged the old woman tightly, trying not to cry.

"Let me see!" her mother said softly, as she joined them. "Oh, it's perfect. Absolutely perfect, Paige."

"I think so too." Paige swiped at her eyes. "I don't want Apollo to see it until the ceremony."

"I'll take care of it," her mother said, as Paige took it off again.

"Do you have a ring yet?" Nicky asked.

Paige shook her head. "He wants to surprise me, but I'm wearing this one—" she held out the ring finger where Thespina's wedding band twinkled now that it had been cleaned and polished, "—until the wedding. Then I'm going to switch it over to my right hand, which is where the Greeks wear wedding rings, and put the new one on my left."

"That's so sweet," Nicky sighed.

"He's so romantic," Raegan agreed.

"And hot!" Nicky added.

"Ew, you're talking about my brother!" Melina laughed.

They all giggled.

*E*verything was set for the wedding, so they took the time to do some sightseeing and made a point to allow the families to get to know each other. Sophia had been surly and withdrawn, as usual, and Melina fought a wave of guilt. She hadn't meant to say what she'd said to her the day Paige had first come to dinner—it had been unfair—but she'd been angry. It had been three years; it was time for Sophia to move on. She didn't love Giorgios, there was no doubt about that, and Melina was tired of watching her suffer.

Since she was sharing a hotel room with Sophia and three-year-old Mihalis, she decided to stay behind with her tonight instead of going out with the others. Besides, too many nights watching Mick and Raegan laugh and flirt was making her skin crawl. She'd tried desperately to forget about her brother's blue-eyed best friend, but it wasn't easy.

Sophia came out of the bathroom carrying a wet and sleepy Mihalis in her arms. She'd just bathed him and he was wrapped in a towel, his eyes half-closed as he nestled against his mother.

"*Thea Lena!*" *Aunt Lena*! He squirmed when he saw Melina, reaching out his arms to her.

Sophia sighed, and put the child in Melina's arms. "What are you doing here? I thought you left with the others."

Melina stroked the toddler's silky hair as she absently dried him off. "No. I felt bad that you've been staying in every night so I thought I'd stay too. We can put him to bed, order room service and talk."

"About what?" Sophia fixed her sister with an icy stare.

"Come on, don't do that."

"Look, if you're going to stay in, I can go out." Sophia folded her arms across her chest.

Melina scowled. "Really? You hate me so much that you won't even spend an evening with me?"

"The only reason you spend any time with me is so that you can spend time with him." She motioned to Mihalis with her chin.

"I just said we'd put him to bed so you and I can spend time together!" Melina protested, her chest tightening angrily. "Dammit, Sophia, you've got to stop it!"

"You ruined my life!" Sophia hissed.

"It's not my fault he didn't love you!"

"Shut up!" Sophia balled up her hands into fists. "Don't make this about me! I gave up everything that meant anything to me for you! And now I'm stuck with—"

"Divorce him!" Melina cried.

"*Thea?*" Mihalis' eyes filled with tears as the adults' raised voices scared him.

"I'm sorry, baby." Melina kissed his forehead. "Let's get you dressed, okay?"

He nodded sleepily.

"Just give him to me and go out." Sophia all but snatched the boy out of Melina's arms.

"Sophia, please! We can find a way to—"

"No. Just go have fun with everyone, like you always do. As you like to remind me, I made my choice and now I have to live with it. So go on."

"Is this how it's always going to be? You angry and bitter, blaming me for everything?"

"Yes." Sophia turned her back and walked into the other room.

*M*elina was furious. Grabbing her purse, she stalked out of their suite and took the elevator down to the lobby. Yes, Sophia had made a sacrifice for her, but it wasn't Melina's fault that Sophia's American college boyfriend hadn't been on board. It had been a terrible time for both of them, but no matter how hard Melina tried to make things right between them, Sophia was bitter. Melina would never understand why she'd married Giorgios—it hadn't been necessary—but Sophia had played the martyr and done it anyway. Now she was miserable and took it out on everyone.

Walking outside where a group of men were smoking, she approached one of them with a wan smile. "I don't suppose I could steal one of those?"

"Sure." An older gentleman with a bright smile pulled out a pack of Marlboro Lights and handed her one.

"Thank you!" Melina smiled and put it between her lips, expecting him to light it for her. Instead, a lighter came from her right and a familiar voice said, "Thought you'd quit."

Mick's blue eyes met hers and even after four years, Melina felt her heart skip a beat. "What are you doing here?" she asked, frowning.

"Same as you—sneaking a smoke."

"I haven't had one in over a year," she sighed. "But I just argued with Sophia… She makes me crazy!"

"Why?"

She shrugged. "Sister things. Her husband is an asshole and she can't take it out on anyone else, I suppose."

He nodded, taking a deep drag from his cigarette. "I quit too," he said after a moment. "But that job in Japan sucked the life out of me and they all smoke, so somehow I fell into it again."

"It's bad for us," she acknowledged.

"I know." He paused, meeting her gaze. "We haven't talked in a long time, Lena. How are you? How are you really?"

"Don't pretend you give a shit," she muttered, blowing a ring of smoke in the air.

"Come on, don't be that way. We had an argument and the next thing I knew you wouldn't take my calls!"

"You made it clear you were only interested in one thing," she shrugged. "And that wasn't going to cut it for me."

"I was in college!" he protested. "And you were my best friend's sister—his older sister, no less! I was crazy about you but you were going back to Greece and I still had another year of college! Not to mention, you had a guy back home. You're still with him, aren't you?"

She snorted. "Not really. We go out on occasion, but he knows I'm not going to marry him."

"Why not?"

She lifted an eyebrow. "None of your business?"

He sighed. "You Lakkas women sure know how to hold a grudge, don't you?"

"Fuck off, Mick." She stared out at the night sky, wishing his nearness didn't still affect her and that she hadn't had to come on this trip. She'd known she would see him but hadn't expected it to be so hard.

"Why do you hate me?" he asked softly, moving closer to her, the smell of his aftershave wafting over her. "We had a good thing going. It was just an argument—I'll never understand why you got so angry with me. I wish you'd explain it, Lena." One of his massive hands came up to cup her cheek.

She closed her eyes, reveling in his touch, allowing the pleasure only he could bring her to warm her insides. Just one more second, she thought, as her eyes fluttered open. She stepped out of his grasp and put out her cigarette on the trash receptacle. "If you'd loved me, you'd know the answer to that. But since you didn't, it doesn't matter anymore. I'm going for a walk and I don't want you to follow."

"Lena, wait…" He reached for her hand but she kept it out of his grasp.

"It's better this way, Mick. Really. Let it go."

The following morning was Sunday and Paige's parents hosted brunch at the house. The wedding was in five days—on Friday—and Paige and Apollo would leave on their honeymoon the following day so they'd planned a final, informal gathering for both sides of the family this afternoon. Raegan and Mick were there too, of course, and the house bustled with activity. Paige's mother, Angela, Maria and Thespina were in the kitchen making omelets and putting out pastries while Paige made sure everyone had coffee, tea or juice. Raegan and Mick were laughing about something, as usual, while Apollo, Dimitri and Seth talked about the upcoming football season. Sophia had overslept this morning so Nicky had gone to get her and Mihalis, and they arrived just as everyone was sitting down to eat.

Sophia hadn't been very social since she'd been in Las Vegas so it was the first time some of them were able to meet Mihalis, and Angela and Raegan were fawning over him.

"Oh my God, he's gorgeous!" Angela gushed, holding out her hand and leading the little boy into the kitchen.

"He's beautiful," Maria agreed, beaming. "The most beautiful grandchild in the world!"

"And those eyes," Raegan laughed. "He's going to be breaking hearts all over Greece in a few years, Sophia!"

Sophia smiled. "I hope not for a while!"

"Are his father's eyes blue?" Raegan asked, gazing at the dark-eyed woman.

"Er, yes," Sophia nodded. "Not so blue like Mihalis', but still blue." She turned to Paige. "You have milk for him, please?"

"Yes, of course. Let me get some!" Paige reached into the kitchen as Sophia watched.

Paige pulled a carton of milk out of the refrigerator and put it on the counter as Sophia pulled a plastic sippy cup out of her bag and filled it before handing it to the little boy.

"He's really well-behaved," Paige said with a smile, watching him.

"Thank you. I'm very lucky—he's never a problem."

"Hey, Paige?" Raegan hobbled up to her on crutches. "Can I talk to you for a minute? Alone?"

"Sure." Paige turned to her with a smile. "What's up?" She followed Raegan to her room and Raegan shut the door. They sank onto the edge of the bed and Raegan gave her a grin.

"Mick offered me a job."

"He did?" Paige's eyes rounded. "Doing what?"

"As his virtual assistant. He desperately needs someone who can be flexible because he'll be working in Santorini the next six months or so and his assistant in San Francisco works nine to five, which is essentially nighttime in Greece with the 10-hour time difference. I mean, he doesn't expect me to work from midnight till dawn or anything, but I'm usually up late anyway so we can talk at different times and I can do things during the day while he's asleep. He'll pay me 20 bucks an hour, Paige, and I don't have to leave the house!"

"That's wonderful!" Paige nodded. "I mean, that's really great! I'm so happy this worked out for you!"

"And he said when I'm better, he might fly me to Santorini for a few weeks to be there for the project unveiling."

"Yay!" Paige laughed. "That'll be awesome." She paused. "You're not falling for him, are you? You need a job more than you need a man, Raegan!"

"No way!" Raegan shook her head. "He's got it bad for…well, this girl he knows, who doesn't return his feelings, so we're just friends. Besides, you're right—I need a job way more than a new boyfriend!"

They giggled together for a few minutes, excited about the future and all the changes in their lives.

"This is going to be so great," Paige said softly, hugging her.

"I'm so glad you found Apollo," Raegan answered. "You were never the same after you met him. Now you're pretty much the happiest girl in the whole world. It's all over you!"

Paige wrinkled her nose. "It doesn't look bad, does it?"

Raegan shook her head. "Hell, no—you wear it like a woman in love!"

"I *am* a woman in love!"

EPILOGUE

*P*aige had no idea where Apollo's mother had found a Greek priest, a *pappas*, on such short notice, but there he was. They weren't having the ceremony in the church; they'd opted to rent out the clubhouse in her parents' subdivision and have both a short ceremony and fun reception at the same place. It saved on time and money, since they were already legally married, and Paige hadn't argued when Maria had brought up having the ceremony overseen by a priest from the Greek Orthodox Church. Being blessed by the church seemed to make Maria happy, and Paige's family didn't care one way or the other since they weren't religious; she was happy to do something so simple that would keep her in Maria's good graces.

"Why am I nervous?" Paige asked Raegan as they got ready for the ceremony to start. "We're already married—this is dumb!"

"Your hands are shaking!" Raegan said softly, gripping them and gently squeezing.

"I know! It's dumb!"

"It's not dumb," Raegan smiled. "You've never been a fan of being the center of attention, and that's exactly what this is. Just remember you're already married, this guy adores you, and you're about to embark on the very best adventure you could ever imagine."

"I know, I know!" Paige took a deep breath. "It's just…what if it doesn't work out? What if he doesn't love me?"

Raegan rolled her eyes. "You're a dork. He could have signed those papers and let your skinny behind leave Greece forever. Instead, he courted you, asked you to stay with him forever, and then followed you halfway across the world to keep you. I'm pretty sure you guys have a good chance of things working out. There are no guarantees, but from the outside looking in, you guys have a lot going for you."

"Yeah." Paige gazed down at the gorgeous diamond on her left hand. He'd given it to her last night as the family had looked on. They'd found matching wedding rings they both liked and they would exchange those during the ceremony. She'd already moved Thespina's ring to her right hand and looked down at it now with a smile. She was so glad his grandmother had made the trip to the U.S. to be here with them. It was a lot of fun spending time with her, and her own grandmother—her mother's mother—who'd also flown in for the ceremony, had been attached to Thespina at the hip.

"Everyone is here," Melina poked her head into the small ante-room. "Are you ready?"

"As I'll ever be!" Paige nodded.

Melina stepped out and there was a quick knock before Mick stuck his head in. "Ready?" He grinned at Raegan, who nodded.

The wedding was somewhat informal, and since they were already married, they were dispensing with traditions like having her father walk her down the aisle, a big wedding party or even reading vows. Essentially, Mick would walk with Raegan, who was on crutches, and then she would sit down while Mick held on to both wedding rings. Paige would walk down the makeshift aisle by herself, the priest would say a prayer in both Greek and English, and then they would eat, drink and dance. Hopefully, it would be short and sweet, just as they'd planned. She had no interest in a long-drawn-out ceremony or extended speeches. Though she had no trouble when it was work-related, in her personal life she really disliked having the attention of a room full of people.

"Let's do this!" Raegan blew a kiss at Paige and gratefully accepted her crutches from Mick, who also helped her up. They'd become fast friends and seemed almost as inseparable as the two grandmothers.

"I'm ready." Paige got up and wiped her damp palms on her dress. In a minute or so, she would be standing next to Apollo and then she wouldn't be nervous anymore.

She watched from the door as Mick solicitously walked beside Raegan, who moved slowly with her crutches. She caught a glimpse of Apollo standing next to the *pappas*, as handsome as she'd ever seen him in a gorgeous suit his mother had brought from Greece when she'd come. He'd gotten a haircut too, and she smiled to herself, thinking about all the times he'd mentioned needing one. Obviously their wedding was a big enough occasion for him to do it!

As she took the first step towards where Apollo was waiting for her, Paige felt her step falter and she breathed in deeply, steadying herself. She caught a reassuring wink from Thespina and felt warmth flood her, finally able to put one foot in front of the other. Though she'd had the occasional glimpse of memory from their legal wedding nearly three and a half years ago, as Apollo reached out his hand to her, she got a wave of pictures that flashed through her mind with such clarity she was momentarily startled. She'd been wearing her favorite black miniskirt, a low-cut red top that showed off her modest cleavage and high, high black pumps. Apollo had been wearing jeans and an untucked button-down black shirt, the sleeves rolled up to his elbows. He'd been smiling, just like he was now, and she couldn't help but move against him with a combination of love, nostalgia and relief that she was with him again.

"Welcome!" The *pappas* spoke in a deep, booming voice in perfect English. "We are here today to celebrate the love of Apollo and Paige, who will be—"

"I do!" A loud voice interrupted the priest as Tom stumbled into the room. His hair was sticking up as if he'd just gotten out of bed, his tie was askew and his shirt wasn't tucked into his slacks. He had a bottle of what appeared to be tequila in one hand and his speech was slurred.

"You do what?" the priest asked, clearly not amused, his eyes narrowing.

"Didn't you ask if anyone has a reason these two shouldn't get married?" Tom looked befuddled.

"I did not," the priest answered primly. "They're *already* married, so that would be a ridiculous question."

"But you can't marry him!" Tom cried to Paige, weaving through the middle of the room in her direction.

"Not today, my friend," Mick stepped in front of him and put a big hand on his shoulder. "The only thing you're going to accomplish here is to make a fool of yourself."

"But I loved you!" Tom was trying to peer around Mick's large form and they appeared to be doing a kind of dance as Mick blocked him.

"Oh, Tom." Paige was mortified, but this wasn't her fault. They'd broken up, she'd told him she was married to and in love with someone else; she felt bad that she'd obviously hurt him, but he needed to let this go.

"All those years together!" he cried. "We did everything together! How can you love him?"

"Let's go." Mick nudged him towards the door.

"No! She loves me! Ask her!" Tom was flailing his arms as Mick continued to back him towards the door.

Nicky's date, an old family friend named Dan, got up and

joined Mick, talking in a low voice to Tom as they tried to move him out the door.

"Paige!" Tom was wailing now and Paige groaned.

"Tom, enough!" Seth stood up and glared at the younger man. "She doesn't love you and she's married to someone else. Now stop this nonsense!"

"She's spent more time in my bed than his!" he roared, reaching around Mick as though he could get to Paige that way. "She's mine, damn you! Mine!"

Before Apollo could react, Thespina rose from her seat like a whirling dervish in black. With her small sequined handbag swinging wildly, she approached Tom amidst a torrent of Greek that Paige was almost glad she didn't understand. She swatted at him repeatedly, cursing a blue streak that had Paige's family frowning in amusement and Apollo's unable to contain their laughter. With Mick's continued assistance, Thespina prodded Tom out the door until no one could see them anymore.

"I love your grandmother," Paige whispered to Apollo, though tears had begun to spill from her eyes.

"Don't cry, *koukla mou*," he whispered back, his fingers brushing them away. "Think of how funny this will be 20 years from now."

"Most fun I've had at a wedding in years!" the *pappas* whispered, discreetly winking at her. "This isn't your fault. Now, dry your eyes—I have a blessing to perform!"

"Should someone get *Yaya?*" Apollo asked, glancing over his shoulder.

"I've got her," Mick called out, coming back in the room with the older woman holding on to his arm as though she was royalty.

"As I was saying," the priest continued as though nothing had happened, "we're celebrating the reaffirmation of Apollo and Paige's vows..."

Fifteen minutes later, Paige breathed a sigh of relief when Apollo pressed his lips to hers and the room filled with cheers.

Laughing and smiling, all thoughts of Tom long gone, Paige felt a kind of happiness she'd never experienced before. As memories of their first wedding ran through her mind like a kaleidoscope of disconnected videos, she focused on the handsome, loving man at her side.

"Welcome to the family," Maria said with a smile, hugging her tightly.

"Thank you." Paige hugged her back. "I'm so sorry my ex-boyfriend almost ruined everything."

"Ruined?" Maria's eyes twinkled. "This is the most fun my mother-in-law has had in a decade! Did you see her attack him?"

Paige snickered. "It's pretty funny...now! I almost died of embarrassment as it was happening!"

"Forget it!" Maria waved a hand. "He's a *ksekoliaris!*"

Paige just grinned. "I think so too!"

*D*inner was set out—a huge mishmash of Greek and American food served buffet style—and the 40 guests attacked it with gusto. Paige and Apollo hung back, watching their friends and family celebrate. His fingers stroked the skin of her forearm, the gentle touch causing gooseflesh to break out. They sat close together, thighs rubbing as they enjoyed the feeling of actually being married. The ceremony had somehow changed their perception and suddenly everything felt so much more real, more intense and even more intimate.

"Today has been a good day," he said softly.

"It's wonderful," she nodded. "And I remembered..." She cut off, almost embarrassed.

"Remembered what?" He turned to her in surprise.

"Our first wedding. Not all of it, but enough bits and pieces to create the visual in my mind's eye."

"I remember what you were wearing," he admitted. "Some sexy red top and these really high heels..."

She grinned. "What else do you remember?"

"I remember the wedding night…" he murmured, nibbling the back of her ear. "I remember the nights before the wedding too."

"I'll bet you do!" She closed her eyes against the way his touch affected her, letting it flood her senses, a veritable blanket of comfort coupled with the deep-seated feeling of everything being just right.

"How long until we get the wedding night do-over?"

"Not long." She nudged him. "But definitely not until after I eat! It smells wonderful!"

Eating wasn't in the cards for her just yet, as Mick clanged a fork against the rim of a glass to get everyone's attention.

"As the best man," he spoke loudly, "I'm supposed to make a speech. I know everyone is enjoying the wonderful meal that's making my stomach growl, so I'll keep it short. First, I want to congratulate my best friend and his beautiful bride—I'm glad you guys decided to have a ceremony because I was kind of ticked off that I missed the first one!"

Laughter rumbled through the room as he continued. "The year they met, Apollo was determined to go to Vegas for spring break, and I was headed for the Bahamas. It was the first time in four years we didn't spend spring break together, but he wanted to see Vegas before he went back to Greece so off he went. Next thing I know he's pining away for some girl, telling me he might have married her…I thought he was crazy, and to be honest, I basically ignored him because—who gets married and doesn't remember or find out for sure?!" He turned to glare at Apollo and Paige, who were chuckling along with everyone else. "Three years later I get this phone call—he really did marry her, she'd come to Greece to divorce him but he was falling in love with her. I got my butt on a plane to Greece as fast as I could because I had to meet this girl—and she left the day I got there. I really didn't know what to think, but my friend asked me to come with him to the States to get his wife back…so what's a guy to do? I put my butt back on a plane, this time to Vegas." He glanced at Paige and smiled.

"Then I met her. She had these big hazel eyes and was staring up at Apollo like he'd hung the moon just for her—and I knew it was all over. My best friend's bachelor days were a memory; he was totally hooked on this girl and she on him. They were going to ride off into the sunset together and go on all these adventures…"

He said a few more things but Paige was looking at Apollo with a frown. "You told him about me wanting to go on adventures?!" she demanded, somewhat frustrated. "That was private!"

"I didn't tell him!" he said, shaking his head, a little perplexed. "I swear on all of our future children, I never told him that."

"Then how did he know?"

"It seems, *koukla mou*, that your desire for adventure is written all over you." He lovingly stroked her cheek.

"It is?" She looked a little confused.

"Apparently. But you know what?"

"What?"

"I'm going to spend the rest of my life giving you as much adventure as you'll ever want or need."

"That's the most wonderful thing anyone's ever said to me." Her eyes sparkled as she moved into his arms.

* * *

Thank you for reading Adonis in Athens—get ready for the next book in the series, Smitten in Santorini! Read the first chapter on the next page…

Melina Lakkas was having the mack daddy of bad days. She'd quit her job after getting yet another pay cut, her car was in the shop needing major repairs, and her sister had left an ominously cryptic voice mail for her. She was almost afraid to call her back. The way this day was going it couldn't possibly be good news.

Once she got home, she sank onto the couch and pulled out her phone. It was probably better to get this over with.

"I'm getting a divorce," her sister Sophia said in greeting.

"You're what?" Lena froze, her heart sinking.

"Everyone has been thinking I should do it for years and now it's time."

"I don't know what to say."

"There's nothing to say, but I wanted to let you know."

"Are you moving in here?" Lena lived with their parents and paternal grandmother. They had a guest room, but that meant Sophia and her three-year-old son would have to share it.

"Short-term, I don't have a choice," Sophia said quietly. "Giorgios doesn't have any money and although I've gotten a job, I can't afford to rent an apartment on my own without digging into our dividends from the company."

"What kind of job did you get?"

"At a café," she responded. "Just on the weekends. I can make a hundred Euros in a weekend, maybe 400 a month, enough to pay for my phone and contribute a little to the household. The payouts we get from Lakkas will keep me going and until the economy turns around, and anyway, what choice do I have?" Lakkas, International was their family shipping company and both she and Lena got quarterly payouts.

Lena swallowed hard, a million things running through her mind as she tried to process what her sister's divorce might mean. "Will Giorgios keep his mouth shut?"

Sophia sighed. "I don't know. He hasn't said anything yet, but you know it's going to get nasty once I contact a lawyer."

Lena started to pace, the phone at her ear. "What are we going to do?"

"I don't know."

"You can't work it out?" Lena hated how pathetic she sounded.

"You know I love you, but I can't be married to him anymore. He's always been a little bit of an asshole, but his outbursts used to be rare. Now it's almost all the time and…" She hesitated, taking a breath. "He hit me."

Lena gasped. "He *hit* you? Oh my God."

"That's what pushed me over the edge. I heard the usual nonsense about how it won't happen again, but I know it will, and I won't live that way."

"No, of course not." Lena paused. "Did you tell Apollo?"

Sophia snorted. "No. Why would I? So he can go to jail? And you'd better not either—that won't help any of us. Apollo runs the company and is probably going to wind up supporting us, so keep what I told you to yourself."

"I'm so sorry, Sophia. You never would have married him if…"

"I would have married him," Sophia said impatiently. "We were together for years and it was comfortable. I was never brave enough to truly take a chance on someone else, no matter how much I wanted to."

"This means we're going to have to tell the truth," Lena groaned.

Both women were quiet for a few minutes, ruminating the different possibilities. Before they could say anything, however, the front door opened and their brother Apollo was calling out to Lena.

"Lena? Are you home?"

"In here!" Lena called back. "I'll call you back," she told her sister, disconnecting.

"*Kalispera!*" *Good afternoon.* Apollo's wife, Paige, had only been living in Greece a few weeks but was taking the task of learning the language seriously.

"*Kalispera!*" Lena smiled at her, glad to see her brother and his pretty wife so happy.

"I need a favor," Apollo said after kissing her on both cheeks.

"What's going on?" Lena asked.

"It's Mick—he needs our help."

"*Mick?*" Lena tried to keep her voice neutral.

"There's been a fire at the construction site and he needs someone who speaks Greek to help with translation. He doesn't trust his foreman and after being gone for over a month, I can't take any more time off. Can you go? I know you quit your job, so you have the time, and he'll pay you."

"He…what?" Lena's heart hammered painfully in her chest.

"He needs your help. Will you go?" His eyes met hers intently. "It would mean a lot to me. I'd go myself but…"

"Don't worry about it, of course I'll go." Lena sighed, accepting her fate and wondering how she'd survive being around the only man she'd ever truly loved for any extended period of time.

"Look, I'm not stupid," he said softly. "I know you two had a thing, but no matter what happened, it couldn't have been such a big deal that after all this time you can't be friends again?"

Lena didn't respond as she turned and headed towards the kitchen. "Tell him I'll be there tomorrow. I'll book a trip on the ferry—the airport is a hassle."

"Thanks, Lena!"

She barely heard him as she shut her eyes and tried to breathe. Damn, her day had definitely gotten a whole lot worse. Being around Mick wasn't going to be easy. In fact, the whole thing was going to be a nightmare. She'd barely been able to keep her distance from Mick at Apollo and Paige's wedding last month—how could she possibly do it while working for him? There was no way to gracefully get out of this because short of telling the truth, she had no excuse. She was unemployed, vocal in her desire to have something to do other than work retail, and the money would be welcome.

Apollo had figured out there had been something between them, which surprised her. *Shit.* Her carefully constructed world was slowly crumbling and she had no way to keep the pieces from scattering. Things were going to go south quickly and she needed a plan; the problem was that she'd been trying to come up with a plan for almost four years and still didn't have one that was viable. She was pretty sure she wasn't going to come up with one overnight either.

To find out what happens, buy "Smitten in Santorini" at the retailer of your choice!

www.KatMizera.com

www.ingramcontent.com/pod-product-compliance
Lightning Source LLC
Chambersburg PA
CBHW060358310726
48976CB00003B/862